CONAN THE BARBARIAN

THE BARBARIAN

MICHAEL A. STACKPOLE

BASED ON A SCREENPLAY WRITTEN BY THOMAS DEAN DONNELLY & JOSHUA OPPENHEIMER AND SEAN HOOD

BERKLEY BOULEVARD BOOKS, NEW YORK

THE BERKLEY PUBLISHING GROUP
Published by the Penguin Group
Penguin Group (USA) Inc.
375 Hudson Street, New York, New York 10014, USA

Penguin Group (Canada), 90 Eglinton Avenue East, Suite 700, Toronto, Ontario M4P 2Y3, Canada
(a division of Pearson Penguin Canada Inc.)
Penguin Books Ltd., 80 Strand, London WC2R 0RL, England
Penguin Group Ireland, 25 St. Stephen's Green, Dublin 2, Ireland (a division of Penguin Books Ltd.)
Penguin Group (Australia), 250 Camberwell Road, Camberwell, Victoria 3124, Australia
(a division of Pearson Australia Group Pty. Ltd.)
Penguin Books India Pvt. Ltd., 11 Community Centre, Panchsheel Park, New Delhi—110 017, India
Penguin Group (NZ), 67 Apollo Drive, Rosedale, Auckland 0632, New Zealand
(a division of Pearson New Zealand Ltd.)
Penguin Books (South Africa) (Pty.) Ltd., 24 Sturdee Avenue, Rosebank, Johannesburg 2196,
South Africa

Penguin Books Ltd., Registered Offices: 80 Strand, London WC2R 0RL, England

This is a work of fiction. Names, characters, places, and incidents either are the product of the author's imagination or are used fictitiously, and any resemblance to actual persons, living or dead, business establishments, events, or locales is entirely coincidental. The publisher does not have any control over and does not assume any responsibility for author or third-party websites or their content.

CONAN THE BARBARIAN

A Berkley Boulevard Book / published by arrangement with Conan Properties International, LLC

PRINTING HISTORY
Berkley Boulevard mass-market edition / July 2011

Special thanks to Simon Varsano, on-set photographer

ISBN: 978-0-425-24206-3

BERKLEY®
Berkley Boulevard Books are published by The Berkley Publishing Group,
a division of Penguin Group (USA) Inc.,
375 Hudson Street, New York, New York 10014.
BERKLEY BOULEVARD and its logo are registered trademarks of Penguin Group (USA) Inc.

PRINTED IN THE UNITED STATES OF AMERICA

10 9 8 7 6 5 4 3 2 1

To the memory of
Robert E. Howard

ACKNOWLEDGMENTS

The author would like to thank the following people for their help on this project: Fredrik Malmberg and Joakim Zetterberg of Paradox Entertainment, Howard Morhaim, Ben Bova, Kat Klaybourne, Thomas Dean Donnelly, Joshua Oppenheimer, and Sean Hood.

CHAPTER 1

CORIN, BLACKSMITH, SON of Connacht and, like every other Cimmerian, a warrior, watched the young men of his village. He measured them with a careful eye, aware that soon he would be fashioning for each a sword. It would match them in length and personality, becoming a part of them. In the south it was said Cimmerians were born with swords in their hands, but Corin knew that this was not true.

We are born with the courage to wield a sword, as Crom grants. He smiled. *A Cimmerian needs little else.*

A dozen young men, some showing only the first wisp of a beard, practiced with the fellows in a circle of hard-packed snow. Two warriors circulated among them, snapping order. The youths' swords came up and flashed out, high cuts and low. Warriors lashed the youths' bellies when their charges displayed sloppy guards, and tipped elbows up and kicked feet into their proper place. Smiles betrayed boys who thought learning the deadly arts was but a game; and harsh cuffs disabused them of that notion.

Only survivors earned the right to smile after the grim work of swordplay was done.

The youths moved in unison—some clumsy, some certain, some bold enough to add a flourish to a cut. They watched each other, being impressed and trying to impress. Clusters of giggling girls standing on the shadowed side of huts increased their desire to preen and sapped their focus.

Corin shook his head slowly, a lion of a man with a thick mane and beard. Despite the late-fall chill, he wore no tunic, only a leather apron. The smith's strong arms displayed thick muscles over which a tracery of pale scars played. A few were the marks left by hot metal from the forge. The rest had been earned in battle.

The boy's grunt caught Corin's attention, but he did not turn toward it, not immediately. Had he done so, he would have smiled and his smile would have been seen. The boy needed no encouragement, but Corin, remembering his own childhood, saw no reason to discourage either.

Slowly he glanced over, and there, opposite the circle where the young men fought, his son, Conan, aped their movements. The stick his imagination had transformed into a Cimmerian broadsword slashed the air with a whistle. The boy ducked and twisted, then brought the stick around in a fluid riposte that would have cut a throat. Another twist, then a downward stroke to break a shin. The stick whirled up and around, both hands on the hilt, and came down in a beheading stroke.

Conan's father ran a hand over his beard to hide a smile. Conan's movements did not *ape* those of the young men; if anything, his fluidity mocked their stiff awkwardness. Where they were slow and tentative, he moved quickly and with certainty. Though battling at shadows much as they were, Conan was winning, whereas they would die easily.

Pride swelled Corin's breast, but the soft voice of his wife came to him. Her dying words echoed inside his skull. In their wake came a weariness of the soul, and an ache that reminded him of old wounds. He composed his face, his brows narrowing, and turned to face his son.

"Boy, what are you doing?"

Conan froze, stick quivering in an aborted thrust. "Father, I was—"

"I sent you to gather firewood, Conan. My forge grows cold."

The boy pointed at a stack of wood. "But I . . ."

"That's a thrust *near* the heart, Conan, not *in* the heart." Corin shook his head. "I give you a simple task and then find it half done, and you playing with a stick like one of those Aquilonian sorcerers in your grandfather's stories."

Conan dropped the stick as if it were a viper. "Father, I wasn't . . . that wasn't a wand. I was watching the others and . . ."

Corin waved his son to him. "Conan, those young men are being trained as warriors because they have earned that right."

"Only by being older than I, Father."

"Which means they are closer to death than you." Corin cupped the back of his son's neck in a hand. "You have it in you to be a great warrior *someday*, my son, but not *today*."

"But I'm already taller than Eiran, and he's only just started shaving . . ."

"Conan, enough."

"But, Father—"

"Enough." Corin pointed to the small pile of wood his son had gathered. "Double that, stack it inside the woodshed, then I want you to go check your trapline. You'd best be quick, too, since winter's stealing up on us, and night will be on us soon enough."

"Yes, Father." Conan's head tipped forward, but he looked up through black locks with those icy blue eyes. "It is just that I want to be ready to defend our village."

Corin raised an eyebrow. *Aggressiveness that will be welcome in a warrior is a nettle in a headstrong son.*

Conan, well used to reading his father's expression, said no more and set about his tasks.

Corin, satisfied, returned to his.

CONAN'S ANGER WITH his father had all but dissipated by the time he'd run far enough into the hills that the ringing of Corin's hammer on the anvil could not longer be heard. In leaving the village, he'd almost picked up the stick, but his father's suggestion that it was some sorcerer's wand tainted it. Instead, armed only with a small skinning knife, Conan departed on his appointed chores, running across snowy fields and up into the forested hillsides of Cimmeria.

His father's suggestion that it would be some time before he became a warrior melted beneath the intensity of his youthful fantasy. Out in the forest, away from the bemused smiles and sharp glances of adults, Conan grew into the man he knew he would become. Though already tall for his age, he grew taller. His arms and legs became as stout as his father's and twice as powerful. His effortless stride ate up yards, and by the time he vanished within the trees, his transformation was complete.

No longer was he Conan the smith's son, sent to gather rabbits from snares. No, he'd become a full warrior. He didn't seek puny animals, but greater prey. Somewhere in the forests there might be Pictish scouts—Raven Clan or Otter, perhaps—probing Cimmerian lands before a raid. Or, worse, Aquilonians could have again come north, pushing their borders into lands on which they had no claim. His grandfather had fought them at Brita's Vale, and he always said they'd return. Perhaps that was the more realistic threat.

It really didn't matter which to Conan. Either required him to move swiftly and quietly through the forest, stepping carefully so the crunch of snow underfoot would not betray him. He moved from point to point, slid down into the wind-blown bowl around evergreen trunks, and peered through snow-laden boughs at the forest around him. He watched the shadows, because in them you could see the Picts; and he listened, because the clanking of the Aquilonians' armor would betray their presence.

Though Conan knew he was playing at a game, for him it became so much more. The child delighted in the thrill of see-ing something half hidden in snow and transforming it in his mind into a Pictish ambush. But the part of him that was closer to being a man narrowed his eyes and looked past the fantasy. He watched to see why he'd thought a Pict might be lurking, then studied the land to make certain it was no illusion.

None of the other children in his village had that inten-sity. For that reason they seldom invited Conan to join in their games of make-believe. Elders had said, and children had passed on their words, that Conan had an old soul and a vital one. They all knew why.

I was born on a battlefield.

For so many, that fact defined Conan and set their expec-tations of him. He was destined to be a great warrior, and he wanted to prove himself worthy of that destiny. His mother had died there, giving him birth. Though he had no memory of her, he had been told that with her last breath, she had given him his name. His greatness would honor her and his family, perhaps even all of Cimmeria. The name *Conan* would strike fear into the hearts of Picts, Aquilonians, Vanirmen, and anyone else who believed Cimmeria could be theirs.

The youth slipped from behind a tree, carefully watching his back trail. Moving from point to point, he worked his way over to a rock wall. He could have easily followed the game trail at its base, working around and up the hillside to the top, but instead he leaped up. His fingers caught a handhold, but only for a second, then he tumbled down into the snow.

Another child might have laughed, but nothing about failure amused the young Cimmerian. He rolled to his feet again, brushing snow from his wolfskin cloak. He eschewed using the footholds that had started him up the rock wall before. He leaped again, caught the rock, and clung to it fiercely with his right hand. He steadied himself with his left hand, then began his ascent. Keen eyes picked out a clear path, and in less time than it would have taken him to follow the game trail, he reached the top.

And I have left no sign of my passing. He smiled, then shrugged. *Aside from that hole my bottom dug.*

The forest opened before him, revealing a long oval meadow split by the dark scar of a stream. Conan kept to the forest's edge, studying the expanse of largely undisturbed snow. When he came close to a set of tracks, he'd crouch and study them. He looked not only to see which animals had passed that way, but how the tracks changed over time. Years of study enabled him to read sign both of men and animals. Had Picts or anyone else been through the area, he would have known how many and how long ago they had passed.

Though no invaders had marched through the meadow, small game had. Conan checked the dozen snares set around the area and gathered two hares. Both appeared to be dead, caught by the neck in a loop of sinew. He broke their necks to be sure, then gutted them, tossing the entrails out where eagles and hawks might feast. He reset the snares, and moved two others closer to trails that led to the stream.

The quickest way back home would have been the path he chose to reach the meadow, but that way was barred to him. Not that any barrier had been erected, or that the cliff would have been too difficult to descend. Not that any invaders had taken up positions to ambush him. No, for Conan, that way would not work simply because to return by that same path would be careless. It would *invite* ambush. It could lead an enemy to his home, and it was the duty of every warrior to see that such a thing never happened.

Conan continued through the woods. He'd left his village to the north, and two days earlier he'd reentered from the east. This time he turned west, working his way through the forest. He paused on a hilltop that overlooked the trade road running toward the setting sun. He had traveled on it a short ways previously, before turning north to visit his grandfather, but today the empty road held no interest for him.

Instead he looked beyond it, toward the mountains to the south, and the lands beyond. The name *Aquilonia* had become common enough that it no longer inspired over-whelming awe when he heard it. But places like Ophir and Koth and Shem, dark Stygia and far Khitai . . . all of them sounded so exotic. Men had always said that his grandfather was a great warrior; but they also said he was a greater storyteller, and in his tales these places to which he had roamed, in which he had raided, became miraculous realms of wonder.

Of course, being eleven years old, Conan knew that his grandfather exaggerated. After all, it was not possible that a place like Shem might exist, a place so hot year-round that it never saw snow, and where the sand itself rose in great blizzards. Or that uncharted jungles, teeming with feral, manlike beasts and horrors from before time, might exist—this just was not possible. Those were stories to scare children and slacken the jaws of the foolish. Conan had grown beyond such wild tales.

What fascinated him about old Connacht's stories had been the people and their odd ways. Conan wondered at their need for legions of gods and for massive temples raised in their honor. The stories made it clear that the personal sense of honor that each Cimmerian treasured was but a commodity to be bought and sold—quite cheaply, too—in the land beyond the southern hills. He would never call his grandfather a liar, but a part of him would never believe until he had seen those things for himself.

The Cimmerian youth drew himself up and smiled as he looked south. He would be a warrior. As Crom wished, he would make the most of the courage and wit with which he was born. He would use them to protect his homeland.

"And," he said to the wind, "if civilized men dare trespass here, then, by Crom, will I make them pay."

CHAPTER 2

CORIN DID NOT look back from where he squatted at the hearth. "Was it Picts this time, Conan, or shining knights of Aquilonia?"

The crack of the door banging shut almost eclipsed Conan's sigh. "I was being careful."

"Practice, or was there reason?"

The boy set the rabbits on the table at the hearth's far side. "If I had seen anything, I would have told you."

Corin smiled and stirred the cauldron of stew hanging over the fire. "You can hang them up, let them season a day or three. Ronan's eldest speared a buck. They gave me a down payment on a sword for him. I've cut some up, added it to the stew."

"Ardel is going to get a sword?" Conan snorted and tied the rabbits' hind paws together. "The buck must have been trapped in a snowdrift."

"Ardel may be slow, but he throws a spear well."

"Cimmerians are swordsmen."

"And what if a Cimmerian loses his sword?"

Conan's eyes tightened as he hung the rabbits from a peg near the door. "He would sooner die than do that."

"And likely will, if he does, and *if* he cannot handle any other weapon." Corin ladled thick brown stew into a pair of wooden bowls. "A warrior may describe his skill with a blade when he's talking about a battle he has survived; but to survive there's not a one of them that wouldn't use anything that came to hand as a weapon."

The boy shook his head. "You can't use just *anything* as a weapon."

"Yes, you can." Corin handed his son a steaming bowl of stew. "There, for example, your supper. You could use that as a weapon."

Conan's brow furrowed as he studied the brown gravy and bits of meat and beans in it. "It's not hot enough to burn. And the bowl is not heavy enough to kill. I don't see how."

The smith stood and set his bowl on the table. He extended his hand toward his son. "Here, let me show you."

Conan, eyes narrowed warily, handed him the bowl.

"Good, now just sit over there." As his son sank to the floor by the door, Corin seated himself at the table and began to eat his stew. The venison cubes could have done with a bit more cooking, and he'd have to trade for more salt before winter ended, but it tasted good. He suddenly wished for a hearty loaf of bread—the kind his wife had been famous for making. He'd never learned how to make it himself, and Conan showed no aptitude for baking. *Not that the boy ever would have indulged himself in anything that didn't lead directly to his being a warrior.*

Conan stretched his legs out.

Corin finished his stew and started in on Conan's bowl.

The Cimmerian boy's foot twitched, betraying impatience. But it wasn't until Conan's head began to sink, his shoulders rise, and glower to deepen that Corin relented and turned toward his son. "So you want to know how this stew could kill someone?"

Conan nodded.

"Not counting poison, the stew would kill the way it is killing you now." Corin pushed the bowl toward Conan's place at the table. "By not having any."

The boy frowned.

"When you hear stories about our destroying the Aquilonians at Brita's Vale, what do you remember?"

Conan's face brightened. "How Connacht slew a centurion and scattered a whole legion of knights."

"Of course." Corin shook his head. "Don't you remember what came before? Why were the Aquilonians at Brita's Vale?"

"The Cimmerians forced them there to fight. They knew they were doomed, so they formed up to defend themselves."

"Good, now I want you to do something, Conan, something very important."

"Yes?"

"You've thrilled to my father's stories as a child. I did the same when I was your age. But now I want you to think of the story with a man's mind." Corin closed his eyes for a moment, remembering when he had learned what he hoped Conan would now learn, and wishing that it had been his father who encouraged him to learn the lesson. "The Aquilonians had come north to punish Cimmerians for raiding along the frontier. They burned villages and slaughtered people as they came north. They were invincible until they reached the vale. How did they become vulnerable?"

The boy's mouth opened for a heartbeat, but shut quickly enough. Blue eyes flashed warily. Conan's face became an iron mask of concentration, and Corin felt pride blossom in his breast. In that moment he saw the man his son could become, and he hoped he had the patience and strength to aid him on that journey.

Conan's gaze darted toward the stew. "Your father described raids on the supply trains coming to aid the Aquilonians. The Cimmerians took away their stew. They killed their reinforcements. They starved them of men, iron, and food. The Aquilonians could go no further."

"Very good, Conan, very good." Corin toed the bench away from the side of the table. "Come, finish your dinner and get more."

The boy, smiling, sprang to his seat and devoured the stew. Corin let him finish what was left of the bowl in silence, then began talking as Conan returned with a second helping.

"You must understand, son, that many a battle is won before the first arrow flies or the first sword is drawn. Brita's Vale was a close-won battle. The Aquilonian general had chosen his position well. Had his troops been a little less hungry, 'twould be some noble's villa on this very spot. The Aquilonians knew us as we know them . . . and to engage any enemy without knowing him is folly."

Conan glanced over, then nodded. "Father?"

"Yes?"

"Why did you never go raiding as your father did?"

"Are you suggesting I did not have the courage to go?"

The boy's spoon plopped back into the stew. "No, Father, no. I've heard the stories. Everyone says you are a great warrior, that just knowing Corin lives in this village is what keeps our enemies at bay. It is just that . . ."

The smith reached out with a scarred hand and gave his son's forearm a squeeze. "I heard no disrespect in your voice, my son. And, like you, the tales of my father's adventures certainly filled my dreams. But I think I am a more practical man than my father. This is why I am a smith. I can take ore and smelt it. I can pour it into a mold. I can fire it and hammer it and temper it. I can test it and sharpen it. I can shape it into something which is real and is useful. I make things which allow others to live their lives more easily."

The elder Cimmerian smiled. "For all the stories of treasure and glory, have you seen a single gem in my father's possession? A medal from some distant potentate? A proclamation from some king thanking him? No. But there is not a single man in this village who does not carry steel I shaped for him. I am content in knowing that I keep this village safe. It is my duty, and a duty I take most seriously."

"But, you know things of war. You could be a great war leader."

Corin sat back and laughed. "There is one tale of Aquilonia which my father used to tell, but I do not think you have heard it. When a general wins a great victory, they parade him through Tarantia in a chariot of gold, drawn by eight white stallions. Throngs line the streets. They throw flowers and gold and offer him their daughters. Everyone adores him."

Conan's eyes brightened. He sat forward, his unfinished stew forgotten.

"But in that chariot, nestled at his feet, is a dwarf. Throughout that parade, through the showers of gold and flowers, the dwarf says but one thing over and over again. 'Remember thou art but a man. As you have slain, so shall you be slain. Glory is fleeting, and you will be but a ghost in a scroll which will turn to dust before you are ever remembered.' "

Conan's expression of rapture dissolved into a look of confusion. "But that makes no sense. Crom wishes us to be brave and fierce. It is for this that we live."

Corin nodded. "So, you know the tale of Britá's Vale. You know its heroes."

"Of course."

"And what of the time before that when we threw the Gundermen back into Aquilonia?"

"I . . ."

"Or the time before that?"

Conan sat straight up and pounded a fist on the table. "No one will ever forget Conan, son of Corin!"

Unable to contain his pride, Corin laughed heartily, then clapped his son on both shoulders. "By Crom, that is a declaration I believe even the gods will honor. Now finish your stew."

As his son returned to eating, Corin got up and crossed the small hut. He reached up and pulled a cloth-wrapped package from atop a rafter, then returned and laid it on the table. "While you were dreaming of glories, I made this for you. Ah, no, finish your meal first."

There could be no mistaking what lay within the gray woolen wrapping. Long and slender, with the obvious projection of a cross hilt, it had to be a sword. Not a great sword or a long sword, but more than a knife.

Conan, showing more restraint than his father would have credited him with, finished the stew, then gathered both bowls and the wooden spoons with which they'd eaten and set them in a bucket. He looked expectantly at his father, clearly willing to do the washing up if the order would be given. Corin hesitated for a moment, then shook his head and smiled.

"Open it."

Conan lifted the sword in his hand, hefting the weapon before its unveiling. Then, slowly, with the same care Connacht had described using when unwrapping a harem wench in Koth, Conan freed the sword from its confines. With a steel blade half again the length of the youth's forearm, a bronze cross hilt and pommel, and a leather-wrapped grip, it clearly was no toy. Though the edges remained dull, and the tip rounded, if needed to kill a man, it would suffice.

Conan reached for the hilt, then hesitated, looking at his father.

Corin nodded. "Understand some things. I hammered this from an Aquilonian short sword a scavenger dug out of Brita's Vale. It's not Cimmerian steel—you'll earn that—but it is better than a stick for practicing."

The youth nodded, lifting the blade, slowly moving it around in lazy circles. He only half listened to his father— Corin really had expected nothing less. The smith knew he would be repeating the rules to his son many times, and that more than once he'd have to take the blade away from him to instill discipline. Still, the care with which the boy studied the weapon's weight pleased him. Any other boy—including those being trained by the warriors—would have first looked for something to cut, then would have run into the middle of the room, fighting phantoms and shadows.

"Conan, you will shape a scabbard for your blade. You will oil it and care for it. You will *not* put an edge on it until I give you leave to do so. Do you understand?"

The boy nodded, then sighted down the length of the blade.

"It is true and straight, my son." *Like your spirit.*

Conan looked up. "Father, I—"

Corin held a hand up. "Do not thank me."

"Why not?"

"Because it is a terrible thing I have done here, my son." *I hope your mother will forgive me.* "Know this. Because of this blade, you will be very angry with me—more times than either of us will care to remember."

"No, Father—"

"Accept that is so, Conan. And this is the other terrible part: in giving you that sword, I will let the man you will become slay the child you have been." Corin took the blade from his son. "A weapon like this is only good for killing men."

Conan smiled. "I shall destroy our enemies."

"So I hope, but you must remember, my son, that this sword cannot tell friend from enemy." Corin flipped it around and offered the hilt to his son. "*And* it can kill the man at either end of it. Sometimes both."

Conan accepted the sword, then returned it to its wrappings. "I shall make a scabbard. I will not sharpen it. And I will train only after my chores are done."

"Very good."

The boy looked up. "Will you train me?"

The question caught Corin off guard. "When the time comes, Conan, the warriors—"

"Father, I see them look to you. They see you as their master." Conan's eyes widened. "You shape the sword to suit the swordsman. I would have you shape the swordsman."

"If you do every chore I set for you, complete every task I give you, then, yes, I will train you." Corin nodded solemnly. "I've given you the means to kill men . . . and I shall train you so you know when to do it, and how to do it well."

CHAPTER 3

CROUCHED IN THE shadow of an evergreen, Conan watched the invaders march through his forest. The weight of his sword tugged at his left hip. His hands, palms leathery with a winter's work with his blade, flexed; their pain forgotten. He kept his breathing shallow, exhaling so his misty breath would dissipate in the branches above. He shifted slowly, allowing no movement, no sound, to betray is position.

Ardel led the other young men through the forest. They'd been sent on a patrol, but it was really little more than a game. Winter had blanketed Cimmeria with deep snows. Even the most determined invader would wait for walls of snow to melt before heading north. The patrol was a fool's errand, but Ardel led the troupe as if he were a king intent on vanquishing a horde. Each of them carried a sword—blades longer by half than the one Conan bore—but he comforted himself with the knowledge that none of them could use the blades as well as he could.

That winter, which should have been intolerable for all the snow, had been glorious for Conan. The snow made some chores impossible, which gave him just that much more time to practice with his sword. He'd spent more time with it in his grasp than out, and the first blood it had tasted had been his from the blisters it raised on his hands.

His father had devised a training routine for him. Conan had expected it to mirror what the other warriors put Ardel and his troupe through. It did not, and Conan suspected his father did things differently simply to challenge his son. Conan became bored quickly, which led to inattention—and that would get him killed faster than anything else. Some of the exercises led to frustration, but every time Conan reached the point of being disgusted, his father gave him another task.

Little by slowly, Conan began to understand what his father was doing. At midwinter, Corin had tasked him with hauling a large block of ice from a nearby pond, then crushing it into thumb-size shards, using the pommel. Conan had beaten the ice for hours, making great headway at first, but slackening as his muscles tired and he grew cold. Then his father had him gather up all the ice chips, place them in a small leather trough, and add water.

And the next morning, when the ice had frozen solid, he commanded his son to break the ice up again. For three mornings running, he gave Conan that job. On the fourth, Conan kept his sword in its scabbard and fetched a hammer from the smithy.

Corin, tall, his massive arms folded over his chest, studied the boy. "What are you doing?"

Conan brandished the hammer. "This is the better tool for that job."

"But I want you to use your sword."

"Why?"

"Because"—his father's eyes narrowed—"in battle you may not be able to find a hammer. If you think that a blade's edge or point are the only useful parts, you might as well go to war unarmed."

Conan set the hammer down and drew his sword. He smashed ice with the pommel, taking care this time to study not the size of the shards that flew off, but the cracks that remained. He shifted his aim, pounding a crack at its tip. A larger piece broke away. Again he struck, and within an hour had reduced the block as instructed.

He entered the forge. "It's done, Father."

"And what did you learn?"

"Some tools are better than others for some jobs, and that the blade is not the only or even best part of the sword for some jobs."

Reddish hell-light played over his father's features. "What else? Why did you finish faster?"

The boy thought. "I learned about the enemy. I learned its weakness and attacked it there."

"Very good, boy."

Conan smiled. "Now, Father, will you fight with me?"

Corin looked over and faintly grinned. "Not yet, Conan. You've learned enough for a day. You have chores."

"Father!"

"Loughlan brought his ax for sharpening." The smith pointed at the wheel in the far corner. "Put a keen edge on it."

"Yes, Father, and then I can put an edge on my sword?"

Corin sighed. "You've barely learned what you can do with the weapon's blunt edge, Conan. When you know that sword as an eagle knows its talons, *then*, and only then, will you sharpen it. For now, however, you'll learn how to put an edge on other things, so you won't dishonor your sword when the time comes."

Conan had wanted to rebel, but his father's reminder about honoring the blade appealed to him. It gave him a reason to be patient, so he was. He performed every exercise a hundred times, then two hundred and a thousand. When Corin pronounced himself satisfied and offered a new exercise, Conan would perform previous exercises to prepare for the new.

Some of the things his father asked of him seemed outlandish. Corin fitted a lead-filled sheath over the blade's tip, shifting the balance and doubling the blade's weight. He ordered his son to trace smoke as it rose through the air, or slash at sparks rising from the hearth. The exercise left Conan bathed in sweat. When he tired and tumbled, soot and dust caked him. But always he got back up and kept doing as commanded until his father called a halt.

Just as Conan was about to complain about the futility of this exercise, Corin slid the sheath from the blade. "One more time."

Conan ran his forearm across his brow, smearing black soot. His father pumped the forge's bellows, launching sparks. The sword whipped out quickly, hitting one, then another and another. Conan, the steel an extension of his arm, whirled and leaped, stabbed and slashed. Even when he stumbled, he cut through a spark, rolled, and came up to impale another.

"Enough, son."

Day after day, and through the long nights of winter, Conan trained. Each exercise built upon the one before it. Once he learned how to do something well, the lead sheath returned, or his father might secure his ankles with a short length of chain, forcing him to maintain his balance. Not yet strong enough to send his blade crashing through another fighter's guard, he learned that a quick cut could be just as deadly as a crushing blow.

Conan worked with two goals in mind. The first was to be granted permission to sharpen the sword. His slash would move faster than the eye could see, and his blade would open throats or thighs, slit bellies, and pierce any flesh his enemies left unguarded. He'd always known he'd grow into a powerful man, but being fast with a razored sword in hand would make him even more powerful.

The second goal—and he acknowledged that his father might grant it before the first—was for his father to spar with him. Corin's refusal wasn't born out of fear. Conan's father didn't know fear. But each refusal suggested to Conan that he was somehow unworthy of being a warrior in his father's eyes. Conan wanted that recognition desperately, and would stop at nothing to earn it.

I have to show him. Conan looked out from around the tree again as Ardel and his patrol plodded along a game trail. The boy smiled, and removed the satchel in which he'd placed a grouse that had been caught by a deadfall trap. He looped the strap over a low branch, then took a handful of snow and packed it down into a ball. He made two more, then slipped from his hiding place.

Remaining low, he moved quickly to a spot beneath the ridgeline, and came upon a rocky outcropping that overlooked the trail. The rocks hid him from the trail below. As Ardel started up and made the turn where the trail switched back, Conan popped up and hurled the first snowball. Ardel, who had slipped for a moment, looked up at the last second. The white explosion obliterated his florid expression.

"It's Picts. We're under attack!"

Conan rose again and threw. The second snowball caught another boy in the side of the head. He'd already begun to turn back down the trail. Unbalanced, he toppled into another youth. They went down in a tangle of limbs, falling off the trail and rolling deeper into the ravine.

"Picts! Picts!" Ardel's orderly band dissolved amid the panic.

Conan, ducking back, and barely able to contain his laughter, gave the call of a raven in the Pictish manner. The sound alone prompted more shrieks, which grew fainter as the youths ran off, back toward the village. Conan chased them with another raven's call, then sat in the snow and laughed.

. . . Until he heard a raven's call himself.

He froze, pressing himself back against the stones. Wary eyes studied his surroundings. Nothing moved. The air remained still, sunlight through trees dappling the snow with white stripes and spots. As far as Conan could see, the snow remained undisturbed save for his footprints and those of Ardel's troupe.

That does not mean they are not out there. Conan rested his left hand on his sword's hilt for reassurance, then hunkered down into a crouch. He wanted to go back for his grouse, but that would involve backtracking. That could lead to an ambush. That realization sent a jolt through him.

He swallowed hard, then took a single step forward.

A raven called again.

Conan looked up to the right.

The large black bird eyed him coldly.

"Are you just a crow, or has a god sent you to watch me?" Conan spoke to smother the spark of fear in his breast, realizing he was speaking as his grandfather did while storytelling. "Which is it?"

The bird, or the god who had sent it, became bored. The raven called once again, then opened its black wings and took to the sky.

Still cautious despite being confident he was alone, Conan circled around to he tree where he had hung the grouse and recovered it. He then went down the hill and cut across the trail Ardel's war band had blazed through the snow. What had been amusement at how easily they had panicked turned to disgust, since they made no attempt to hide their trail or deceive trackers. They headed straight for the village.

Conan paralleled their track, watching to make certain he was not being followed. He only emerged from the forest and followed it after the village's alarm bell tolled. By the time he reached the last hillcrest, a group of warriors had started out, with Ardel guiding them.

And my father leading the way!

Conan ran down the hill and Corin dropped to a knee. "Thank Crom you're unhurt, Conan. You *are* unhurt, yes?"

"Completely, Father."

Corin stood. "Ardel, take Conan back to the village. We can find the Picts on our own from here."

Conan laughed. "There are no Picts, Father."

Ardel's piggish brown eyes blazed. "Yes, there were. A war band. At least a dozen. The Raven Clan. They ambushed us."

Corin caught his son by the shoulders. "What do you know of this?"

"I saw them skulking through the forest, Father. I threw some snowballs and called like a Raven. They went running off."

"He lies." Ardel thumped a fist against his chest. "I know what I saw. I would not run from a child."

Corin released his son. "The trail will tell us what happened. Mahon and Senan, scout ahead. Ardel, you and your friends can return to the village. The rest of us will wait here."

Conan smiled as the older boys headed back down the hill. They retreated, but he was left to wait with his father and the rest of the warriors. *As it should be*.

"Conan."

"Yes, Father?" Conan looked out toward the two scouts. "I wasn't lying."

His father nodded solemnly. "I didn't expect you were. What was the job I gave you this morning?"

"To check the trapline."

"And how does that include tracking and harassing Ardel and the others?"

"It doesn't, Father."

"No, it doesn't." Corin shook his head, his shoulders slumping with evident embarrassment. "Take a look around, Conan. Two dozen men summoned to hold off a Pict war band so the others can prepare to defend our village. All because you decided to play a joke."

"Yes, Father."

"So, you will go back to the village. You'll go to each of their homes, and you'll complete the task they would have been doing but for your foolishness. You'll muck out stables. You'll chop wood. You'll haul water. You'll do what they need." Corin's head came up. "And not a one of you will let him off lightly. My son wishes to be a man, to abandon childhood. He'll not escape punishment because he is a child. Do you understand?"

Each of the warriors nodded grimly. Conan felt himself shrinking at the heart of that circle. He wanted so badly to fulfill his destiny as a man, as a Cimmerian, and yet he had diminished himself in all of their eyes. His stomach knotted up and his throat closed. Tears, born of frustration and shame, brimmed in his eyes, but he refused to let one fall.

"Conan, go, get to those chores."

He nodded, his voice tight and hoarse. "Yes, Father."

"And, Conan . . ." His father held out a hand. "Your sword."

THE SUN HAD been asleep for three hours by the time Conan returned to his home. His father sat at their table. A bowl of cold stew waited for him, but the boy felt no hunger. He'd flown from the hill, thankful that no one could see the tears glistening on his face. He even let himself fall once, face-first, into the snow, so he could rise and rub away any telltale tear tracks. He'd done all the chores and then some, hoping that his effort might earn him back the sword.

But deep in his heart he feared he had lost it forever.

"Sit, Conan."

The boy sank to his knees near the door and studied the floorboards. "I am not hungry, Father."

"You don't have to eat, just listen."

"I understand what happened. I understand why you punished me."

"You'll need to understand more than that, my son, if you ever want to wield that sword again."

Conan dragged himself to his feet and staggered to the bench. "I did everything you asked, Father."

"I know. And more." Corin nodded, stroking his beard. "As I expected. And you should know that there was not a single man who did not tell me, one way or another, that I was being too hard on you. Imagine. Cimmerians suggesting that."

Conan wanted to smile, but mirth eluded him.

"Do you know why they did that, son?"

The boy shook his head.

"They expect big things of you, Conan. You were born on a battlefield. They see you as destined for great things." Corin leaned forward, elbows on the table. "And do you know why I push you as hard as I do?"

"Because I was born on a battlefield?"

"No. Because your mother saw you as destined for *greater* things."

CHAPTER 4

CORIN ROSE FROM the table, poured the cold stew back into the cauldron over the fire, then ladled up a fresh serving. "You were born on a battlefield. As you'll someday learn, a parent waits to hear his infant's first scream. With you, it was doubly welcome. It meant you were alive. And it drowned out, just for a moment, the screams of dying men."

His father slid the bowl onto the table and began to pace. Firelight burnished gold onto Corin's face. His eyes grew distant, as did Connacht's when the old man prepared to tell a tale. "They were Vanirmen, Conan, sloppy, yellow-haired dogs come to worry us. Truth be told, I cannot remember why they came that day. Greed, lust, maybe one of our tribe had just happened to slay one of their kinsmen. The cause of that war—as with so many others—is hardly as important as the result. Had they won, some Vanir would be telling his son a tale of glory this night."

Corin looked down at his son, his hand resting on Conan's shoulder. "Eat, boy, this is a tale long in the telling."

Conan nodded and found hunger overwhelming shame.

"We had little warning—even less than Ardel afforded us after your trick. The Reivers came from north and south. I led the defense in the south. Your grandfather, were he there that day, could have told you which ax clove which head, which spear impaled which warrior. He'd have kept count of his cuts taken and given, but I've never had that gift. I've never had the desire to remember. All I do know is that steel flashed and rang. I took pride in the fact that my sword, crafted by my hand, rang purely and notched Vanir steel. It whittled spear hafts and harvested fingers. It chopped men down and chopped them up."

Corin paused by the hearth, leaning against it with both hands, staring into the flames. He fell silent for a moment. For reasons he could not explain, Conan felt his own throat tighten.

When his father began speaking again, his voice was low and thick. "Your mother, Conan . . . your mother was a true Cimmerian woman. You have her eyes, the blue, but your black mane comes through me by my father. But your mother, so fierce and brave. Though swollen with you in her belly, when the Vanir broke through in the north, she charged out to meet them. She killed one man with a spear thrust, then knocked another down with the haft. Had our warriors not crumbled around her, she'd have held the line. But they ran and a Vanirman stabbed her in the belly, almost killing you.

"She didn't cry out, your mother. Not a sound. She'd not give the Vanir the victory. But I saw her go down. With one hand she held her belly, keeping you within her. With the other she reached for a sword, even as her killer stood above her." Corin snorted. "Stupid man hesitated. I don't know why. I don't care. It just gave your mother enough time to get that sword and drive it into him where he'd stabbed her. And before he could strike and finish her, I split him in half."

Corin's hands tightened on the mantelpiece. His shoulders shook. Conan was certain it was from rage. His father could not cry, and yet as the boy made that determination, a tear rolled down his own cheek.

Corin, his face shadowed, turned toward his son. "Your mother was dying. She knew it. She drew a dagger from her belt and pressed it into my hands. 'Take your son,' she said."

The smith looked down at his hands. "I tried to refuse her—never had before, and never after—but she would brook no resistance. 'I will see my child before I die.' And she watched me, Conan, steadied my hand as I finished what the Vanirman had done. I cut you from your mother's womb and laid you on her breast. She kissed you. You tasted your mother's blood, and never heard her scream."

Corin pressed his hands together. "She knew she was dying and she said to me, 'See that there will be more to his life than fire and blood.' And then, with her last breath, she named you Conan."

The boy set his spoon down.

Corin turned his face toward the door and the village beyond it. "What they remember of your birth is that it came on the day of a great victory. Born on a battlefield, destined for glory. Suckled on blood, not milk. A wolf, not a dog, meant for wonders and miracles. You remember my father telling you stories of heroes and kings, where their scribes claimed they were born of virgins, or strangled monsters at birth, or made up any number of legends to make these men seem greater than they were. So our people have done with the truth of your birth.

"And yet, had one more Vanirman had breath left in his lungs, had he slain me as I held you, then all the wonders and miracles would have been soon-forgotten tragedy. A life of great destiny may be nothing more than a life that avoids serial tragedy." Corin sighed. "But I see the day of your birth differently. I knelt in the snow, my beloved Fialla dead, her naked child so fragile, nestled in hands covered in blood: that of the Vanir and of your mother, mayhap even some of mine. I knelt on a battlefield where dying men wailed as if infants and called for their mothers—and you remained silent, and your mother would never answer your call. I heard men cheer victory and praise the gods for their survival; yet 'twas your mother's wish that filled my head. For you, more than fire and blood."

Conan's confusion drew his brows together. "Are you saying she did not want me to be a great warrior?"

Corin laughed and rested his hands on his son's shoulders. "Even as she died she knew there would be no preventing that. But she sensed in you, and I have *seen* in you, the potential for more. You can be the best warrior of your generation. You could be the best warrior of our village. You could make men forget that Connacht ever existed. But those are foothills, and you are destined for mountains, Conan, and the stars. Others see you as born to a great destiny, and I know you are born to great responsibility."

"What responsibility, Father?"

"Responsibilities you will acquire when you are a man full grown. Nothing to worry about at the moment, but there will come a time . . ." Corin came around and sat at the table, stretching out his legs and facing his son. "What you did today was irresponsible. It caused panic, and some of those boys, since panic was their first reaction, will always react that way. We may train that out of them, but you've made it that much harder."

"Yes, Father."

"The first lesson of a great leader, Conan, is not to expect his followers to do what he can do, but to learn what they are capable of, and teach them to do it as best they can. You shamed these boys. Your shame may push them to try harder to redeem themselves. So, this is what you will be doing from now on: you will continue your chores for me and the people in the village. You will not complain. When they tease you, you will hold your tongue and your fist. You will shame them into being better men than you are, and when they fail, you will say nothing."

Conan frowned deeply. "Yes, Father."

Corin laughed, slapping his hand on the table. "Your mother had that look. I only saw it once directed at me and vowed never to earn it again. Restraining yourself will not be the hardest thing you do in life, Conan; just the hardest thing you've done up to now. Aggression is a warrior's virtue. Restraint is a leader's. You must promise me to do this."

"I promise, Father."

"Good." The smith nodded. "You have half a bargain to keep, and I will offer you the other half. Tomorrow morning you'll find your sword in the smithy. You'll put an edge on it, only a hand span from the tip down."

The boy's face lit up as his heart began to pound. "And you will train me. We will fight?"

"We will, Conan, we will. I have much to teach you, but not immediately."

Conan's shoulders slumped. "Why not?"

"It's very simple, my son." Corin met his son's blue gaze. "You're growing, and soon will outgrow that Aquilonian toy. It's time you learned to forge a blade, a proper Cimmerian blade."

The boy stood, weariness forgotten. "Crom made me to wield swords, not to hammer them."

"Crom has shaped you, as he shapes us all, to his own cold ends." Corin shook his head. "But if you want a blade to be part of you, if you want it to live in your hands, then you're going to help bring it to life."

OVER THE NEXT six weeks Corin marveled at the fact that his son had not bristled or broken, had not cried or complained. The smith had no desire to see his son break; nor did it surprise him when Conan pushed himself beyond where Corin wanted him to go. The boy learned quickly, and while little mistakes and little frustrations might coax an oath from him or a glower, he always returned to his tasks with a singular determination that Corin had never seen even an adult display.

The smith had not been easy on his son. He sent Conan out to the nearest mine to gather iron ore to smelt for the blade. Corin had borrowed a mule to aid him. Conan returned with two baskets of ore strapped to the beast, and another smaller one on his own back. The boy crushed the ore and prepared it for smelting, then worked the bellows until the iron became a red-gold river of molten metal.

Corin watched Conan's pride rise to his face, lit by the iron's backglow as it poured into the mold. The boy gathered wood while the metal cooled, and chose leather to wrap the oak on the hilt. The boy helped Corin pour the bronze for the pommel cap and cross hilt. Then the boy took the cooled steel and plunged it into the forge, burying it in charcoal.

He pumped the bellows until the blade glowed, then brought it to the anvil to begin the shaping.

Here Conan encountered his greatest challenge, and watching him tightened a fist around Corin's heart. The boy intended the sword to be perfect, but had no understanding of how much work that would entail.

The hammering on one side had to be matched equally on the other. Stretching the metal made it too thin. Cracks appeared. Pieces broke off. And while the metal could always be reheated, and the pieces folded back in, frustration led to hard blows where subtle were required . . . and subtle always seemed to take too long.

A boy forging a man's weapon. Corin smiled as he watched, remembering his own first clumsy efforts. Connacht hadn't been terribly patient with him, but that was because his father had assumed Corin intended to travel and see the world. Though Connacht had his reasons for remaining in Cimmeria, more than once, when he told tales, Corin was certain his father would vanish again if the slightest chance arose.

Corin's father had been surprised when he realized the nature of Corin's goal: it was not to create a sword he could take into battle, but to create *the* sword that was meant to be his in battle. Connacht could never understand that about his son, but at least he respected it. He was as proud of everything Corin did as he was of his own youthful adventuring.

Conan plunged his sword into a trough. The water bubbled and steamed. He pulled the blade out again, rivulets running. Corin felt certain that his son was seeing blood.

"Is it finished, Conan?"

Conan looked over at his father, then nodded.

Corin rose and crossed to the anvil. He took the blade

from his son and turned it over. The boy had shaped it well. The forte would turn blades. The tang would not sheer off, yet was not so heavy as to unbalance the blade. It tapered to a point, but not too sharp a one.

"Nicely done, boy."

Conan smiled, his soot-stained face streaked with sweat trails.

"But let me ask you this: Which is most important when forging a blade? Fire or ice?"

The boy snorted. "Fire."

Corin raised an eyebrow as he continued to study his son's handiwork.

"Ice?"

"Are you certain?"

Conan nodded, but hesitantly.

The smith smashed the blade against the anvil. It rang dully, then shivered into fragments. Conan stared down, his shocked expression mirrored in the metal shards. His expression darkened as he looked up at his father.

'Tis a lesson best learned now, my son. "We'll begin again, Conan." Corin knelt and began gathering metal shards. "You'll learn what makes a great sword makes a great warrior. By the time you know that, you will be ready to wield the blade we shall make together."

CHAPTER 5

CONAN WATCHED EXPECTANTLY as his father studied the blade. The boy had hoped it would be finished three weeks previously, but his father had made him rework the blade. "You're growing too fast," Corin had complained. He redesigned the blade, lengthening it, making the tang and forte more stout so it would be a worthy sword for the man Conan was to become.

But Conan wanted it now. "What do you think, Father?"

"Close, very close." Corin bounced the blade on the anvil. The metal quivered and rang sweetly. He stabbed it into the fire again and nodded to his son. "A little more heat."

Despite the aching in his limbs from all his chores and all the training, Conan pumped the bellows with all the vigor he could muster. Sparks flew and heat blossomed. Using tongs, his father turned the blade over amid the glowing coals, then drew it out. "Get the small hammer."

Conan did as he was bidden and shaped the weapon

where his father pointed. "Gently, boy, but firmly. A smith, a swordsman, must maintain control of his tools. Smooth that out. And there, and there."

The boy hammered carefully, relishing the peal of metal on metal. Something about it bespoke strength. So unlike the hiss and skirl of steel on steel in battle, where strong blades became vipers. The sound coaxed from the sword and anvil by the hammer meant that he need never fear the blade betraying him. This he had come to understand.

Corin inspected his handiwork, then glanced at the cooling trough. "Go get more ice."

Conan ran out and chipped ice from a block, then carried it back into the forge and dumped it into the trough. "When you asked me which is more important, fire or ice, you never told me the answer."

Corin raised the blade, and in the shadows beneath the forge's roof, the metal still glowed dully. "A blade must be like a swordsman. It must be flexible. A sword must bend, or it will break. And for that to happen, it must be tempered."

The smith plunged the sword into the trough. Ice melted, and water bubbled and steamed with the hiss of a thousand snakes. "Fire *and* ice. Together. This is the mystery of steel."

"Is it done, Father?"

Corin nodded. "Yes, but you're not."

"But you have taught me much."

"Do not misunderstand me, Conan. You have learned much—more than boys half again your age. But it is not in what you know, but how you apply it, that we will see how great a swordsman you will become." Corin folded his arms over his chest. "Do you remember when I asked you that question? When I shattered your sword?"

Conan's face flushed. He had been so proud of what he'd

done, and then found it was worthless. In an instant he had gone from victorious to defeated. "I remember."

"Did you think the question fair?"

The boy shrugged.

"Did you wonder why I had let you proceed without giving you the answer, and telling you something so important?"

Conan glanced down. "You wanted me to learn to hammer before I could make a sword?"

His father leaned back against the anvil. "In part, you are correct. But there is something you need to know, about men, about yourself. Men learn in one of two ways. Some observe, ask questions, think and act. Others act and fail, and if they survive their failure, they learn from it. Clever though you are, my son, you do not ask questions. You think of your ignorance as a failure.

"So you failed at your first attempt to make a sword. Have you learned from it?"

Conan could not bring himself to meet his father's gaze. He considered the man's words and wanted to deny their truth. He couldn't, at least not about men in general. But Conan wanted to be more. He was destined to be something special. Great warrior and more, as his mother desired. And yet his father was right. He didn't like asking questions just in case he revealed ignorance about something everyone else knew.

Does that make me weak? Conan frowned. *Maybe just stubborn.*

He looked up. "Which were you, Father?"

Corin roared with laughter. "Your grandfather was a man of great passions and tempers. He did not reward failure in himself or anyone else. So I would watch. I would maybe ask a question—though, I admit, with him I asked for a story to hide my intention. I learned to do things correctly and sought never to fail. When I have, however, I survived and have learned."

A certain melancholy had entered his father's voice. Conan's eyes narrowed. "Is this why you have never taken another wife?"

Corin folded his arms over his chest. "Your mother, and her death, were not a failure. We have you as proof of that. But when she died, my heart ached terribly. I survived. It may make me a coward, but I never dared love again. When you find that one woman, Conan, the one who fires your heart, who makes you feel alive and makes you want to be a better man than you are, never let her go. I was that fortunate *once*. It would not have been fair to hold anyone else up to comparison with your mother."

Conan's father fell silent, and the boy said nothing to break the silence. He'd seen his father turn reflective before—often while watching him, but at times when Conan didn't think his father knew the boy could see him. His father had always displayed serenity and wisdom, but this time pain creased his brow. Conan did not see this as weakness, however. To *surrender* to it would have been weakness.

Survive. Learn. The boy nodded solemnly. "I will make you proud, Father."

Corin's expression lightened. "You already have—even though there are times you disappoint me."

"Father, I won't ever again."

Corin crouched and looked up at his son. "Don't make promises you cannot keep, Conan. We all disappoint others. If we never do, it's because we never take a chance, we never live. What your mother wanted, what I *want*, is for you to live and live wonderfully large."

The smith rose to his full height and tousled the boy's hair with a scarred hand. "You're not yet the man for that sword, but tomorrow we begin getting you there."

* * *

OVER THE NEXT month Corin began training his son. "The first thing you must remember, Conan, is that men call it 'sword fighting' but it is really 'man fighting.' A blade is only as keen as the mind driving the arm."

To make his point, Corin extended the sword they'd made full out, resting the tip at the top of his son's breastbone. "Cut me with your sword."

The black-haired boy, eager, thrust toward his father. The man's longer reach, and the length of his sword, brought Conan's effort up short. The boy ducked away from Corin's sword, but Corin merely retreated a step and again pressed the tip to his son's chest. The boy's eyes narrowed, then he beat Corin's blade aside with a great clang and clash of metal.

Yet before he could get close, Corin had slipped back again. He met every harsh parry with a retreat, every bull-like rush with a sidestep. Conan's face flushed. Lips peeled back from teeth in a feral snarl. The boy knocked the blade aside, then spun, but Corin likewise pivoted, then slapped the boy across the buttocks with the flat of the sword. Conan slipped and flew headlong into a snowbank.

He came up sputtering, spitting out snow. "You're not fighting fair!"

The smith stabbed the blade into the ground and rested his hands on the pommel. "Do you think anyone you ever face across a blade will fight fairly?"

"Men fight honorably."

"No. If you choose to believe that, you'll die in your very first battle." Corin shook his head slowly. "Men who *survive* tell other men that they fought honorably. They lie. Remember all the tales your grandfather has told? Has he ever mentioned a Kothian or Gunderman or Shemite who fought honorably?"

Conan shook himself like an animal, flinging snow off his clothes. "No."

"And you do think anyone who survived fighting against him ever described him as honorable?"

"No."

"If you remember nothing else, my son, remember this: it's not the man who slays the most who wins a battle; it's the man who *survives* who wins it."

The boy, frowning, rubbed his bottom. "And what if I kill them *all*?"

"Then you are the only survivor." Corin pulled the blade from the snow. "So, first I shall show you how to survive, then I shall train you in how to kill."

Conan watched him warily, but did as he was told. Corin began by showing his son how to retreat and keep his footing. He showed him the four gates—up-right, up-left, down-right, down-left—that would block all slashes. He showed him the five sweeps to turn lunges and the brushes to guide blades wide.

The boy's natural speed and agility made him adept at all of them, but his impatience to strike back diluted his focus. More than once, when Conan tried a clumsy riposte, Corin bound his sword and knocked him to the ground. The boy would bounce up again, fury blazing in those blue eyes, and would come on. Because of his size, skill, and reach, Corin never feared injury. He knocked his son down again and again, until the boy could no longer rise—which took well into the night on some occasions.

Corin stood over him one night as large snowflakes drifted down. "Do you know why I keep beating you?"

Conan spat blood from a split lip. "Because you will not teach me to attack."

"It takes no skills and no intelligence to stick something sharp into someone. A scorpion can do it. A wasp. An elk." The smith sighed. "All the times we have trained, what have you learned?"

"You don't fight fair."

"The whispers of ghosts bother me not at all. What have you learned?"

The boy sat up in the snow, his sullen eyes covered in shadows. "You have a longer reach than me. You move too quickly for me to close."

"And what does that tell you?"

"I have to be quicker. I have to be stronger."

"No, son." Corin shook his head. "It means you shouldn't be fighting me with a sword."

The boy blinked.

"Every man you face will have his strengths and weaknesses. Every group of men. Every army—anything you will ever fight will have strengths and weaknesses. If you attack his strengths, you will lose. If you bring your strength to bear on his weakness, you will win."

Conan scowled. "You don't have a weakness."

Corin sank to a knee and rested his hands on his son's shoulders. "I do have a weakness, Conan. You don't see it as such, but I do. It's not one you'll ever be able to use against me, but it is there."

The boy looked up. "Then I will never be able to beat you."

"You will." Corin smiled. "Tomorrow, in fact, I shall teach you how."

CORIN MOVED ONTO the sheath of ice that covered the river and waved his son out after him. Winds had scoured the ice clean of snow, so he spread his feet carefully, setting himself. "Two weeks you've spent learning to attack, Conan. Do you really think you've earned this blade?"

The youth nodded, setting himself.

"Then come take it. Take it and it's yours."

Conan's eyes widened for a moment, then he darted forward, roaring a war cry. He slashed low, but Corin blocked low-left. The smith brought the hilt up, deflecting the quick high slash, then shoved.

Conan, off balance, scrambled to keep his footing. He went down hard, but never lost his grip on the sword. Ice cracked beneath where he'd fallen, but the boy bounced up again and drove at his father. High cuts and low, thrusts and feints, the boy began combining things he'd been taught in ways Corin hadn't imagined he'd figure out so quickly. And the blows came fast, forcing Corin to dodge more than he ever had before.

Conan's effort made no difference. Corin never tried to attack, but concentrated on fending off his son's blows. Whenever Conan tired, whenever he hesitated, the smith would bind his blade and shove him back, again and again spilling him to the ice.

"You are *still* all fire, boy."

Snarling, Conan regained his feet. His eyes narrowed, his face tightened. He charged forward, his sword aimed to deal blow that would split a man up from down.

Corin ducked back. "No. Slow down. Find your footing!"

The blow's vehemence spun Conan around, and Corin knocked the boy off his feet. He landed hard, but came back up, blade low, murder on his face.

"Enough."

The boy came for him, not the least glimmer of reason in those blue eyes. Corin fended off two blows, then sent the boy flying back.

"Enough!" As the boy charged forward again, Corin stabbed the great sword into the ice. The sheath of ice began to crack. Muttering a brief prayer to Crom, Corin levered the blade forward. Ice shifted and split.

Conan, his charge unchecked, plunged into the shallow river.

At least he did not lose his sword. Corin shook his head slowly. "You are not ready for this sword."

The boy, having dragged himself from the frigid water, looked up aghast. "But, Father . . ."

"The sword has been tempered, Conan. You have not been. All fire, no ice. You will not bend, so you will break." Corin slid the great sword into its scabbard. "Someday you will be ready for this blade—*worthy* of it. Until that day, your possessing it would only get you killed."

The boy shivered. "Does this mean you won't train me anymore?"

Corin sighed. "No, my son, it means I have to train you even better."

CHAPTER 6

CONAN, HIS LUNGS burning, cut around a large hut. Snow flew as he sprinted past a knot of giggling girls. He brushed off his brown tunic's sleeves, ridding them of the last of some chicken feathers. He ducked under a skinned elk carcass, narrowly avoiding the loss of an ear as he dashed between the butchers.

Already he could hear his father's voice from the heart of the village. "When a Cimmerian feels thirst, it is the thirst for blood." Corin's bass voice made those words into commands, yet Conan had heard them uttered as cautions. The same words he used to encourage the boys like Ardel he'd employed to focus Conan.

On the boy sprinted, weaving his way past warriors who sparred or sharpened swords. "When a Cimmerian feels cold, it is the cold edge of steel."

For a heartbeat it surprised Conan that his father's words didn't evoke the sense of having a sword in his hands. The boy smiled, just briefly, realizing that he *had* learned some of the lessons his father taught him. He caught his first adult glimmer of the depth of his father's wisdom, and that drove him yet faster. He wanted to surprise his father, not disappoint him, for surprise and faithfulness to his teaching would earn Conan more responsibility and opportunity.

Ahead, a line of youths stood facing Corin. The smith held a small bowl from which he plucked turquoise eggs mottled with brown—raven's eggs, which Conan himself had gathered as part of his chores earlier that week. Each young man opened his mouth, and Corin solemnly placed an egg on his tongue.

Conan dodged a lunging dog, then skidded to a snowy stop at the end of the line, his chest heaving. His father saw him, but gave no sign. Then he spoke. "But the courage of a Cimmerian is *tempered*. He neither fears death nor rushes *foolishly* to meet it."

Conan bent forward, struggling to catch his breath. He cast a sidelong glance at the larger young men and could see they understood little of what his father was saying.

Corin gave the last youth an egg. "So, to be a Cimmerian warrior, you must have cunning and balance as well as strength and speed."

Conan straightened up. His father had given him a long list of chores that morning, all of which were meant to eat up time. He sent him to chop wood for old Eiran, and requested that the old man dull his ax before Conan could do the job. And then Deirdre had wanted a chicken killed—not one of the ones in the coop, but the one that had escaped from it. So it went with tasks that had him crisscrossing the village—or would have had him doing this if he had not realized that they could be done with a greater economy of effort. *Cunning won the day that strength and speed alone could not.*

Corin looked at his son. "I gave you chores, boy."

"Finished, Father." Conan could not help but smile.

The smith regarded the others. "The first to circle the hills and return, his egg unbroken, earns the right to train with the warriors."

The young men broke ranks and sprinted in a pack for the hills.

Conan watched them go, astonishment slackening his jaw.

Corin peered into the bowl, then tossed his son an egg. "By Crom, boy, what are you waiting for?"

Conan popped the egg into his mouth and ran off, letting his shock and anger speed him. As he pressed to catch up, he saw the first of the others slip and fall, broken yolk and blue shell staining his chin. The young man spat disgustedly and tossed snow at the boy who had knocked him down, but the others did not notice.

Cunning. Tempering. Conan's blue eyes narrowed. The race wasn't just about speed, but about completing the circuit with the egg intact. The boy who fell, had he not broken the egg, could have gotten back up again. *So the egg is everyone's weakness.*

Ardel, never having been the swiftest of the youths his age, had also figured this out. As he and others worked their way up the hills, then along the grand circuit, he jostled the competition. He swept one boy's legs, plunging him face-first into the snow. Egg erupted from his mouth. Ardel even swung a fist at Conan, but the younger boy ducked.

Cunning. While the other boys smashed against one another, Conan cut off the trail. The extra duties his father had assigned to him over the winter had given him a familiarity with the area that none of the others came close to possessing. He leaped over rocks and ducked beneath fallen trees. He cut diagonally across a hillside, using saplings to slow and redirect himself. When he returned to the trail, he'd passed the largest boys. He raced ahead, leaping and cutting, their snarls forcing him to smile.

Then he caught it. Movement through the forest around them, pacing them. For a moment he thought wolves might have come hunting them, so quickly and furtively did the figures move from shadow to shadow. Then he caught a flash of foot here, a hand there, a motion only a man could make.

He slowed, instinctively raising a hand to warn the others. *Picts!*

The other boys stopped dead. One of them cried out, then choked on his egg. As four Pictish scouts, heads shaved at the sides, hair stiffed with porcupine quills, emerged from the forest, the other boys turned and ran.

Conan, his nostrils flaring, stood his ground, balling his fists.

A bola whirled in one Pict's hands. It spun through the air, the leather laces tangling Conan's ankles, drawing them together and dumping him to the ground. The boy turned over, wiping snow from his face, as the quartet of Picts drew slowly toward him. They didn't seem to fear him—rather, they viewed him as more of a curiosity than anything else, and this dismissal kindled anger in Conan's heart.

Conan looked past their tribal paint and the double axes they bore. Their wariness came tinged with weariness. The Picts were far from home, had no supplies, and had a haunted look on their faces. They had no idea what to make of him, and began discussing his fate in their harsh tongue.

One pointed back toward the south, then again to the west and the Pictish homelands. The others gesticulated wildly. Their tattoos and paint suggested they were Otters, who usually raided down near the Aquilonian border. What they were doing so far north and east Conan didn't know, but clearly they were up to deviltry.

While their discussion distracted them, Conan dug fingers into the leather lacing that bound his feet together. He resisted the urge to struggle, since that would only draw the leather thongs more tightly together. He turned one foot, then pushed on a lace. He tugged another. Then, as the Pict leader grabbed a handful of Conan's hair and jerked his head back to stretch his throat for the skinning knife he held high in his hand, Conan slid his feet from his boots and brought one of the bola's weights up in a short, sharp arc.

The leather-wrapped stone caught the Pict on the right side of his face. His cheekbone cracked and an eye socket crumbled. The man spun, blood spurting, his face misshapen, and crashed down beside the barefoot Cimmerian boy.

Conan tugged the ax from the downed man's belt and threw himself backward. The second Pict's ax blow would have crushed his skull had he been a heartbeat slower. Conan somersaulted backward, then came up. He ignored the cold as his feet dug into the snow. All that was important was that he maintain his balance.

The third Pict charged him, ax raised for a blow that would split him from crown to crotch. Conan brought his ax up in the high-right guard, blocking the blow. The Pict's eyes widened and he raised the ax again. But Conan rushed forward, slipping inside his guard, and smashed the ax into the man's knee. The blade sheared through leather leggings and flesh. The knee buckled and the Pict went down.

Conan's next blow slammed into the Pict's breastbone, shattering it. Spitting blood, the warrior crashed onto his back. Conan spun away from a feeble swipe at his legs, then brought his ax up high left. He blocked the fourth Pict's blow, then spun beneath his arm. He used the man's body to shield him from the last Pict, then tripped him.

The second Pict closed quickly, but the Cimmerian was quicker. Conan kicked out, catching him over the right hip. The Pict leaped back, steadied himself. His eyes widened for a moment, then he lowered his shoulders and bull-rushed the boy.

All of Corin's training kicked in. The endless hours of repetition slowed time for Conan. The Pict meant to overwhelm him, to use his size advantage, though not great, to bowl the boy over. All the man had to do was to block any blow Conan might deliver, then weight and speed would grant him victory. He'd knock Conan down, then dash his brains out.

Conan stabbed the ax toward the Pict as if to fend him off. The warrior slashed to batter the ax out of the way, but Conan dipped his ax beneath the other man's. The Cimmerian took a step forward and to the left, twisting like a suddenly opening gate to let the Pict rush past, bringing his ax up to his left shoulder. Conan backhanded the ax through the Pict's line of attack, catching him solidly in the spine, just above his hips. His legs died and he stretched limply on the snowy ground.

The last Pict had gathered himself, brushing snow from a furious face. As the death throes of the man with the broken spine slackened, Conan spun away from him and engaged his last foe. The Cimmerian ducked beneath a wild ax stroke at his head, then buried his own ax in the Pict's belly.

The man collapsed around it, slamming into the ground face-first. He sagged to the side, desperately trying to suck in breath. He lifted an arm to ward Conan off, but Conan snapped it with an overhand blow. Another blow crushed the back of the man's skull, and the battlefield became silent save for the rasping breath of the third Pict and the scolding call of a raven.

Conan crouched and studied his surroundings for any other movement. He saw nothing, then recovered his boots. By the time he'd pulled them on, the third Pict had stopped breathing.

Conan bent down and recovered the skinning knife that had been intended to drink his blood.

And he set about some very grim work.

WHEN THE FIRST of the young men returned, dejected, chins stained with broken egg, Corin felt no concern. That was normal, and the boys would learn. He took pride in the fact that Conan was not among them. But then, as the largest boys came running in, eyes wide with panic, fear began to coil in his belly.

Then Ronan stopped one of the boys—his son, Ardel—and glanced back at Corin. "Corin! Picts in the woods. They hunted the boys."

Corin scanned the back trail. "How many, Ardel?"

"Too many." The young man looked up, ashen-faced. "There were too many."

"And you came straight here? You led them back to us?"

Ardel sank to his knees. "Too many."

Corin turned to summon more warriors, but saw a human form emerging from the forest to the south. He started in that direction, then stopped, waiting.

The form began to jog toward the village. Conan, his pace steady, his breath coming in thick vapor, wended his way to the center of the village. Covered in blood, he paid no attention to what the others were saying, to their gasps or their encouraging nods. He did not look at the other boys, but instead continued on, his face half masked by his hair but his blue eyes burning fearsomely.

He tossed the Picts' severed heads at his father's feet, then spat out the egg. He looked up into his father's eyes. "The only thirst I know is for blood. The only cold I know is the cold edge of steel. My courage is tempered. I fear not death. I do not rush foolishly toward it. Speed and strength, cunning and balance. I am ready to train as a warrior."

Corin smiled. *You are indeed ready, my son.* "How many?"

"Four, only four." Conan toed a head. "Exhausted, no supplies, so they have a camp somewhere."

Corin looked around at the warriors. "I want warriors to scour the hills. Go!"

"Me, too, Father?"

Corin nodded. "Yes, my son, I called for warriors, didn't I?"

"Yes, Father." Conan beamed and the sight of his joy warmed his father's heart. The boy turned to run off back the way he'd come."

"Conan."

"Yes, Father?"

"Go get your Aquilonian sword." Corin nodded solemnly. "You're a warrior, by Crom, and I fear, by the end of this day, your blade will have drunk its fill."

CHAPTER 7

CONAN, SWORD BARED, ran into the hills west of the village. The other scouts had fanned out toward the south, but the boy headed toward where he had killed the Picts. He could start from there and then backtrack.

Pure joy bubbled through him. He imagined himself—now properly armed—killing a dozen of the painted savages. Maybe the four he'd slain were the vanguard of a war band! While he knew this wasn't true, given their ragged condition, he could wish it were true. It would make for a better telling of the story.

That thought sobered him. Though he cared only for what his father thought, he couldn't help but notice the looks on the other faces. Ardel and the other young men looked shamed—as well they should—and resentful. They'd given in to panic while a younger man had not. Even at that young age, Conan recognized that they would eventually forget their shame, and instead revel in remembering that they had been present when Conan brought his trophies to the village.

The others—the warriors—their reactions had been easy to read as well. Some refused to believe. Some of them had been in combat, but had never killed an enemy. Others, knowing just how difficult that was, couldn't believe so young a man had done it alone. But the vast majority remembered the omen of his birth. For them, his return, his accomplishment, only confirmed their belief in his destiny. While this made most of them happy, a few had looked away from him, believing that such a great destiny would afford Conan a life poor in peace and happiness.

Had he been older, he would have understood that sentiment, but even if he had, it wouldn't have mattered. Crom gave men courage. Crom meant for men to survive by their wits and the strength of their arms. Crom guaranteed nothing more, and certainly no peace or happiness. Conan was a Cimmerian warrior, and a warrior's life he would lead.

Conan cut through the forest and scaled the rock face leading toward the meadow where he had placed his traplines. As he clambered to the top and crouched to rest, he heard the jingle of tack and the creak of leather. Below, along the track at the cliff's base, came a half-dozen riders, armored in leather and light mail. Conical steel caps covered their heads and bloodred scarves half hid their faces.

Conan crouched behind a fallen tree. He'd never seen such men before, not even on the trip south with his father to visit a market town. Even so, something about their swarthiness and the shape of their helmets struck a chord with him. His grandfather had spoken of such men from his travels. *Zamora? Zingara?* It was someplace distant and exotic.

The riders slowed as they cut across his track. The leader

glanced toward the rock face, where the tracks ended, and shook his head. Then he studied Conan's back trail, but the forest and hills, with their deep drifts of snow, provided no easy passage for horsemen. With the wave of a hand and a harsh command, he started his men farther down the game trail that would, a mile or so farther north, cut across a road that led to the village.

Outrage, contempt, and fear warred in Conan's breast. That such men would dare come into Cimmeria infuriated him. They had to be very foolish, though a small part of him imagined they might have come north to settle some generational blood feud with his grandfather.

The way the lead rider studied the tracks and didn't even bother to glance up at the top of the cliff fortified Conan's suspicion that they were stupid. Sure, the size of his track, the length of his stride, suggested that he was still a boy, but to so casually imagine that a rock face could not be climbed was folly. *Steppes dwellers!* Conan spat disgustedly, then cut down and around off the hill. Though going back down the cliff face would be faster, if the horsemen returned, he'd be trapped.

He picked his way across the horsemen's back trail, stepping only in the tracks they'd left, then plunged through brush and cut slightly south. If he ran fast, if he encountered no trouble, he could reach the village before the horsemen and warn his father. Noting that he'd heard no blasts from the signal horns the other Cimmerians carried, he felt a surge of courage—not because he had a desire to be a hero, but because he did not want to leave his village unprotected.

At no point had it occurred to him that the riders might be innocent travelers. They'd had the look of hard men about them. They had no remounts or pack animals in tow, which meant they'd entrusted those things to others. They had to have known his tracks were fresh, yet they did not call out in a friendly manner. And the trail they rode branched off from the larger trade route to the south, which would have afforded them a direct and easy path to the village.

No, he was certain that they were part of something larger and, worse yet, imagined they were part of a cordon to make sure no one got away. His grandfather had talked about having had such duties, but had never said too much or anything good about them.

Conan burst from the woods, his lungs burning, aghast at the sight of his village.

Flaming arrows rose from the south, arcing down like falling stars. They landed among the southernmost huts, sticking deep in thatched roofs. The huts began to burn. The breeze swirled dark smoke through the rest of the village, washing it over the Cimmerian defensive lines.

And there, at the center, stood Corin, magnificent, the great sword he'd forged for his son held high. He directed the defenses, pointing men and women to their places in the lines. Conan instinctively understood what his father was doing and desperately wished he were at his side. A couple hundred yards of snowy fields separated him from the village, so he rose to sprint.

A loud metallic hiss to his right stopped him. Armored men in closed ranks were stepping from the forest. Aquilonians, surely, for Conan had seen their like before. The short swords they unsheathed in unison were not unlike the sword he bore. And their shields, tall ovals, were standard in Aquilonian legions, though he'd never seen the crest before. A human face, or so it appeared, with tentacles writhing around it—the very sight of the crest set Conan's flesh to crawling.

The Aquilonians began a measured march toward the

village. Two drummers paced behind them, hammering out a rhythm to which the soldiers marched. Conan's heart pounded double time to that beat, and he sprinted twice as fast, quickly outdistancing the Aquilonians.

Then trumpets blasted and horsemen broke from the wood lines, racing across the snowy fields. No lightly armed scouts these, but heavily armored cavalry, with horses encased in layers of steel armor. The warriors bore curved swords with heavy points, equally suited to slashing or stabbing. The warriors would have towered over Conan were they on foot, but in the saddle, they became juggernauts of destruction.

Hoofbeats thundered despite the muffling snow. Conan ducked and dodged to avoid being trampled beneath steel-shod hooves. He spun to the ground, escaping the last of them, ending on his knees, facing away from the village. He struggled to his feet and started to turn, but the center-most Aquilonian ranks parted as if they were a curtain, and a lone warrior came riding through.

It would have been easy to mistake him for one of the cavalry, for his horse had been similarly armored and his sheathed sword bore a resemblance to the scimitars the others carried. But something about him, about the way he sat tall in the saddle and studied the battlefield with a hawk's serene gaze, marked him as different. He, too, bore a shield with the tentacled mask on it, but less as a tool of war than as a proud emblem.

Conan didn't know who he was, but he knew he was dangerous. He spun and sprinted for the village, certain that if that man reached it, no one would be left alive.

The young Cimmerian warrior plunged headlong into the furious battle, hyperaware of everything going on around him. Sounds sorted themselves into the harsh din of metal-on-metal impact, or the wet crack of sword cleaving bone. The hiss of air from punctured lungs differed from the wet gush of entrails flowing from a slashed belly. Men shouted. Some gave orders, others begged for mercy. Words came in hard, guttural tongues and in the more familiar Cimmerian. Light flashed from blades, blood splashed red and filled the air with a tang that erased the scent of smoke.

Conan caught the first glimmer of the knowledge that would keep him alive: combat appeared to be chaotic, but, in fact, had an order and flow. Currents ran through it, strength channeled against weakness, and weakness ebbed until it could attack greater weakness. Lines surged and collapsed, voids opened and were filled. To move with the energies was to survive. To hesitate or defy them was to be drowned in a river of blood.

More arrows sped through the air, launched by female warriors. Conan grabbed the arm of an Aquilonian warrior and spun him around, using him as a shield. Three arrows thudded into his chest, but Conan slipped from beneath his falling body, then slashed another Aquilonian across the hamstrings, crippling him.

Hulking warriors whose skin was so dark it almost appeared purple, with round shields and long spears, rushed through the village, impaling victims. Before Conan could finish the Aquilonian, one of the Kushites knocked him to the ground. Conan leaned away from the thrust that should have pinned him to the earth, then stabbed up. His blade opened the man's belly and he ripped the sword free. Blood sprayed and the warrior fell, but Conan was already up and away.

He ran toward where he'd last seen his father, but the Cimmerian lines had been shattered. Arrow-stuck bodies lay everywhere. The black shafts had spared no one. Ardel lay curled up around one in his middle; his head connected to his body by a slender ribbon of flesh. His father, Ronan, lay not far away, impaled on a Kushite spear. A half dozen of the enemy lay at his feet. Elsewhere other Cimmerians lay, similarly surrounded by the enemy dead, but where the Cimmerians were only a village, the enemy seemed composed of nations.

The massacre would spare no one.

Look where he might, Conan could not find his father. He cut through the village, slashing and stabbing, too quick to be hit, too small to be followed, and too easily lost in the smoke to be hunted. A bloody-handed raider staggered from one hut, a red hand held high to display a necklace of copper beads. Conan slashed her knee, then took her head with the return stroke before he'd even noticed she was female. It mattered not to him. She was an enemy, he was a Cimmerian warrior, so no greater consideration of circumstances need be given.

He gained the smithy and felt relief, for the fires consuming the southern half of the village had not yet reached it. He slipped past the open doorway, seeing a number of figures inside, and made his way into the woodshed. He closed that door behind him and crossed to the smaller inside door by the forge. The crack between door and jamb gave him a perfect view of the interior.

What he saw made his gorge rise, but he kept the vomit down.

Corin stood within a circle of the enemy, his shoulders slumped with weariness. His father's clothes were soaked in blood. A black-shaft arrow had pierced the right shoulder. One of the archers, regal in her leather armor, smiled grimly, leading Conan to believe that her bow had sped that arrow. *For that I will kill you.*

The others gathered there likewise appeared to be leaders

of the various contingents that still swarmed over the village. A corpulent Aquilonian general with unkempt hair and armor remarkably clean of blood watched Corin with piggish eyes. Another man, even larger and clearly sharing bloodlines with the heavy cavalry, had supplemented his armor with a sheaf of chains. The Kushite chieftain carried a massive war club festooned with metal shards and sharpened bones. The last man bore facial tattoos that Conan could not recognize, yet would never forget, and studied Corin the way a cat studies a dying mouse.

And there, standing tall among them, was the man who had ridden through the Aquilonian ranks. Corin evinced no fear of him, but the others did. Conan smiled with pride for his father, but his blue eyes glittered with cold contempt for the others.

The leader, hand resting on the hilt of what appeared to be a double-bladed scimitar, paraded before Conan's father with the air of prince. "There is no shame in kneeling before Khalar Zym. All these fighters have surrendered, left their lands, and sworn their allegiance to me." The man inspected his fingernails, then picked up the Cimmerian great sword. "They've done so because they know I will one day be a god."

Corin's eyes narrowed. "God or not, one day you will fall."

The leader rolled his eyes, then with a wave of his hand summoned forth a robed figure from the shadows. The acolyte bore a mask that looked exactly like the crest on the invaders' shields, save that it was missing a piece. The brown-gold of aged bone, covered in a scaly flesh, the mask appeared unspeakably ancient and evil. Conan stared at it, entranced and revolted at the same time.

The bandit leader glanced at the mask, then smiled at its

reflection on the sword's blade. "You know, of course, what this is. The Mask of Acheron. One piece is yet missing. You have it here."

Corin's face betrayed nothing to the outsiders, but Conan could read his expression well enough to know that the bandit spoke the truth. This sent a jolt through him, for he knew of no mask, knew of no secret. Perhaps it was something known only to warriors, and so his father had not yet told him. That had to be it; there could be no other explanation. *It is the responsibility of which he spoke.*

The bandit chuckled. "I do have an appreciation for bravery, Cimmerian, but I have a great *need* for the last piece. You can give it to me now . . . or die, and I shall find it myself."

Corin smiled, his expression coming as much with ease as it did with defiance. "I prefer death."

The bandit leader nodded. "I thought you might. Lucius, to you goes this honor."

The Aquilonian general drew his short sword and approached, raising it to behead the smiling Cimmerian.

CHAPTER 8

CONAN BURST FROM the woodshed. The short sword came up in a sharp, vicious arc. It lopped Lucius's nose off. The Aquilonian stumbled back, hand rising to stem the bleeding.

Before the nose could hit the ground, Conan twisted and drove straight at Khalar Zym. The bandit leader whirled. The great sword came up, deflecting Conan's strike. Khalar Zym kicked the boy in the chest, sending him back into the arms of the bandit's Kushite confederate. Corin took a step toward Zym, but the large man in chains smashed him to his knees with a forearm shiver across the shoulder blades.

Khalar Zym turned away, his left hand coming up to his right ear. His fingers came away bloody. His eyes widened with shock, then he smiled. "Is that your son? He must be your son. I *like* him."

Conan snarled and almost pulled free. The tattooed man grabbed him as well.

"Much fire in that one, Cimmerian. You're clearly proud of him, as any father should be of a dutiful child."

Corin said nothing, and Conan followed his father's example.

"Alas, a child can sometimes be as much a heartache as a delight. Or a weakness."

Khalar Zym barked an order in a tongue Conan did not recognize, but that rasped like a file over his brain. The Aquilonian and the chained man wrestled Corin over to the forge and there bound him with chains. The larger man walked out into the village and returned with a bucket-size steel helmet, which he filled with scraps of iron. He looped chains around it and fastened another chain to Corin. He arced another chain over a rafter and prepared to hoist the helmet into air above Corin.

Khalar Zym waved the acolyte forward. The sorcerer reached out and traced a finger over a patch of helmet. A gold sigil writhed there for a moment, then died, but a glow grew from within the helmet itself. Conan watched aghast as with that simple gesture all the nightmare stories whispered around fires about magick became real.

The large bandit hoisted the helmet clumsily as the acolyte withdrew. A golden droplet of molten steel splashed down to burn Corin's thigh. The smith grit his teeth. The flesh tightened around his eyes, but he did not struggle or shift from beneath the helmet.

Khalar Zym shrugged. "You can cry out. I shall think no less of you."

Corin said nothing.

"As a smith, I thought you might appreciate what can be done with a whisper and magick. For you to make metal fluid, it would be hours with the bellows. For him, a caress. Just think of the power I would share with you when I become a god."

Corin snorted. "Cimmerians have no use for sorcery."

"Pity. You would profit by it." Khalar Zym frowned and looked at his subordinates. "Well? Find it!"

Lucius bowed his head. "Exalted one, it is not like finding the other shards. There is no temple, no sanctuary."

"Fool." Khalar Zym pointed around him with the great sword. "Cimmerians do not pray. They have neither priests nor preachers. This, here, this place of fire and steel, this is what matters to them. This is their church. It will be here."

Khalar Zym's subordinates, save for the Kushite who knelt on Conan to restrain him, searched the smithy. Though not terribly active in their search, they checked all the places where one could expect to find something that, if Conan figured correctly, could have fit easily inside his clenched fist. *Father hid it well. They will never find it, and he will never reveal its location.*

Father and son looked at each other in that moment, in silent agreement. They were Cimmerians. No matter the pain, no matter the torture, they would say nothing. Khalar Zym would never let them live, and a life granted because of surrender to a tyrant would not have been worth living. Conan could not give the secret up, and with a nod he let his father know he would happily die beside him to protect it.

The tattooed man sank on bended knee before Khalar Zym. "The bone shard is not here."

"Can you do nothing right?" Khalar Zym inspected his ear again. The bleeding had stopped and he nodded. He turned to Corin. "Your son has courage and talent. He is so like my daughter."

The bandit looked toward the smithy's corner. "Marique, I have need of you."

A small slender girl in a long, shimmering purple cloak of fine fabric emerged from the shadowed corner where she had waited, silent and unseen. Because her father had likened them one to the other, Conan stared at her. A shiver ran down his spine. Though she appeared to be only a year or two older than he, her eyes stared off into the distance as if she were remembering, or seeing, an entirely different scene than the one that was happening around her. Her hair had been gathered into a mass of dark braids, save for bangs that barely hid her forehead. Her flesh had a corpselike pallor. It surprised Conan that she did not stink of the grave.

"Yes, Father?"

Khalar Zym smiled. "These fools tell me the shard is not here."

"They just don't know *how* to look."

Her father smiled. "Will you find it for me, Marique?"

The girl bowed her head obediently. "As you desire."

One hand emerged from beneath her scaly purple cloak. Silver talons sheathed her fingers. She waved them through the air as if plucking the strings of an invisible lyre. Something thrummed through Conan's chest. The Kushite's weight shifted, not enough to free him, but enough to let the boy know that the black giant had felt it as well.

The others drew back as the girl began to circle the smithy. Her path spiraled outward, her dark cloak swirling about her. Although she did not move swiftly, her movements were quite deliberate. She cocked her head as if she were listening for something. She must have heard it because the pattern of her movements shifted, narrowing, leading her to a shadowed corner.

"There, Father, I have it."

She gestured casually and a wooden plank peeled back as if a leather flap. She reached down into the dark recess and removed a golden box. Bearing it in both hands, she approached her father. On bended knee, with her head bowed, she raised the box to him.

Khalar Zym set his great sword down and reached for the box with trembling hands. He removed the lid and stared. His eyes glistened. His mouth hung open for a heartbeat. He grasped the thing in the box and raised it up with the gentle reverence of a father holding his child for the first time.

"You have served me well, daughter. Your mother would be proud."

The girl's head remained bowed, but she smiled most contentedly.

Khalar Zym rubbed a thumb over the fragment of bone lovingly, then his eyes narrowed and his visage became cruel. "Oh, Cimmerian, you could have saved me much trouble. As I would have given you glory, so shall I now give you pain. But how? Oh, yes, yes . . ."

He gazed at his daughter. "Marique, would you like a brother? We can take this Cimmerian, bend him to our will."

The girl shot Conan a venomous glance, then smiled up at her father. "As you wish."

"My lord, you cannot." Lucius shook his head, a bloody cloth held to his face.

" 'Cannot,' Lucius? Did you say I *cannot* do something?"

The large man blanched. "No, my lord, I meant . . ." The Aquilonian drew his short sword. "I meant that I hoped you would give me the honor of dispatching this barbarian."

"While that might give you satisfaction, Lucius, it will do nothing to give my Cimmerian friend pain." Khalar Zym tapped the bit of mask against his chin. "No, I know what we shall do. Remo, Akhoun, more chains. The rest of you, gather the men, fire the rest of the village."

At Khalar Zym's instruction, his henchmen attached another chain to the helmet and looped it over a rafter. This they placed in Conan's hands in the middle of the forge floor, while they hung a counterbalance above his father's head. The boy hung on tightly. The first quiver of his arms had sent a droplet of burning metal sizzling into his father's shoulder.

Khalar Zym crouched beside Corin. "This is the only way which I may punish you, Cimmerian. You do not cry out with pain. You fear no insult to honor. The worst I can do to you is to let you watch your son die trying to save you. And we both know, you and I, as fathers, that is precisely what shall happen."

Zym stood and led his men from the forge. Torches thrown on the roof and laid against the walls from outside started fires that greedily consumed the building. Marique lingered, studying the great sword. She smiled at her reflection in its blade, then picked it up. She hesitated, and in the reflection her eyes met Conan's.

She spun, watching him warily. "It is a good thing you die here, Cimmerian. Were you to live, you would prove troublesome." She gazed after her father, then strode quickly to Conan's side and licked sweat and blood from his cheek. Her voice became a whisper. "Not that this might prove wholly unwelcome, but we shall never know."

In a swirl of cape she departed. From outside, men cheered their great victory, but the rising crackle of flames swallowed all sound of their retreat.

Corin met his son's gaze. Though collared and chained to the helmet, begrimed, bloody, and exhausted, he did not look defeated. "Conan, you cannot save me. Save yourself."

Already the chain had begun to get hot, but the boy shook his head. "A Cimmerian warrior does not fear death."

"Nor does he rush foolishly to embrace it." Corin raised a hand to the chain on his collar. "Let go of the chain, boy."

"I'm not afraid to die." A fiery coal fell from the ceiling, burning Conan's cheek. It smarted fiercely, but to brush it away would be to doom his father. Conan snarled against the pain, but held on.

"Conan, *look at me.*"

The boy looked up into his father's eyes. "Your mother . . . she wanted more for you in this life than fire and blood. As do I." Corin's grip tightened on his chain. "I love you, son."

Corin yanked and his body fell. The chain ripped free of Conan's grasp. Molten metal poured down over the smith, outlining his features in red-gold as the forge's light had often done, then liquified them.

Conan darted toward his father, but the blast of heat from the metal drove him back. A rafter cracked, cutting him off. The heat forced him to the doorway. The boy stumbled through, expecting a spear thrust or an arrow. He tumbled into a snowbank, burying his face and hands. The snow cooled his seared flesh but could do nothing to erase the image of his father's death.

The boy rolled over and looked at his blistered hands. Each link had left its mark on his flesh. He tried to remember his father's hands, so big, so callused, and yet so gentle when circumstance required. Already that memory had begun to fade within the liquid metal pool that had consumed his father. Conan pressed his hands into the snow again and waited for numbness to swallow the pain.

He had no idea how long he lay there. Though he did not fear death, in that moment he was not so certain that he was fond of living. He knew that if Crom meant him to live, he would live—the courage and strength to do so would have been born in him. But there, with the forge burning and the stink of roasting flesh filling the gray smoke, Conan saw little reason to move.

Then he heard something. Not a random sound like fire's crackle or the hiss of bubbling water. A voice. A voice free from pain and full of joy. In this place, at this time, that could herald only one thing.

Conan rolled to his feet and looked about warily. There, through a swirl of smoke, he saw two things. A raider, one of the heavy cavalry, kneeling over the body of a woman. He grabbed a double handful of her hair and pulled back, stretching her throat and opening her mouth in a silent scream. Then he pressed the edge of his sword to her hairline and, in one swift stroke, harvested her scalp.

And, halfway between the raider and Conan, a Cimmerian sword had been stabbed into a snowbank, forgotten.

Swiftly and silently, fluidly, the last Cimmerian warrior ran forward. He grasped the sword's hilt with his left hand, mindless of the pain of bursting blisters. He splashed through a puddle of snowmelt that he could have run around, because he wanted the raider to know he was coming.

The man heard the sound and half turned toward it. His right hand came up to ward off the sword, but Conan's first cut separated wrist from arm. Before the raider could scream, a second blow dented his helmet. He sagged to the side, dazed, and stared up.

Conan buried the sword in his throat and watched the light flow out of his eyes.

Conan sat down beside the dead raider and looked at the burning village. The boy he had been that morning would not have wanted to cry, but could never have held back the tears. The man he had become understood the desire to weep, but could never let him give in to weakness. Crom cared not for the lamentations of mortals, and Conan, determined to be make Marique's comment into a prophecy, had no time to mourn.

As night came on and the warmth of fires faded, he freed the sword from the raider's throat, took a knife from his body, scavenged meager supplies, and set off to find his grandfather.

CHAPTER 9

CONAN AWOKE WITH a start. He couldn't feel his hands. He pulled them from beneath the heavy aurochs skin that was all but smothering him. They'd become as large as hams, or at least the cloth wrapping them was. And when he tried to tense his fingers, he couldn't move them much, but something inside the cloth squished and a noxious scent poured out.

A stick clacked against the foot of the bed. "Boy, if you pull those poultices apart again, I *will* let your hands rot off."

He looked and could only see a silhouette moving through the hut's darkened interior. Still, there was no mistaking the voice. "Grandfather?" Conan meant to ask the question forcefully—befitting a warrior—but it came out as a croak, and a weak one at that.

"No *other* fool would take you in, Conan." The old man stirred coals in the hearth, then tossed on more wood. A little blaze began to flare. Connacht, leaning heavily on the stick, walked to the bedside and peered down at the boy. He placed a hand on his forehead. "Good. I think the fever's broken. Death wanted you, boy, but we cheated him, we did."

"Water?"

The old man helped Conan sit up and drink. He didn't let the boy have too much, or drink it quickly. With his bandaged hands he couldn't have managed the cup anyway, so Conan drank at the dictated pace. He nodded when done.

"How long?"

"A week, though now's the first you're right in the head." Connacht shook his head. "Came in fevered. Burns on your hands all infected. Had the blood poison. Lucky for you I remembered what a Shemite healer did for me once. Had to use bear fat instead of goat. Smells worse, seems to work the same."

Conan stared at his hands as they lay like lifeless lumps in his lap. "A week?"

"Came crashing through the bush wild-eyed and burning up."

My father burned up . . .

"Weren't in your right mind. Went for me with your sword, you did."

Conan's eyes widened. "I didn't . . . ?"

"Hurt me?" Connacht laughed. "You were too weak to break an egg with a hammer, boy. How in the name of Crom did you get here?"

Conan closed his eyes. *Is my father really dead? Are they all dead?*

"Conan?"

The young Cimmerian shook himself. "Raiders destroyed the village. I was the only one who survived."

Connacht's face became graven. "I know you didn't run, boy."

"I wasn't a coward, Grandfather. But . . ." Conan's throat closed.

Connacht poured more water. Conan drank, both because he was thirsty and to soften the lump in his throat. Yet even when his grandfather took the cup away, he couldn't say anything.

The old man nodded slowly. "Seen a lot of people die. Many of them friends. Had more than one in my arms, just talking to him, easing the passage. Never an easy thing."

Conan shook his head.

"My son?"

"I . . . I tried to save him."

"And he wanted you to live."

Conan nodded.

"You think he was wrong? You think he was stupid?"

The young Cimmerian looked up horrified. "No."

"If there weren't no saving him, and there was a chance of saving you, he did right." Connacht scratched at his throat. "Like as not, you won't see that, but it's true."

"I killed some of them, Grandfather." Conan remembered the last raider. "One was a big man, cavalry. He was taking a scalp. I took his knife."

The old man crossed to where a belt hung on the wall and drew the dagger from its sheath. "Turanian. Long way from home."

"Kushites, too, and Aquilonians. And female archers."

"Easy, son. Excite yourself and the fever will come back." Connacht's eyes narrowed. "All those people this far north. Taller tale than I've ever told."

Conan snarled. "I'm not lying."

"Didn't say you were."

"They wanted something. A piece of a mask. Ashuran, I think. Is there such a place?"

Connacht returned to the stool by the bed. "Not Ashuran. Acheron, maybe, but it's long-ago gone. Thousands of years."

"They found it. They found what they wanted."

"Who?"

Conan frowned. "Klarzin. He has a daughter, Marique. And there is an Aquilonian named Lucius."

Connacht laughed. "There's hundreds of Aquilonians named Lucius, boy."

"This one has no nose."

"Don't know that narrows it down much."

"I took his nose. Cut it right off."

"Did you, now?" His grandfather nodded solemnly. "Taking the nose off an Aquilonian makes any day a *good* day."

Conan smiled, then remembered why it had been so terrible a day. He shivered and sank down again in the bed.

His grandfather brushed a lock of black hair from his forehead. "You've told me enough for now. You'll be telling me the rest later. We'll figure it all out."

"Good." Conan stared at his hands. "When we do, I'm going to kill them all."

CONNACHT REPACKED THE poultices over the next week and a half, and Conan didn't fight him. He didn't have the strength. The boy wanted to be up and tracking his enemies, but it was all he could do to throw off the auroch hide and sit up when his grandfather brought him broth. After several days of that, the old man switched him to stew.

Aside from eating, all Conan could do was sleep. Sometimes nightmares had him crying out in the middle of the night, but Connacht was always there by his side. He'd listen to Conan, then tell him a story. Not quite the same stories he used to tell during his visits to the village—these were a bit more gentle—but the sound of his voice was enough to allow Conan to drift back into sleep.

A couple of times Conan woke up during the day, and on one of those occasions, he thought he heard his grandfather talking to someone outside the hut. Later that afternoon he asked if he'd been right.

Connacht nodded. "Aiden came up from the south to tell me your village is gone. The tribes had some skirmishes with your horde. They backtracked to the village. They burned all the bodies, hauled what they could away. They brought me some things of your father's; said they didn't find you among the dead."

"Did you tell them I was alive?"

"He didn't ask, but likely knew. No matter. No one else will."

"Good. They won't expect me."

"Conan, you are not even certain who they are."

"How many march under the crest of the tentacled mask?"

"None."

Conan frowned. "What?"

"I have traveled the lands, Conan. No nation bears such a crest."

"What of this Acheron?"

Connacht brought his grandson a bowl of stew and loosened enough of the bandages to slip the poultice out, but left enough to cover the burns. "Feed yourself and I'll tell you of Acheron."

"You've been there?"

The older man laughed. "I'm not that old, Conan. Acheron fell in ancient days, before there was a Cimmeria. It was an evil place, so they say. Swing a dead cat, you'd hit a necromancer or three. Put four of them in a hut together and you'd have a dozen plots hatched. An evil people wanting to take over the world. So they went and concentrated and made this thing of power. A mask. And they gave it to their god-king or whatever they called him. He and his hordes cut a swath . . . well, from what you and Aidan said, you know. But imagine kingdoms falling, Conan. Nations just wiped from the face of creation."

The boy nodded, watching his grandfather's face for any hint of a lie. He spooned stew into his mouth, chewing unconsciously, wiping the spillage on the back of his hand.

"As the tales would have it, men from the north took exception to the rise of Acheron. Was a close thing, but armies from across the world banded together, and led by northerners, they shattered Acheron's power. They took the mask and broke it into parts. Each contingent got one and hid it away. They hoped no one would ever be able to assemble it and create such misery again."

Conan crunched a piece of gristle. "How could anyone know of the mask?"

"You'll find, boy, that there are always people nosing about in places they shouldn't, learning things not meant to be learned, and then developing quite a problem keeping their mouths shut." The old man grew silent for a moment, then grunted. "You'll run afoul of a number of them in your life."

Conan's spoon froze halfway to his mouth. "Are you now a seer?"

"No, I just benefit from having seen much." Connacht shook his head. "People seek power, and there are some who hunt for Acheron's secrets. Your Klarzin might be one. Have to hope if he's up to deviltry, the devils will take him before he can shed more blood."

"Not devils he has to worry about." Conan handed the empty bowl to his grandfather. "More, please. And a favor."

Connacht returned from the hearth with more stew. "I'm your grandfather. What would you be having me do?"

Conan took a deep breath. "I cannot go and kill Klarzin."

"Now you've returned to your senses."

"I need your help. My father taught me much. You taught him more. I need to know it all."

Connacht raised an eyebrow. "Even knowing all I taught him didn't keep your father alive."

"If you will not teach me, I will find another sword-master."

The old man thought for a moment. "There is no dissuading you?"

"I will have my vengeance."

"You'll do everything I say, as I tell you to do it?"

Conan sighed, hearing his father's words come out of his grandfather's mouth. "Exactly."

"Very well. In another week we'll begin." Connacht stood. "Finish your stew, then sleep. Sleep as much as you can. When you become my student, you'll have no time at all for that nonsense."

Had Conan entertained the thought that his grandfather was joking, the old man disabused him of the notion immediately. He established a routine that had Conan waking before dawn, crawling into bed well into the evening, and if the boy stood still at all, it would only be during some odd exercise to build strength or maintain balance. Very little of his training actually included holding a sword in hand, which irked the boy until he figured out what his grandfather was doing.

For the first two weeks, things focused on his getting his strength and endurance back, as well as keeping his hands healthy. Conan had always been slender, but his illness had reduced him to skin and bones. Connacht had him hauling water, shifting stones, running ever-longer distances, then having him sprint—all the while increasing his weight by adding rock-filled pouches or bits and pieces of old armor to his attire.

The greatest care was lavished on Conan's hands. The blisters had long since burst and the infection had been defeated. His grandfather mixed up a foul-smelling unguent out of fish meat, bear grease, and a variety of dried roots and leaves, then had the boy work it into his palms. Conan continued to wrap his hands and don gloves for anything involving lifting. Connacht also forced him to flex his hands hundreds of times throughout the day.

"You'll always carry scars from that day, Conan, but you can't be crippled by them."

The combat drills Conan hungered for came at last, but not in the way he'd been expecting. His grandfather still wouldn't let him touch a sword. "Sword's just a metal sting. A warrior's weapon is his body. Can't use that, doesn't matter how sharp the sword."

The old man then proceeded to teach his grandson every aspect of infighting that he'd learned from a lifetime of adventuring and brawling—and Conan suspected that he made up a few on the spot. Connacht, despite being four times his grandson's age, tossed him around as if he were a raggedy doll. Conan vaguely remembered having accused his father of not fighting fairly, but Corin had been the soul of sportsmanship compared to his father. Kicks, punches, head butts, and elbow strikes knocked Conan all over the yard before the hut.

Connacht even bit him once!

Conan would have protested, but he remembered Klarzin parrying his sword cut, then kicking him full in the chest.

Corin had been right. Fighters might talk about fighting fairly, but in their storytelling they left out certain details. He couldn't remember a single of his grandfather's stories that included his having bitten anyone, but the old man was a bit too practiced at it to even suggest that it had never happened.

Conan gave back as much as he could, and occasionally landed a fist or a kick on his grandfather. He never hurt him, though, but not because he pulled his punches. Connacht still moved quickly enough to slip most blows, and certainly knew enough to anticipate Conan's next moves. Still, as the weeks wore on, Conan's hits became more consistent than misses, and his ability to block attacks improved greatly.

One day Connacht called a sudden halt to their fighting. "Good. You've learned well."

Conan, doubled over, catching his breath, glanced up. "Is this how you taught my father?"

"Corin, the size of him? No. I had a different way with him." The old man straightened up. "I want you to haul twenty buckets of water from the river to fill the cistern, then I have one more thing for you. Accomplish that task, and tomorrow we begin working with a sword."

Conan smiled and ran off. The sooner he perfected his sword fighting, the sooner he'd be able to avenge his village. While thoughts of revenge filled his mind, he hauled water and saw nothing of his grandfather. He did hear some pounding from within the hut, but attached no significance to it.

Finally the cistern brimmed over and Conan returned the buckets to their place near the small forge his grandfather maintained. The young Cimmerian stepped into the hut and found his grandfather sitting by the hearth. The meager furnishings had been cleared out of the center. An iron plate had been bolted to the floor and four feet of heavy chain attached to it. The chain ended in an iron shackle.

Connacht nodded to it. "Put your right ankle in there. Lock it shut."

The young man sat on the floor and secured the shackle around his ankle.

His grandfather got up, took Conan's sword from where it hung on the wall, and stood beside the doorway. "You're a good fighter, Conan. You learn quickly. You're determined to go after Klarzin, aren't you?"

Conan nodded.

"There's nothing anyone could do to stop you, is there?"

The boy shook his head.

Connacht tossed Conan's sword out into the yard. "Go get your sword. When you get it, you'll be ready to get Klarzin."

CHAPTER 10

CONAN STARED AT his grandfather, waiting for an explanation.

Connacht walked out the doorway and let the hide flap slide across to eclipse the sun.

The young Cimmerian shook his leg. The heavy chain dragged at the shackle, digging into his ankle and grinding against bone. He grabbed the chain and tugged, hard, but it didn't give at all. More importantly, the short chain didn't allow him to move to where he could brace himself against something to use his legs in trying to pull free. The best he could do was to lay a foot on the eyebolt sunk into the middle of the plate, but unless he could snap the chain, that effort would be useless. And without some leverage, actually ripping the plate out of the floor wouldn't work.

On hands and knees he crawled over and looked at the plate, chain, and eyebolt. All were solid steel and without being softened in the forge's fire, they'd resist his efforts to break them. He examined each link in the chain, but could find no weak ones. He rubbed a link against the plate's edge, but his grandfather had rounded off the edge, so wearing a link down would take days.

Even the shackle was stout enough to frustrate his attempts to pry it open. He had nothing with which he could force the lock. Conan instantly understood the desire of a trapped fox to gnaw its own foot off to escape a trap. Not only was he not flexible enough to do that, he had no desire to cripple himself.

There has to be a trick to it. Conan's icy eyes narrowed. *No, if my father had done this, there would have been a clever way out. Not so Connacht.*

The boy yanked at the chain, then howled in frustration. He whipped the chain back and forth, hoping some hidden weakness would shear the bolt off, but no such luck. He wrapped the chain around the eyebolt and yanked, hoping to bend it. It resisted his best efforts. In no time he sat in a puddle of his own sweat, no closer to freedom than he'd been before.

Snarling, he pounded the chain against the floorboards and made some headway. He peeled away wood, biting out the splinters that lodged beneath his fingernails. He tore at the wood, hoping to rip the whole plate free. As he dug down, however, he discovered that his grandfather had secured it around one of the floor's crossbeams.

Even this fact did not discourage Conan. He continued to rip away wood, hoping that he could loosen things enough that he could rotate the plate around the crossbeam. That would loop the chain around the crossbeam, and he could then haul back on it to use the chain to saw through the crossbeam. Large heavy links and seasoned hardwood would make the job difficult, but he'd get through.

Then he learned that his grandfather had bolted the plate to the crossbeam on the underside, which made the plate immobile and his plan irrelevant.

The boy tossed pieces of wood at the hide flap. He wanted to provoke a reaction from his grandfather. A laugh at his predicament, a curse at the destruction he was causing, a reproving stare and a comment he could think on. Anything. But all he got in return was silence. It was as if he was completely alone in the world.

That thought flushed frigid fear through his belly. What if he *was* alone. What if Klarzin had tracked him to his grandfather's hut and sent an assassin after him? What if Lucius No Nose was coming to finish what Klarzin hadn't let him do at the village? Conan grasped a piece of wood with a pointed end because he refused to think of himself as helpless, but with four feet of chain hobbling him, he'd be slaughtered, weapon or no weapon, in a heartbeat.

He moved around to the far side of the plate, let the chain play out, and sat with his shoulders and head against the wall, watching the doorway. The rattle of chains reminded him of Klarzin's allies, and of the chain he'd failed to hold on to back at the village. He looked at his hands, the scars visible but the flesh pliable. There he sat, trapped by chains as his father had been, as vulnerable as his father had been, and the last seconds of his father's life played through his mind over and over again.

At some point the sun sank below the horizon, leaving Conan in perfect darkness. His stomach growled but he couldn't get anywhere near his grandfather's larder. He heard nothing of the old man and the sounds he usually associated with the coming of night in the forest remained elusive and distant.

He grabbed the chain and smashed it against the floor

several times, relishing the din. He pulled at it some more, then slumped onto his side and curled up around his empty belly to sleep.

He awoke in the middle of the night and looked around, but nothing had changed. His grandfather had not slipped into the hut to take his bunk. He'd not brought the boy a sleeping hide, or water, or any sort of food. Conan rubbed his hands together, as he might have done to work his grandfather's salve into the scars. He grabbed the chain, intent on yanking it, but saw the futility of this and stopped. He let the chain slip from his hands and fell back to sleep.

He awoke with the dawn and found a bowl of water within reach at the far side of the chain's range. He leaped toward it, crouching, then watched, wary. The door flap had been pulled back. He imagined his grandfather waiting for him to begin drinking before he sprang in and beat him with a stick. *Or maybe the water is not good water, and will make me sick.* He waited, watchful, but burning thirst convinced him to hook the bowl with a finger and pull it within reach. He retreated to the hut's rear wall and drank carefully. He made sure no water slopped down his chest.

Before he knew it, the water was gone.

He thought about smashing the bowl or hurling it out the doorway, but he didn't give in to the impulse. His grandfather might not give him another bowl. Instead he placed it back on the spot where he'd found it, then returned to where he'd slept. He shook his bound leg a couple of times, but the chain had become no less strong, and he'd become weaker. He didn't intend to doze, but he did, and awoke to see his grandfather sitting on a stool just inside the doorway.

"Do you want to be free, boy?"

Conan nodded.

"I don't mean free of the chain."

The young Cimmerian frowned. "What?"

Connacht pointed at the chain. "That chain is revenge. It's Klarzin. If your goal is to become the man who can destroy him, you might succeed. But he *will* destroy your life. Because the man who could defeat him needs to be the man who will learn to fight out in my yard there. The boy who remains trapped will never be that man."

"But he killed my father. He killed *your son*."

Connacht nodded. "I know. Blood calls for blood. But blood feuds never solve anything. You know why I live here, in the north, away from others, even though I'm from the tribes of the south, yes?"

Conan shook his head.

"A blood feud. Spirits, a spirited girl, and hot words led to blood flowing. I killed a few more of those who wanted revenge, but they would never stop coming. So I walked away."

"But Klarzin is not a Cimmerian. It won't be like killing one of our own."

"But all you will become is the man who knows how to kill Klarzin, which means you have no use after you've done that." His grandfather shook his head. "Since you were born, we knew you were destined for great things. I'd rather see you die here of starvation, chained to the floor, than for you to hobble yourself because of some idea that you will avenge your father. It won't bring him back. It won't bring any of them back. It won't even make them feel better about dying. And you will have wasted your life."

Conan's chin came up defiantly. "So the man who killed my father and destroyed my village is allowed to live as if he did nothing?"

"You haven't listened to me." The old man glanced out toward the yard. "I told you, out there you will learn what it takes to kill this man. You will learn what it takes to kill *any* man—which makes you very useful. And in the big world, you will see many wonders, and have many adventures, that will make you forget Klarzin. Imagine that instead of him and his horde, it had been an avalanche that wiped out your village while you were hunting. Would you go to war against it? Would you look to slay avalanches or mountains?"

"I will never forget him."

"And you would never forget the avalanche, but you wouldn't spend your life hunting avalanches. You would learn to spot them, you would learn to deal with them, to survive them. You would make sure that an avalanche would never hurt you again. If you could, you would act to stop an avalanche from hurting others. But vengeance? Life is too vast to allow it to be focused on so tiny a thing. You want to live, to slay, to love; these are what you want, not to hunt down a single man who likely has no more memory of you and your village than you do of the first snowflake you ever caught on your tongue."

Conan snarled and kicked out. The chain rattled, but the weight and the grinding against his anklebones underscored the reality of his grandfather's words. As much as he wanted to dismiss them as nonsense, the chain reminded him of how limited his goal really was.

"What if I find him, Grandfather? What if our paths cross?"

The old man smiled venomously. "Then the man who killed my son will admire the training I gave my grandson. Klarzin's life will splash in red rivers from his rent body. You'll kill his demon-spawn daughter, too . . . and the world will be better for it. To be able to make that all happen, Conan, you will have to learn some lessons. Very important lessons."

The boy frowned. *I want Klarzin dead, but I am not yet the man who can kill him.* He nodded slowly.

Connacht stood. "That decision is the first you've made as a man."

Conan looked up. "How does a man get out of a shackle?"

His grandfather laughed. "Depends on the shackle. Been caught by a few myself, never cared for it, especially when taken by slavers." The old man tossed him a fist-size rock. "Now, that shackle there lets a tongue slide into the lock and catch in place. The key pulls the latch back."

The boy looked at the rock. "This is not a key."

"But the trick of this kind of shackle is that a small spring holds the latch in place. A sharp blow, right there beside the keyhole . . ."

Conan scooted forward, pulled his ankle in, and hit the shackle where his grandfather indicated. It took three tries before the shackle slipped a little, and two more before it gave enough to free his foot.

Connacht applauded. "If they do your wrists up with them, just slamming one shackle into the other usually works to have you out of them quickly."

The youth smiled. "So, I have learned my first lesson."

"No, Conan, that's your second lesson."

The boy frowned. "Then what is the . . . Oh." He smiled. "Never stick yourself in a situation unless you know how you're going to get out of it."

"Very good, though I expect you'll need to be reminded of that lesson from time to time." Connacht stroked his own unshaven chin. "And there are more shackles I'll teach you to escape from. I suspect you'll find that information useful."

Steadying himself against the wall, Conan stood. "Fine. I will learn everything you would teach me. But please, out in the yard." He brushed the chain aside with a foot. "I am done with children's games."

CHAPTER 11

IN THE THREE years Conan lived with his grandfather, the name *Klarzin* almost faded completely from his memory. The horrific acts that destroyed his village and slew his father did not. Sometimes they came back to him unbidden but consciously; in dreams and nightmares more often. The latter occurrences enhanced the surreal quality of that day and softened the sharpest of the memories. Had it not been for the traces of chain scars on his hands, he might have forgotten most all of it.

Connacht did not give the boy time to remember much of anything. He worked Conan hard, both because he was proud of his grandson, and because he felt guilty about Corin's death, guilty that his son had been slain by outsiders. He'd centered the blame on Lucius, the Aquilonian, only because Aquilonians were familiar enemies, and because of Aquilonia's proximity, the chances of avenging Corin were far greater.

Being men and Cimmerians, neither Conan nor Connacht spoke of their feelings, dreams, or fears. They would have denied having any of the latter, and barely acknowledged the existence of the others. Still, in the way Connacht watched him, Conan recognized his own father's love, and assumed his grandfather saw the same emotion in him. Connacht's guilt would flare up when the boy failed to grasp a lesson. When that happened, the old man would push and push until the boy mastered whatever skill his grandfather was teaching, at which point another lesson would begin.

For another boy, this existence with a grandfather whom others shunned would have been a lonely one. Connacht's swift punishments for failure would have had others howling in pain, or vowing to run or seek revenge. For Conan, these were not options simply because someone born on a battle-field would never run, and a Cimmerian would not acknowl-edge pain. Stripped of the family and life he had known, Conan redefined himself as the man of destiny others had supposed him to be. If he failed, their hopes and expecta-tions would be invalidated. His father and mother's wishes would never be realized. Conan, though given to the occa-sional bout of melancholy, did not dwell overlong on things introspective and instead occupied himself learning all he could of the killing arts.

In Connacht he had a willing and a superior teacher. Connacht the Freebooter, the Far-Traveled, had been isolated because of his past. In training his grandson, he could guar-antee two things. First, his bloodline would not be extin-guished easily. Second, those who had forgotten who and what he had been would learn the truth through his grand-son's exploits. While even the most casual of observers could have seen that Conan would be a great Cimmerian warrior, Connacht intended him to be the *greatest* Cimmerian warrior. He would be the man against whom all others would be measured.

More than once Connacht had told him that. The admission came late at night, when his grandfather finished some tale of how he'd escaped slavers or survived a battle. Conan would stare at him, wide-eyed, with the admiration and love that rewards all the trials of parenthood, and mutter, "Someday, Grandfather, I shall be as you were."

"No, Conan, you will be greater. Men once remembered me as a Cimmerian. They will remember you as *the* Cimmerian."

To Conan, that idea seemed, at first, ridiculous. And then, later on, it became a goal. It became fused with the destiny that had been thrust on him by his birth on a battlefield and by his parents' desire that he know more than fire and blood. If he were to be *the* Cimmerian, he would have to do more than just be a warrior. He didn't know exactly what that meant, but he was determined to find out.

And in his fourth summer with his grandfather, just after he turned fifteen, he gained his first opportunity to become *the* Cimmerian.

THE AQUILONIANS HAD long coveted Cimmerian territory. With every generation, they conspired to steal as much as they could. They pushed into Cimmeria and established the hunting outpost known as Venarium. During the years when it had been little more than a trading post, the Cimmerians had tolerated it. When troops invested it, when stone walls replaced the wooden ones, and when punitive raiders sallied forth from its confines to hunt down Cimmerians who had gone raiding . . . then it became an open sore and could no longer be tolerated.

Cimmerian elders gathered and conferred. They summoned the tribes and clans. They even sent word to isolated villages and single homesteads, suggesting that all had been forgiven and that any animosities must be forgotten in the face of this greater threat to Cimmeria. So it was that Conan and Connacht left the homestead, and went to join the others in an encampment northeast of the Aquilonian settlement.

Conan had never much been given to considering how he had changed since coming to live with his grandfather. He measured his growth not in pounds or inches, but in skills mastered. Yet the way the other men looked at him, and the shock when they learned he was only fifteen years old, left no doubt that he had changed physically. Though he'd not yet attained his full height or weight, he'd gone from being a boy to a six-foot-tall man, lean as a wolf but well muscled, tipping the scales at over a hundred and eighty pounds. A few men said they could see his father in him, and this made him proud. He never smiled, however, and kept his own counsel, for, as both Corin and Connacht had told him, " 'Tis better to be thought a fool than to open your mouth and remove all doubt of it."

While excited to be in the warrior camp, Conan also wanted to get far away from it. Though he was not the youngest there, the other youths had been grouped into support companies. They would be held in reserve, and went through daily drills to prepare them. Everyone knew that if the battle went so badly that the youngest warriors were called upon to fight, they would die. But such was Conan's size and so well developed were his skills that he did not fit with his peers.

The companies of adult men wanted even less to do with him. While all was supposed to be forgiven, the southern tribesmen—whose coloration matched Conan's most

closely—were clearly wary of Connacht and anyone connected to him. The northern tribes seemed reluctant to trust
Conan, both because he appeared to be a southerner *and*
because of his youth.

He and his grandfather fell in with a motley collection
of warriors that the others referred to as the "Outlanders."
While none of them knew Connacht, they knew of him. Like
him, they had ventured well beyond the borders of Cimmeria. Their adventures had taken them to the same faraway
places that Connacht's had taken him. As Elders plotted and
planned, the Outlanders shared stories. They bonded as men
do who have known the same hardships—and as men do
who are destined for more hardships. Not a one of them
doubted that the Elders would form them into their own
company and throw them into the most savage of the
fighting—less because they valued them as warriors than
because their loss would hurt the tribes the least.

Kiernan, the closest of the Outlanders in age to Conan,
was a decade his senior. Though not nearly as tall as Conan,
he had a whiplash quickness matched only by the swiftness
with which he delivered wry comments. He carried a bow—
an affectation he adopted while serving as a Shemite
mercenary—and invited Conan along with him to take a
look at Venarium before the tribes marched.

The two of them slipped over the ridgeline and found
cover high above the valley in which Venarium had been
built. The valley broadened toward the south. The river splitting it would eventually flow into the Shirki and water Aquilonia's central plains. Already forests had been cleared
around the settlement and fields planted with more than
enough wheat and hay to sustain Venarium.

Though Connacht had taken great care in describing the
cities of the south, his stories had not prepared Conan for

his first view of Venarium. The trading settlements he'd visited before had been little more than villages, but Venarium towered above the plains. Stone walls girded it and a switchback causeway led up to the main gate. An inner set of walls warded a fortress at the town's pinnacle, and the high tower, from which flew a half-dozen pennants, commanded a view of the entire valley.

Kiernan pointed toward the fortress. "See there, Conan, how the fort's gate faces south, but the main gate faces east?"

The youth nodded.

"That's so when we breach the main gate, we have to fight our way along and around to the south. The gutters will run with Cimmerian blood."

"And Aquilonian."

"True enough." The smaller warrior ran a hand over his chin. "The Elders will be wanting the Aquilonians to come out and fight like men, but they won't. So we'll prove how brave we are by beating on their doors while they shoot us full of arrows or boil us in oil."

"Connacht has told of siege machines."

"Oh, aye, there are such." Kiernan smiled. "Like as not, we'll soon be chopping wood and lashing things together to form a few, but getting them close enough to work is the trick. On the walls there, on top of the towers, they have their own catapults and onagers. Behind the walls they have trebuchets. All of them will range on what we have."

Conan nodded grimly.

"Now, if the Elders had destroyed Venarium when putting it to the torch was all that was required, we'd not be facing the problem we now are. But the Aquilonians figured to use greed to soften our resolve. Now that stone walls are up, it's a steeper price we're to pay."

"Better to pay in fire than blood." Conan looked at his scarred palms. "This is a huge blood debt."

Kiernan smiled. "There's other coin for reckoning the debt, lad. You always have to assume your enemy is smart. But you get to remember he's a man. And he has men under his command, some of whom won't be so smart. You can use that against them. In this case, if we don't, even the smartest men among us will be dead . . . and Cimmeria will die with them."

The Cimmerian youth frowned. "We cannot do nothing."

"Agreed. But what we'll have to do, in the minds of some, isn't work for warriors, and isn't work for Cimmerians." The older warrior shrugged. "Though I suspect, when recounting tales of victory, some details will go unmentioned, become forgotten, and few will think to complain."

KIERNAN AND CONAN returned to the Cimmerian camp and spoke with the other Outlanders. While no one doubted the courage of any Cimmerian warrior, the Outlanders had all engaged in battles and sieges, whereas their average companion's greatest victory had been a cattle raid. The Outlanders, choosing Kiernan and Connacht as their spokesmen, offered a plan to the Elders. Conan attended his grandfather as the plan was presented, and the Elders accepted it less because it was the wisest plan than because it absolved them of responsibility if it failed.

The Cimmerian host advanced in two wings. One was composed of northerners and invested itself in the valley directly opposite Venarium's main gate. The southern contingent came in from the north and placed itself beside the northern force, with a gap of three hundred yards between them. The Cimmerians made no attempt to surround the city. They posted a few pickets well outside the range of Aquilonian archers and siege machines. The camps showed little organization and less discipline, with fights regularly breaking out in the gap between forces.

A contingent of Elders from the northern force approached the city and met with an Aquilonian envoy. Among the many things they demanded, including the dismantling of the walls were rental fees and three hundred cats. Not to be outdone, a southern party of leaders demanded four hundred rats and five hundred bats. The Aquilonians, who sent messengers south to summon reinforcements, agreed to meet these requests and within a week delivered the tribute to the Cimmerians.

Many of the Cimmerians viewed all of the talking as nonsense, but Conan benefited from his association with Connacht and Kiernan. The Aquilonian commander could look out from his tower and see two Cimmerian forces split down the middle. If the southern troops wished to go home, they would have to go through the northerners. The battles in the gap proved there was little love lost between the two groups. While the Cimmerians were creating some siege machines, they were too small to effectively batter the city into submission before reinforcements could arrive from the south. As far as the Aquilonian commander was concerned, all he had to do was keep a watchful eye on the barbarians and wait for others to rid him of his problem.

Then came the night of no moon.

Venarium depended upon wells to draw water in, and sewers to drain waste away. The sewers flowed together toward the south, into a series of irrigation canals that used water from the river to flood the fields with night soil as fertilizer. The Aquilonians had barred and gated the sewers, but only to keep men out. Their preparations could not stop cats or rats or bats, especially when those creatures were released with burning embers lashed to their tails and legs in woven, green-grass baskets.

The animals fled to safety in Venarium, pouring into the city through the sewers or winging their way above the walls and into towers and attics. As the first fires ignited, after the animals had chewed their way free of their fiery cargo, ala-rums sounded. Troops tasked with guarding the sewers   a duty never given to the most elite of troops—fled to other posts to fight the fires. It took very little for the Outlanders to crash through the sewer gates and pour into the city, all but unnoticed in the chaos.

And once they reached the main gates and opened them, Cimmerian rage consumed the town more swiftly than the flames.

The Aquilonian leader was not a stupid man, nor did he lack courage. Whether from his tower he saw the Cimmerian Outlanders advancing on the gate, or he assumed that the gate would be a target, he donned his armor and led his personal cohort through Venarium's smoky streets. His force hidden behind tall shields, bristling with spears, slammed into the Outlanders' flank and drove them back against the gates they so desperately wished to open.

Many of the Outlanders drew together and back, hoping to buy time for the others to come to their rescue, but Conan was not among them. Clad in a blackened mail surcoat, he burst from the Outlanders' midst and, with one, double-handed blow, split a shield and took the arm of the Aquilo-nian holding it. As that man looked down, terror on his face, his lifeblood pumping in black jets from his severed limb, Conan struck off his head.

Conan waded into the Aquilonians' midst, perhaps for a

heartbeat transported back to his village, imagining himself there, destroying those who had killed his people and slain his father. Good Cimmerian steel clove Aquilonian bone, spraying blood and brains. Aborted screams and cries for mercy filled the night, rising and falling within the din of metal clashing with metal. Conan moved with the battle and through it, Connacht's training allowing him to understand it and master it. Spear points caught on mail, short swords split rings and tore flesh, but never enough to slow the Cimmerian youth. Every cut he returned a hundredfold, every drop of blood he reaped in gallons.

And then the other Cimmerians boiled through the gates and over the walls.

Venarium fell screaming beneath a cold, unfeeling sky and stars that glittered as ice.

THAT NEXT MORNING Conan stood beside Kiernan and Connacht at the vantage point from which he'd first seen Venarium. What had once been grand and imposing was now nothing more than a smoking ruin—home to ravens and other consumers of carrion. Cimmerians still occupied the plains, filling carts with loot, chaining slaves into long strings, making mounds of skulls toward the south to chasten and taunt the Aquilonians.

And not a single Outlander was among them.

Conan frowned. "Do they not see that they invite the Aquilonians to invade?"

Connacht shrugged. "They do not wish to see."

The other Outlander nodded. "That is the Outlander curse, Conan. Having seen the world, we see a future others cannot imagine. They think Cimmeria is immortal, but it is no more so than Atlantis or Acheron or any of the nameless empires that slumber beneath distant sands. Cimmeria may always be remembered—I know it will be thus—but that is not the same as being immortal."

Conan nodded, leaning heavily on the sword that had drunk deeply of Aquilonian blood. He loved his nation. He loved his people. But his destiny lay far from the snow-capped Cimmerian mountains, and once he left his homeland, his return would be a long time coming.

CHAPTER 12

THE CARAVAN WENDED its way along the Zingaran coast, moving slowly in the bright sunshine. Bound for Messantia, it traveled overland because pirate predation had made shipping far too risky. Though Bêlit, the Queen of the Black Coast, had vanished, her second in command, Conan, had joined with Artus and his band of cutthroats, terrorizing any ships that dared slip down the coastline.

Navarus, the caravan master, once again looked toward the sea. The road hugged the coastal hills. The receding tide had created a flat, sandy expanse between the breakers and the slope leading up to the road. The Argosian merchant had no doubt that the beach was truly quicksand, and as good as a wall to protect them from marauding pirates, but even an absence of raiders and the lack of a single sail between him and the horizon did not make him comfortable.

The caravan would take a week to travel the distance a ship could make in two days. While this did give him a greater opportunity to sample the delights of the female slaves in their cages, it forced him to load wagons and pack animals with food and water for his human merchandise. For the men it hardly mattered. They would pull the wagons into Messantia then get sold in lots to Lucius to work his mines. They were not expected to live long, so fattening them up on the road would be pointless.

The women, on the other hand, had to be handled more delicately. He shaded their cages so the sun's angry kiss would not blister their soft flesh. He brought casks of fragrant unguents so they could oil their skin. Fruits and watered wine would keep them healthy, and the hateful crone who served as his camp cook would boil up a broth that made them pliant and radiant at the same time. The best of the women he grouped with a tutor, teaching them to recite Argosian and Shemite verse so they might entertain powerful men, thus fetching a higher price.

One of the mercenaries he'd hired to guard the caravan came running forward. "The coast is clear, Master Navarus."

"Very good, Captain." Navarus wrinkled his nose at the stench rising from the man's armor. "How long until we reach the camping place?"

"We're making good time. Two hours, leaving us two hours shy of dusk. We could push further, but there's fresh water there . . ."

"Yes, yes." The Argosian flicked at a fly with a horsehair stick. "In early, up before dawn."

"And away before the pirates notice. Yes, Master."

HIDDEN IN SHADOWS of the inland hills, Conan and Artus crouched to study the approaching caravan. "By Bel, you're right, Cimmerian. Naravus thought to steal from us by traveling overland."

Conan, a dozen years removed from his homeland, allowed himself a wolfish grin. He need say nothing, for Artus knew him as well as any man alive. The massive Zingaran—born of Kushite slave parents on a Thunder River vineyard—had crossed the Cimmerian's path a number of times down through the years. Never enemies, but not always friends, mutual respect and intrigue bound them. When Conan returned from the Black Coast, he found Artus's company less irritating than solitude, and a solid friendship blossomed between them. It rendered Artus, whose dark hair had been gathered in long braided rows, immune to Conan's sullen bouts of temper.

Conan's blue eyes narrowed. Lying languorously upon a daybed, Navarus rode in an open cart at the head of the caravan, a parasol of the same green silk as his robe shading him. The little man had positioned himself to study the sea, which Conan regretted, for he wished to see the man's face when the pirates attacked.

Artus nudged Conan with an elbow. "Do we let him live this time, or put an end to it?"

"Let the gods decide." Conan didn't care if Navarus lived or died, but as long as he lived and Conan was able, he would bedevil the man. One of Navarus's agents had once drugged wine and fed it to the Cimmerian, thinking to take Conan and sell him into a noble's stable of pit fighters. Fortunately the Cimmerian's constitution and the trick about shackles he had learned from Connacht had thwarted that plan. Conan had killed his abductor, but had never really brought himself to care enough about Navarus to wring his scrawny neck.

"We'd best get to our horses."

Conan nodded and slipped back through the shadows with the lithe grace of a great cat. Taller and stronger than he had been at Venarium, with more scars to mar his flesh and mark his adventures, the barbarian warrior had met no equal among men in combat. Wearing a surcoat of mail with the ease of a virgin wrapping herself in silk, he mounted his horse and drew his sword. He raised it aloft, and from their places on the hillside, the Zingaran pirate crew acknowledged the signal.

The sword fell.

The pirates, who had spent the night digging and levering great boulders into place, knocked away pins, hauled cables, and pushed. The stones rumbled down the hillside, picking up speed. Some bounced. An oblong one began wobbling, its ends pounding the ground, first one then the other. The rocks bounded into the caravan, smashing through wagons laden with fruits and trinkets. Crates of oranges exploded into the air. Burst pomegranates spewed glistening seeds. Shattered urns gushed olive oil, and stale bread loaves tumbled through the dust.

Even before the stones had hit the caravan, the Cimmerian had spurred his horse down the hill. Behind him rode Artus, whose lusty war cry bellowed loudly. Conan kicked out, shattering the first mercenary's jaw, then whipped his sword around to spin another man to the earth, bleeding. Artus cut past, his sword striking sparks from another. With a quick twist of his wrist he sent his foe's blade flying, then stabbed the man in the throat.

Chaos reigned over the caravan. The stones had passed through and, in a couple of cases, had crushed warriors who had been guarding the oceanside. The survivors of that contingent faced an uphill assault against screaming pirates and angry slaves. No matter what Navarus was paying them, it was not enough for them to rush to certain death. They retreated toward the ocean and the northwest, banding together to discourage pursuit.

Artus stood in his stirrups, waving his sword high. "Come back and fight, you pink-bellied, stub-cocked goat lovers!"

Conan reined up beside him, laughing. "You insult them."

The Zingaran raised an eyebrow. "Slavers?"

"Goat lovers."

Artus roared with laugher, but another roar, utterly mirthless, mingled with panicked screams from slaves. One of the mercenaries raised a bloody spear on high. At the hooves of his horse lay a half-dozen slaves and two of the pirates. The mercenary, his brows beetling, muscles bulging beneath hirsute flesh, grinned crookedly. From his expression there could be no mistaking the fact that he counted himself as dead. His only purpose was to take as many people with him as possible.

Conan looked at Artus. "Your joke angered him."

"But he's looking at you."

"He's yours by right, Artus."

"I cede him to you, Conan."

"Are you sure?"

The Zingaran smiled. "I insist."

Conan dug his heels into his horse's flanks. The beast leaped forward into the fray, hooves thundering on the roadway. The mercenary's mount sidestepped free of the corpses, almost daintily, then its nostrils flared and it plunged forward. The mercenary made to couch his spear as if it were a lance, but his grip shifted as he closed with his opponent. His eyes tightened, and as their horses closed, he thrust at Conan's face.

Conan turned his head just enough to avoid the spear,

though blood from it painted his ear. His sword arm came up. The glittering steel came over and down, then through. The horses shot past each other, the riders still in their saddles.

But the mercenary's head spun in the air, the flesh gray, the eyes already milky. It hit the ground, spinning to a stop on its left ear a heartbeat or two before his body crashed into the dust.

Conan reined around and grunted as the larger portion of his foe twitched.

Artus dismounted and toed the head. "As clean a cut as you've made in months."

The Cimmerian slid from the saddle and wiped his blade on a dead mercenary's trousers. "I've made cleaner."

"And you shall again, my friend." Artus sheathed his sword and patted Conan on the shoulder. "Come, we have someone to attend to."

As the rest of the pirates swarmed over the caravan, gathering loot and freeing slaves, the two of them worked to the caravan's head. The caravan master's cart had been crushed by a stone, but he had somehow escaped death. Navarus crouched behind his overturned daybed, his face bloodied and streaked with dust. He held his parasol as if it were a shield, and brandished a paring knife. "Stay back. I am warning you."

Artus looked at Conan. "The gods have spoken."

The Cimmerian grunted.

The Argosian looked up at the two giants towering over him, then sagged back and began to sob. "You rob me at sea. You rob me on land. Why won't you let me alone?"

Artus sank to a knee. "It's simple, Master Navarus. You try so hard, and you're so clever. If not for you, we should be bored unto death."

The caravan master stared, agape. "You are doing this for *sport*?"

The Zingaran shrugged. "Well, we do profit from it, but in your case, it *is* primarily the sport. Isn't that so, Conan?"

The Cimmerian nodded slowly. "You make us laugh."

"Laugh. I make you laugh." Navarus dropped the knife and tears washed tracks through blood and dust. "I can't . . . I don't . . ."

Artus stood and the two of them laughed aloud. This did little for Navarus's disposition. The rest of the pirates joined the laughter openly, and the freed slaves cautiously. A number of the latter, with rocks in hand and blood in their eyes, made their way toward Navarus.

Conan waved them off. "The gods have spoken."

If any of the slaves thought it curious that the pirates would leave Navarus alive, they said nothing. Instead, empty-handed, they turned to helping the pirates gather up loot and repair what carts they could. A handful of pirates returned up the hill and lit a signal fire, which sent a plume of dark smoke into the blue sky. The smoke and the tide would bring their ship, the *Hornet*, into the cove opposite the road.

Artus nodded as he surveyed the scene. "It is good to have you back, Conan."

The Cimmerian looked at him, his face impassive. "You have a good crew, Artus."

"*We* have a good crew, my friend." Artus smiled carefully. "Don't think I don't know how to read men, Conan. They're loyal to me, is the *Hornet*'s crew, because I plucked every one of them from a gibbet before the hangman could drop a noose around his neck. A fair pirate crew they were, too, more cutthroats than sailors, but passable at both. But it's you that have made them into a band of men who fight together."

He waved a hand at the hill. "You thought of attacking from the land while he expected us from the sea. Those sea dogs would have mutinied had I suggested such a plan, but you they would follow into the depths of the Stygian underworld. You're special, and they know it—and knew it 'ere they saw you swing a sword in combat."

Conan grunted.

Artus laughed. "I, too, know you're destined for greatness. Knew it when we met. Knew it when I heard you were shipping with Bêlit. I thought someday to find you, see if you remembered me."

"I do no forget friends, Artus." Conan did not turn to look at his friend, but instead focused on the sea. In his life, Conan had not made many friends—he could count them on the fingers of one hand, and those among them who yet lived were far fewer. Of the dead, one loomed the largest, having left a void in his life that he could barely comprehend, much less begin to fill. In it, he discovered the hole his mother's death had left in Corin's life.

"I know you don't, Conan. And losing friends . . . no sharper pain." The Zingaran nodded slowly. "And I'm not much for the wisdom of the gods, especially as displayed today. But I rendered Bel's share when I was thieving, and don't mind giving the sea a jug of wine and as much flesh as will sink. If we amuse the gods, they might let us live a bit longer."

"And if we are tortured, this amuses them the most." Conan shot Artus a sidelong glance. "So better to torture than be tortured?"

"No sense in hiding, is there?" The Zingaran looked over to where Navarus sat, his daybed righted, his parasol lashed to the haft of a spear. "He hides, and look at the good it does him. 'Everything that was hidden will be found.'"

Conan nodded. "Is it your goal to save me from myself?"

Artus slapped the Cimmerian on the back. "Just to remind you of the reasons we cling to life."

A commotion arose among the pirates and slaves below. Conan and Artus marched into the heart of the crowd.

Artus planted his hands on his hips. "What is the trouble?"

One of the male slaves knelt and groveled at the pirate's feet. "Master, we know not what to do."

Artus shook his head.

Conan drew his sword. "Go. You are all free."

One of the females, a doe-eyed beauty with long golden locks and longer legs, peered up at him. "But . . . but your crew has gathered all the food and water. They have taken the loot and left us defenseless. Where would you have us go?"

Conan surveyed the desolate coastline in the sun's dying light. "You are right. You men, go there, take that fruit, that bread, and two carts for water casks. That will see you back to Zingara."

The slave at whom he pointed frowned. "But, Master, that's hardly enough for our number."

"I know." Conan smiled. "That's why the women will come with us."

CHAPTER 13

THICK AND CLOYING, smoke swirled through the Messantian alehouse's dark reaches. Equal parts the tang of human sweat, the empty promises of opium, and the sharp scent of spilled ale, the heavy air muted laughter and dulled the flash of bright eyes. Women swirled, smoky tendrils caressing them, as they danced free from one pirate's embrace and into that of another. Hungers of all manner would be sated there, thirsts quenched, hearts inflamed, in a celebration of life and victory.

Two men remained detached. Navarus languished in a hanging cage once reserved for house slaves. He still wore his finery and clutched his parasol. He struggled to maintain his dignity while the women he had enjoyed on the road taunted him and tempted him. Pirates ridiculed him, tossing him grapes and scraps of meat with the same carelessness— but less frequency—that they tossed the same to cautious curs slinking between tables. Navarus made no attempt to gather the food with which he was pelted, but occasionally plucked a morsel from a fold in his robe.

Opposite him, in a darkened corner, Conan sat cloaked in shadow. He'd drunk enough ale to soften his grim expression—but had not softened it enough to tempt women to join him. He watched the others abandon all pretense of civilization, not descending into the savagery they would attribute to a barbarian such as himself, but regressing into childhood while coveting adult pleasures. It was not that the Cimmerian could not understand their abandon, or that he'd not seen barbarian tribesmen from Nordheim to the Black Kingdoms similarly indulge themselves. He had on countless occasions, and yet those celebrations had been different.

They are honest.

Those who did not lay claim to the veneer of civilization felt no need to justify letting it slip away. Plunder was for the strong, and there was no vice in taking it. Women were for the strong, and taking them ensured pleasure and the future. The strong earned the right to these things through courage and cunning, speed and daring and skill. Barbarians knew this and respected it. While there were still the craven who might scheme, a strong arm and a sharp mind would see through their subterfuge and put an end to their plotting.

But Conan did not look upon the *Hornet*'s crew with contempt—instead it was the mild amusement of an adult watching children at play. Though the caravan's guards had largely run off, heading back toward Zingara, the crew had worked hard and some had died. And the slave women, now freed, celebrated that freedom by sharing that which would have been taken from them. Slavery had reduced them to little more than beasts. Liberation had granted them their humanity again, and the desire to celebrate that resurrection should have surprised no one.

Artus rose from his place at the centermost table, nearly spilling two half-naked women to the floor, and spread his arms wide. "Is there no one who can best me? Are there no more arms to wrestle?"

Across from where he had been seated, a burly pirate sidled away, one shoulder lower than the other. He grabbed a tankard of ale and downed it quickly while a shipmate grabbed his wrist and yanked his shoulder back into the socket. The pirate roared, spewing froth to the rafters, then joined the other in laughing at his predicament.

Artus pointed at Conan. "Come, Cimmerian. Show these others what it is to be a man."

Conan shook his head. Artus needed no other opponents. He did not need to prove himself to those assembled. The second someone offered him a tankard, or one of the women began to nibble on his ear, he'd pursue other delights. Thus had Artus always been—at least for as long as Conan had known him.

The Zingaran shook his head, his long locks slithering back and forth across his broad shoulders. "Has the time away from ice and snow softened you, northerner?"

The Cimmerian sat forward. He knew what Artus was doing, trying to draw him out. Not in the way of men who have something to prove, but in the way of men seeking to save a friend. Conan had always been content to sit quietly and keep his own counsel, but to Artus's mind, he had been doing that far too much since his return.

Is he right? Conan could not answer that question. He truly felt no different than he had before. Still, there were times when the quiet did press in on him, when a sense of something missing stole over him. It did not make him feel weak, but unbalanced, as if at any moment he could fall and fall forever. *That* was not something that he'd known before he'd met Bêlit and before he lost her; and it was nothing upon which he wished to dwell.

So he rose and stretched, massive muscles twisting beneath flesh darkened by the southern sun. Pirates looked up, muzzles dripping sour ale. Most impressed, more fearful, and a few with smiles proud and confident. Women also stared, half-lidded eyes studying him and the fluidity with which he moved. They'd all seen ample evidence of his power and skill in combat, and wondered if he had talents of similar magnitude in other areas of life.

Artus laughed aloud and snagged two ale mugs from a passing wench. "The lion emerges from his den to learn a lesson."

Conan raised an eyebrow.

The Zingaran bowed as if he were a noble and slid around the table. He offered Conan the seat that would afford the Cimmerian an easy view of the alehouse doors. The Cimmerian sat and rested his right elbow on the ale-soaked table. One of the women, tall and slender, perched herself on his left thigh, her folded hands capping his shoulder.

Artus took up the spot opposite. "Shall we wager, Conan?"

All around them the clink of coins newly won and the whispering of odds being offered and taken encouraged that idea. "I have nothing to wager."

Artus reached out and caught a giggling girl around the waist. He pulled her into his lap. "Mine against yours, winner take both?"

Conan glanced at the woman on his thigh. He caught the hint of a smile before she cast her eyes downward. "A fair bet."

The two men joined hands and eyed each other. Artus smiled cautiously. "Are you ready, barbarian?"

Conan grunted.

Muscles bunched as the two men strove against each other. Artus started hard, aiming for the lightning-fast victory he favored, but Conan met him strength for strength. The Cimmerian felt his muscles knot, the burn up and down his arm. He did not grit his teeth as others might do, but he did lock his jaw and his eyes narrowed. His lips pressed into a flat line, he exerted himself.

Bit by bit their quivering hands shifted position. Artus's initial burst of strength had forced Conan's hand down slightly. Conan brought them back even, then steadily pressured Artus's hand toward the tabletop.

Artus's lips peeled back from his teeth in a snarl. He pushed, winning an inch. Some men cheered; others groaned. The women shifted in anticipation. Gold coins rustled and clinked, but then Artus's hand began to sink again.

Sink too quickly.

Conan guessed his friend's intent. Artus *had* matched his strength against that of many men that evening. He was bound to be fatigued. The smart money was against his winning. If he lost, no one would think it unreasonable. Conan would take the prize and in that night's enjoyment might be drawn further back from the abyss.

Conan laughed. "You're done, Zingaran!" He broke eye contact with Artus and took a long lick up the throat of the woman clinging to him. "Better she know me than disappointment."

As well as Artus knew Conan, Conan knew Artus. The man's dark eyes flashed dangerously. He bellowed angrily, then heaved mightily. Conan's hand slammed down hard enough to slosh ale from tankards. Artus roared, victorious, and rising, thrust both fists in the air.

Then he realized, as he caught Conan's smile, what had happened. His eyes tightened and he pointed a finger at the Cimmerian. "You always were the clever one."

Conan worked his right arm around and massaged his biceps. "And you the strong one."

Artus sat back down and invited both women to join him. "When I first met Conan, he was just a scrawny little rat, picking pockets in Zamora. But even so, it was he who stole the Elephant's Heart and slew the sorcerer, Yara."

The woman Conan had lost to Artus stared at him with open admiration. "That was you?"

Conan drank, then wiped foam on the back of his hand. "Go, Artus, you've won your prize. Enjoy."

Artus stood. "I won't forget this, barbarian."

"Just make sure *they* won't, Zingaran." Conan smiled and looked around. "Who's next?"

The pirates roared laughter to answer his question, but none came to take him up on his offer. Then a small man in a tattered robe and eye patch ducked through the crowd and sat opposite the Cimmerian, his head bowed. Had it not been for the heavy clink of chains linking the manacles on the man's wrists, Conan would have shoved him away.

The Cimmerian looked around the room. A half-dozen men entered in leather armor, wearing an ensign that Conan did not recognize. They were not of the Messantian Guard or any Argosian company, yet they carried themselves as if they had that much authority or more. Out of place in the alehouse, they became objects of interest, but Conan's interest in them faded as their captain entered.

Something struck the Cimmerian as familiar about the incredibly corpulent man. He didn't immediately recognize the face because of the odd mask that covered the man's nose—or what should have been his nose. He realized he'd not seen this man per se, but the man he had once been, only slightly less bulky, and still possessed of a nose.

A nose I took.

The captain pointed toward the crowd and waved his men in to search while he himself retreated back into the night. As the soldiers began to cut through the crowd, the man opposite Conan made to get up. The Cimmerian clamped his hand over the smaller man's, causing that man's single eye to widen with panic.

"They'll take us both to the mines if you don't let go."

"Who are they? Who is the man without a nose?"

"He's an Aquilonian. Lucan, something . . ."

"Lucius?"

"Yes, yes, I think that's it." His other hand grabbed Conan's. "Please, let me go."

"He oversees mines?"

"Lead mines, north of Messantia." The smaller man quaked. "Please. The reward for my capture is small, but I will repay you that and more if you let me go."

Conan did not release him. "I have business with Lucius."

The guards had fanned out through the crowd and approached the table where Conan sat with the smaller man. The pirates drew back, fingering their weapons. Conan shook his head, leaving many of them puzzled.

A guard laid the flat of an Aquilonian short sword on the small man's shoulder. "This one is ours. Release him."

Conan looked up, aware that three of guardsmen had taken up positions behind him. "A reward."

The man behind Conan laid a heavy hand on the Cimmerian's neck. "You've earned ten lashes. Care for more?"

Conan stood abruptly, smashing the back of his head into

a guardsman's face. Bones cracked and blood gushed from
a shattered nose. The guard opposite the table lunged with
his short sword. Conan twisted to the right. His left hand
fell on the guard's wrist and plunged the sword into the belly
of another guardsman. The barbarian jacked his elbow back
into the face of the man who had tried to stab him, then
backhanded a fist to the side of another guardsman's face.

He turned to face the last two of the guards, a bloodied
short sword now in his hands. "I captured him. He said your
captain would pay a reward. Will you cheat me of it as these
men would have?"

The guards' new leader cleared his throat. "That would
not be my intention."

Conan sneered. "Your men are weak. Your master should
have more men like me." He deliberately slowed his speech
and thickened his accent. He recalled the lesson of Venarium, and allowed the Aquilonian to think him nothing more
than a stupid savage. He even pounded a fist against his chest
to emphasize that impression. "He should make me your
captain."

The Aquilonian held up open hands. "I think you are
quite right, Vanirman. I've placed you, haven't I?"

Conan grunted.

"Well then, with a sign of good faith, I would take you
to our master. I'm certain he will hire you immediately.
Provided you prove good faith."

The Cimmerian frowned heavily. "Good faith?"

The guard nodded, pointing toward the moaning men on
the floor. "Your capacity for violence speaks well of you,
but this also demands caution."

Conan nodded slowly, as if considering the words. Then,
smiling, he stabbed the short sword into a rafter. "Good
faith."

"But you never used the sword on any of these men." The Aquilonian sighed. "Such a boon you would be to our master, yet you would not be allowed to approach if believed a danger. If there was a way . . ."

The Cimmerian narrowed his eyes. "Your master pays well?"

"Very."

Conan crouched and came up with a pair of manacles pulled from the belt of a moaning man. He snapped one end around one wrist, held the other out to the Aquilonian. "Take me to this master who pays well. In good faith."

The Aquilonian smiled. "A wise decision, Vanirman, very wise indeed."

CHAPTER 14

"STUPID BARBARIAN. HAD to hold on to me for a reward." The one-eyed man spat in the dust. "Only reward you're getting will be steel in your belly. And you are just too stupid to understand that, aren't you?"

Conan, who to this point in the long walk to the lead mines had kept silent, looked down at his companion. "Stupid enough to know that a scrawny Shemite dog like you would be worthless in a lead mine."

"What?"

"And no man would send six guards after an escaped mine slave." The Cimmerian chuckled. "Why does he want you?"

The little man's mouth gaped in shock. "You *must* know who I am. Why else would you have delivered me to my enemies?"

Conan shook his head.

The small man pressed a manacled hand to his breastbone. "I am Ela Shan, the world's greatest thief. There is no lock which will not yield to me."

Conan rattled his chains. "Your bracelets have locks."

"Yes, well, I lack the proper tools at the moment." Ela sniffed. "Nonetheless, my accomplishments speak for themselves."

The Cimmerian raised an eyebrow.

Ela sighed. "You have, perhaps, heard of the Tower of the Elephant? Home to the Elephant's Heart?"

"You stole it?"

"Not precisely. Yara, its master, had a small villa which I located after his demise and from which I deftly liberated certain treasures."

"You are a scavenger, a jackal."

"I am a *thief*." Ela shrugged. "I simply choose to ply my trade in places where the passing of aeons blurs the provenance of those items I collect."

Conan smiled. Had the little man claimed to have stolen the Elephant's Heart, the Cimmerian would have considered strangling him on the spot. The fact that he did not claim the feat that Conan had performed, and the delicacy with which he chose to describe his career, amused the larger man. Given Ela Shan's current state and lot in life, he could not be a terribly successful thief, but that he had gotten to his age and had only lost one eye did speak to his survival skills.

Before Conan could press him on why Lucius had put a bounty on his head, the dusty canyon through which they had been walking opened into a vast expanse. To the right, two holes opened like nostrils into the side of a hill. Men bent beneath leather hods stuffed with ore hauled their cargo to where other men with sledges pounded large rocks into smaller ones. Yet other slaves shoveled the small rocks into carts that carried them to the smelting ovens. Black smoke rose from them, distantly reminding Conan of his father's forge.

All the way to the left stood a makeshift garrison building composed of large stones and mud walls. The guards guided Conan and Ela toward it.

Ela glanced at the Cimmerian. "Do you honestly believe Lucius will reward you for my return?"

Conan shrugged easily.

The thief frowned. "No, you cannot be that stupid."

As they entered the garrison, an effete man rose from a table and smiled. "Gave us a chase, Ela Shan. My master is disappointed."

The guards pointed Conan to a stool and indicated he should sit. He did, remaining silent. The two guards behind him and the one man before appeared to be the only soldiers on station. Overpowering them would be as nothing, but the effort would be fruitless without knowing where his quarry lay.

Lucius's bailiff sniffed. "And what is this?"

"He disabled four armed men. He came seeking a reward for capturing the thief."

"Why is he in chains?"

The Aquilonian with whom Conan had bargained smiled. "A show of good faith. He hopes our master will employ him."

"Oh, yes, of course." A sly smile twisted the bailiff's features. He grabbed Ela Shan by the scruff of the neck and started marching him deeper into the garrison building. "Once our master has dealt with the thief, he will have time for you."

The two of them disappeared around a corner. Conan caught the buzz of murmurs, but could make no sense of them. Bolts clicked as they shot back, and a door creaked, then the bolts returned to their sockets. The bailiff, his smile now more cruel than clever, returned to his desk. He picked up a triangular stylus and held it poised above a soft clay tablet, but did not begin to make impressions until Ela's first muffled scream filled the hall.

Conan looked up. "Where is your master?"

The bailiff regarded him curiously. "So, the hill ape can speak. As you might surmise, our master is currently . . . otherwise engaged."

The thief cried out again, clearly in pain.

The bailiff made impressions with the stylus, then pointed it at Conan. "Don't worry. You'll get your chance with him very soon."

"I would rather it be *now.*"

Conan smashed his manacles together and the left one popped open. Coming to his feet, the Cimmerian shouldered one guard into the wall and dropped the other with a fist to the face. As the first guard rebounded, Conan kicked him in the chest. That slammed him against the wall again. He bounced harder, then collapsed on top of his companion.

The bailiff, horror on his face, had risen and turned to run. Conan pounced, looping the chain around the man's neck, and yanked the bailiff back against his chest. "You will take me to Lucius now."

"You'll never get in. The door is locked from within." The bailiff clutched at the chain. "They will only open the door for me."

IN RESPONSE TO the insistent pounding on the chamber's stout door, a guard slid back the peephole cover. The bailiff stared at him. Cursing, the guard closed the peephole then slid the bolts back. "He does not want to be disturbed."

Conan delivered a heavy kick to the door, driving it into the guard's face. He reeled back, stumbling into a table and upsetting it. Dice flew along with the coins being wagered on the outcome of throws. Before the other three guards could rise, the Cimmerian had entered the room and flung the bailiff's severed head. It caught one guard full in the face, spilling him backward. A quick slash cut one man down, a thrust opened another's throat, and Conan gutted a third. He left the blade in that man's belly, then caught the door guard by the ears. With a quick twist, the Cimmerian snapped his neck.

Before the body hit the floor, Conan burst from the ante-chamber and into Lucius's den. The fat man, who had been bent over a table, tightening screws on a device that had trapped Ela's wrists, looked up. This close and in good light, there was no mistaking his identity. He was the man from Cimmeria.

Lucius spun away from Ela and reached for his sword, which hung on the wall. Conan reached it first, drawing it in a heartbeat. He drove the pommel into Lucius's forehead, just hard enough to daze him and open a small wound, then shoved the man back into a chair.

Conan pressed the blade to Lucius's throat with one hand while releasing Ela with the other. "Do you remember me, fat man?"

Lucius narrowed piggish eyes. "Should I?"

Conan nodded, then tore away the man's mask, exposing the gaping holes in the middle of his face. "I did this to you."

Blood drained from the Aquilonian's face. "Impossible."

Conan dragged the table with the clamps on it over in front of Lucius. "Fix his hands."

The thief left off rubbing his own wrists and wrestled Lucius's into the torture device. Conan would have bet the little man would have failed, but grim determination contorted his face. He locked the shackle bar over the Aquilonian's wrists, then gave the screw enough twists to elicit a hiss from mine's master.

"Please, Cimmerian, we can be civilized about this." Lucius forced a smile. "I have gold. I can make you rich."

Conan snorted. "I want the man who destroyed my village. I want Klarzin."

"Klarzin?" Lucius blinked. "You want Khalar Zym?"

The Cimmerian's icy eyes narrowed. *Khalar Zym*. Weariness and delirium had contracted the name into Klarzin. Hearing it again brought back memories, sharpening recollections that years and dreams had done much to dull. The cruel face, the hawk nose, the curved blade, and the memory of the blood that Conan had drawn; all of these things came back to him.

"Yes. Khalar Zym." Conan nodded grimly. The name felt like a curse on his tongue, meant to be spat with contempt.

"This is perfect." Lucius smiled and half turned, spitting at a banner on the wall. "There, you see his crest. The tentacled Mask of Acheron. I spit on it."

Ela gave the screw another half turn.

"Stop, stop, I tell you the truth. We are allies, barbarian." Lucius, tears brimming in deep-set eyes, opened his hands innocently. "He was once my master, but no more. I know how you can get him. I know where he is."

Conan nodded. "Speak."

"You have me at a disadvantage." Lucius nodded toward his wrists. "Please."

The Cimmerian nodded at Ela, who loosened the screw.

Lucius smiled carefully. "I will tell you everything I know, Cimmerian. You will find it all useful, but on your word of honor, promise you will not kill me."

Conan nodded. "Speak. I won't kill you."

"You won't regret this, my friend." The noseless man licked his lips. "Khalar Zym . . . he traveled the world and promised us great power. In your village, we found the last piece of the Mask of Acheron. It had been shattered and divided millennia ago. We thought, with it complete, he would become a god. He told us so."

The Cimmerian turned away and found a pair of pliers, which he placed on a small brazier. "You make much noise, but I hear nothing of value.

Lucius looked from Conan to the pliers and back. "Wait. Wait. He said there was another component. Something he needed to activate the mask. To bring it to its full power. I could not wait, so I left his service. But I know he lairs at Khor Kalba. And your friend here, he knows the way through Khor Kalba. With him I was going to steal the mask."

Conan arched an eyebrow.

Ela smiled sheepishly. "What he says is true—half true. I know of Khor Kalba. I have studied it. I intended to enter, but then Khalar Zym took possession." He tightened the screw another turn. "But I was no partner to this one."

Lucius smiled weakly. "We would have reached an agreement, Ela Shan. You needed to take me seriously."

"Is Khalar Zym at Khor Kalba now?"

"No, Cimmerian, no. But I do know where he is. I do."

Conan turned back to the pliers, which had begun to glow a merry red. "Where?"

"The Wastes, the Red Wastes."

"You lie. There is nothing there."

"What is there is hidden, Cimmerian; and what he seeks is hidden well." Lucius smiled. "And he shall return to Khor Kalba through the Shaipur Pass."

Ela nodded. "That is a welcome place for an ambush."

But does Lucius seek to have me ambushed or his former master? Conan picked up the glowing pliers. "What does Khalar Zym want in the Wastes?"

"Foolishness. He and that witch spawn of his seek a girl."

Conan laughed. "The world is full of girls."

"A special one, of special blood." Lucius's eyes focused past the pliers. "Her blood will activate the mask and make the wearer a god."

The Cimmerian shivered involuntarily. He had no use for sorcery, and no inclination to tolerate those who lusted after such power.

He shook his head, leaning in closely, letting the pliers singe a lock of Lucius's hair. "I think you lie to me, Aquilonian dog. You seek to send me into the Wastes on a fool's mission."

"I agree." Ela gave the screw a full turn.

"No, no! I speak the truth!" Tears streamed down the fat man's face. "By all the gods, you must believe me. I hate him as much as you do. I have no loyalty to him."

Your loyalty is only to yourself. Conan stared at the man, lost in distant recollections of their first meeting.

"Please, Cimmerian. I have upheld my end of the bargain. You promised."

Conan nodded. "I did. Ela, the ring of keys on the wall. Find the one that would free the slaves."

Lucius's eyes grew wide. "You cannot. They would riot."

"Calm yourself, Aquilonian." Conan poured ale from a pitcher into a cup. "I will not kill you. I will not free the slaves."

"Here." Ela handed him a small key.

The Cimmerian stared down at where it rested across the scar on his palm, then forced Lucius's head back. The

Aquilonian's mouth opened in surprise. Conan dropped the key into it, then poured the ale down the fat man's throat.

Lucius swallowed, then sputtered, ale glistening on his chin and chest. "By Mitra, why?"

"It's you who invoked the gods, Lucius." Conan flipped the catch, freeing him from the clamps, then hauled him to his feet. "Come."

"Wait, what are you doing?"

Conan's grasp remained firm on the back of Lucius's tunic. He marched the man out into the sunlight. Conan caught sight of only a half-dozen guards, and all he saw was the back of them as they scurried away. Lips twisted in contempt, he tossed Lucius sprawling to the ground as slaves slowly crept closer.

The barbarian pointed at the blubbering fat man. "The key that unlocks your chains sits in this man's gullet."

Lucius, who had scrambled to his knees, stared at Conan. "Cimmerian, you gave your word. You promised you would spare my life."

"I promised I would not kill you." Conan turned and walked away, relishing how the crunch of gravel beneath his feet devoured Lucius's dying screams.

"Northerner . . ." Ela ran to catch up with Conan. "You have earned my gratitude."

"Have I?"

"And Ela Shan is known to be a man who keeps his promises, honors his debts."

"Rare qualities among thieves."

The little man ran in front of Conan and walked backward as quickly as he could. "If you should be so foolish as to pursue this Khalar Zym to Khor Kalba, seek me out in Asgalun. I shall talk you out of it."

Conan nodded slowly. "And you, Ela Shan, if you hear

that the master of Khor Kalba has died in the Wastes, know you have Conan of Cimmeria to thank for clearing your way."

The little thief smiled. "Then may Bel smile on you, Conan of Cimmeria, and may your sword speed Khalar Zym to hell."

CHAPTER 15

TAMARA AMALIAT JORVI KARUSHAN stood atop the monastery's eastern battlement, letting the dawning sun's rays bathe her with their warmth. It had been her habit to do this often in her twenty years. The ritual's regularity instilled a sense of order. The sun's presence reminded her that forces more titanic than she ruled the world. And yet, at the same time, she felt she was a critical part of it, made whole by it as she, in turn, helped make it whole.

As the sun cleared the horizon, she bowed to it, then began her morning exercises. Her years of training as a monk had made her an expert in a variety of combat arts. Primarily unarmed, but she was not unacquainted with a bow or a knife. While she recognized them as useful tools, and diligently studied until she had mastered their uses, she preferred unarmed forms. Knives and arrows, after all, could do serious harm even without the intention to do so. As the saying went, "a falling knife has no handle." Arms and legs, however, feet and fists, could be used to help even more easily than they could be used to hurt.

So, in the early morning, Tamara's slender body moved from one form to another. Her flowing robes easily accommodated her movements. Her long hair had been gathered back and tied with a band. It delicately brushed her shoulders as her exercises continued. As she did each morning, she battled a succession of shadow warriors, turning their attacks back on themselves, using their force and hatred to destroy them.

The simple flowing motion rooted her in the world. Life itself was energy. She recognized it, moved with it. Just as she would use another's energy against them, so she used the world's energy to help her. This was, after all, her role. By doing what she did, she established order in what would otherwise be a chaotic world, fostering peace where there would otherwise be an ocean of misery.

A young novitiate paused at the head of the stairs, then dropped to her knees. She bowed her head, not looking up, unmoving, while Tamara's exercises continued. Tamara had noticed her immediately, more because she had disrupted her routine than because of any inherent interest the girl may have possessed. She hastened to complete her exercises—an action that left her slightly unsettled.

"Yes, sister, of what assistance may I be?"

The novitiate kept her eyes downcast. "Master Fassir, he has summoned you."

"Where?"

"The Pool of Visions."

A thrill ran through Tamara. Master Fassir opened the pool chamber on an irregular schedule. He and his advisers regularly consulted charts of the heavens, drawing lines between planets and stars. They measured the angles and performed complex calculations, which they then compared to horoscopes and prophecies. Most often Fassir walked the chamber's precincts alone, but on rare occasions other monks would be summoned to hear a pronouncement of grave import.

"Thank you, sister." Tamara bowed to her, then flew down the stairs and to the cell she shared with another monk. From a chest in the corner she drew a clean white robe. She fitted a square cap on her head, then draped a gauzy veil over her head and shoulders. Keeping her eyes modestly downcast and steps hobbled by humility, she made all allowable haste to the chamber.

Several other monks, all female and similarly attired, knelt at the long sides of a rectangular granite basin. Sunlight streamed into the room from an open eastern door, but the pool's rippling water reflected none of the light on the opposite wall. At one short end sat Master Fassir, hooded in a white robe, drawing slowly on a pipe. He exhaled fragrant smoke slowly, so it drifted upward like a curtain that further hid his face.

Tamara knelt opposite him and stared down into the shallow pool. She could see nothing but golden tile work at the bottom. She had not expected to see anything, for the pool shared its wisdom with those far older and wiser than she— yet she dared hope that, someday, she would be in Fassir's place.

She felt Fassir's gaze upon her. She looked up into her mentor's face. He had always been old in her sight, but aside from the deepening of lines around his eyes and the corners of his mouth, he had not changed much. True, time had leached his hair and beard of all color, but his eyes retained their kindness. He smiled as he was wont to do, then glanced down into the pool and exhaled more smoke.

"There comes a man, Tamara. I do not see him clearly—he is not yet close enough. There is a journey, sea and sand to be crossed."

"His journey, Master, or mine?"

The old man smiled. "Yes and yes. Two journeys become one. This man . . ."

"Is he a knight?"

Fassir's eyes tightened. "A warrior. A man of destiny. As with your journeys, so shall your destinies merge."

Tamara frowned. *My destiny is to be here. Am I to seek this man and bring him among us?* "What destiny, Master?"

Fassir shook his head, his brow furrowing. "Not what, but which, Tamara. Often there is so little to be seen, but here there is so much, one does not know what to ignore."

Tamara studied him. "Is that all, Master?"

Fassir set the pipe down and rubbed a hand over his forehead. "I fear it is. Things shift faster than expected." He clapped his hands. "Off with you all, to your duties. All save you, Tamara."

The other monks rose and noiselessly exited the dimly lit chamber. Fassir stood and wordlessly led Tamara out through the eastern door. They came out onto a veranda overlooking the monastery's courtyard and gate beyond. The other monks moved about, carefree, attending to their duties.

"You will walk with me, Tamara."

She took up her position two steps behind him and one to the left, as befit her position and his, but he beckoned her forward. "You know well how people come to join us, don't you, Tamara?"

"Of course, Master. Some are born here. Some we seek out as we travel in the world. Some, the most innocent, are able to wander through the wards which keep us hidden. We bring them here and teach them, keeping them safe." She cocked her head slightly. "Is that it, Master? Do you wish me to seek out this man from your vision and bring him hence?"

The older man laughed. "No. Such a man as I saw would not take well to our life. As much as we seek order, he is chaos incarnate. Or, barring that, one who establishes a different kind of order. I doubt you could bring him here, and I am certain he could never find his way on his own."

"I would do all I could, Master."

"This I do not doubt, Tamara. But I did not begin this line of inquiry to elicit a pledge of fidelity to any task I might give you."

"Then why?"

Fassir opened his arms to take in the whole of the monastery. "Why is it that you, of all the monks here, have never inquired about how you came to be here? We all do it. I was but twelve when I did. Others have discussed this with you, of this I am certain. But why have you never asked?"

Tamara frowned. "I have never felt the need to know, Master. I have always felt I was meant to be here. I supposed I must have come from elsewhere, but it did not matter to me. Should it have? Should I have asked?"

"That it is your sense that you belong here speaks great volumes on the propriety of the actions which brought you here."

She looked at him curiously. "You make it sound as if I was stolen from my parents."

Fassir stopped. "You know our purpose here, the purpose of our sister monastery in Hyrkania."

"To maintain order in the world so it does not fall completely to chaos."

"Which we do admirably. And you know that there are times when we send some of our number into the world beyond the wards to further this mission." He sighed, clasping his hands at the small of his back. "I know some of the other monks suggest you are my favorite. It's true, of course, because you are the most dedicated and intelligent of my students. But there is more and here is the razored edge I must walk. Were I to reveal *all* to you, I could trigger a disaster. And yet, to reveal nothing could guarantee disaster. So, I shall tell you as much as I think you need to know. I ask that you trust me, and trust even more in your training and your heart. Between the two, you will find the means and wherewithal to continue your mission."

Tamara shivered. "You are scaring me, Master."

Fassir laughed easily. "It's not a faery tale to frighten children, Tamara. Out there in the world, chaos warps many minds. Men see patterns where none exist. They seek power which is illusory, and their frustration causes them to do things which would curdle a normal man's soul. Just as we might see the first buds on a branch as an augury of spring's arrival, so another man might see a redheaded child as the herald of a dynasty, or a crooked scar twisting flesh as some secret sign of an ancient god's favor. Delusions, all, certainly; but delusions that make men act in ways that do incalculable damage to the world."

He sat the edge of a low wall and bid her to settle beside him. "So you were born into a madman's delusions. You were then and are *now* quite innocent of any connection with him, but *my* master had a vision, much as I did today. He sent me forth to find you. The man who sought you had sent agents far and wide. Some found you and stole you from your parents. Before they could place you in their master's hands, I intervened. I brought you here."

She blinked. "And of my parents?"

"I do not know."

"Did you not seek them out? Did you not tell them I lived?"

Fassir glanced down at his empty hands. "For your sake, it was believed best that they and any who knew you believed you had perished. Yes, I am certain that if your parents lived, this meant great anguish to them—but how much greater the anguish to know that you had become a pawn in the schemes of a madman? And if it were known that you lived, they and any kinsmen you had known could be used as a weapon against you. Here, in the monastery, here with training, we could protect you and prepare you to protect yourself."

Cold trickled down her spine. Part of her knew she should feel anger and outrage, but years of training held an emotional reaction at bay. She had been, and felt as if she *always* had been, part of this world. If she were to hold that belief as valid, then everything leading up to it likewise became valid. Her place here, her purpose, was to prevent whatever havoc the madman intended.

"This man you saw in your vision . . . Is he the madman who is searching for me?"

"No, little Tamara, he is not. He has been touched by the madman, of that I know." Fassir reached out and took her hand. "And I do not see how this will end. What I do know is that your safety is the safety of countless people."

She smiled. "And this is why you have trained me to defend myself and to defend others."

He patted her hand, then let it drop as he stood. Fassir looked out at the courtyard. "Decisions will have to be made, Tamara. Part of me wishes to send you this very moment to Hyrkania. I do feel this is a journey you shall make soon. You must promise me that when I send you forth, you will make it."

"Of course, Master." Tamara nodded solemnly. "I shall even guide this warrior there if that is your desire."

"I fear it is not my desire which will determine the direction of his footsteps, Tamara. It would be fascinating to see which wins out: his will or yours." The older man shook his head. "You will find him a most challenging companion, my dear."

Tamara nodded, then looked up. "And of the madman, Master?"

Fassir shook his head. "As the wards hide you from him, so they obscure him from me. Were he dead, I would know. He is not, so danger still lurks."

"And the paths of my warrior and this madman, they will cross?"

Fassir hesitated for a moment, then looked at her with joy blossoming on his face. With a finger he traced invisible sigils in the air. "You are brilliant, child."

"Yes, Master?"

"Yes. I can see your warrior's path clearly, save in two places. One, in the past, where the madman's path overlays it, hiding it."

"And the other . . . the future?"

Fassir nodded. "I see nothing beyond where they might intersect."

Tamara stood. "You must see *something*."

"I wish I did, Tamara." The old man, his eyes glistening, reached up and stroked her hair. "I wish I did."

CHAPTER 16

CONAN COULD NOT help but smile as he returned to the alehouse. The *Hornet*'s crew filled the public house, their enthusiasm as yet unspent. Navarus slumped in his cage, still alive, but fast asleep despite the detritus flecking his soiled robe. Though the Cimmerian had been gone for half a day, no one seemed to have noticed his absence.

This might have disturbed him save for two things. First, he himself was not likely to have noticed if any of the others had vanished. Such was the nature of life, especially an adventuring life. The sudden desire to return home could end a man's career as quickly as a sharp knife in a dark alley. On the sea, a rogue wave, a snapped mast, or an enemy sword could steal a life and leave fading memories in its place.

And even those memories to which one wished to cling became ethereal and slowly evaporated.

The second reason he felt no alarm was that his return elicited smiles, hoisted ale jacks, come-hither glances, and shouted challenges. Though Conan was not a man who cared about the opinions others held of him, to be welcomed by men with whom he had shed blood did ignite a sense of pride. These were men and women who judged him for what he had done and could do. They cared not for his past adventures. They'd had ample chance to measure his worth, and the sincerity of their smiles reflected how highly they valued him.

Conan found Artus descending from an upstairs apartment, girded for war. "There you are, Cimmerian. Damned if any of these rogues bothered to alert me when you were taken. I just now heard and was going to gather the boys to free you."

"Thank you, my friend, but I *am* free." Conan perched himself on the end of a bench. "I have to take leave of the crew, Artus."

The Zingaran slapped a girl who was sleeping in a corner booth on the rump. "Run along now"

Surprise widened her dark eyes, then she stretched and made as if to resume her place again. Artus spanked her once more and slid onto the seat opposite Conan. "Go, woman. We have serious business here."

Shooting Conan a venomous glance, the woman crawled over Artus. She paused long enough to give the Zingaran a good look at the red mark his hand had left on her pale bottom, then slinked off into the crowd.

Conan watched her go, smiling. "She'll have a knife in your ribs next time you see her."

"Won't be as sharp as the one you just shoved there." Artus leaned forward, his eyes keen. "Why are you leaving?"

"Last night I found one of the men who destroyed my village."

"Caarzyn? You found him?" Artus shook his head. "I remember that once you mentioned him. You were deep in your cups, my friend, and I thought him equal parts bad dream and demon. He's here, in Messantia?"

"No, and 'twas not him I spied." Conan hesitated, surprised that Artus knew as much as he did. Though the Cimmerian counted Artus as a friend, few had ever been Conan's intimate confidants, and he could not think of a one who still breathed. "The master of mines, Lucius, traveled with him. And Caarzyn or Klarzin was not his name. It was Khalar Zym."

Artus's expression slackened. "You're certain of that name?"

"Yes." Conan pulled the banner that had hung on the wall of Lucius's chamber from a small pouch and laid it on the table with the mask crest uppermost. "This was the crest beneath which they destroyed my village. What do you know, Artus?"

"Fell things, Conan. Dark and shadowy things." The pirate sat back. "That name, the man owning it, *is* half nightmare and all demon. A decade ago, two, maybe three, he was a bandit king who commanded a horde. It raided where it would. Cities and towns paid tribute or faced destruction. At times he struck without warning, and none could anticipate him. I never saw him, but my mother told stories of him to keep me abed with fright."

Artus stood abruptly and shouted at the bartender. "Why is my flagon dry? And bring me a bottle of that goat piss you sell as fortified Shemite wine. Two goblets."

His command quelled the party's high spirits and even awakened Navarus. The pirates stared at their captain, awaiting another outburst. When he sat down again, they resumed their celebration, but much subdued. Wolves of the sea, they knew winds had shifted and that they would be sailing soon. Each drink, each kiss, became that much sweeter, as it might be their last.

Artus said nothing until ale and wine had been served. "I'm not afraid of Khalar Zym, Conan, but there are many who are. After he traveled where he desired, his force went away. He was never defeated. No armies found him, no one set torch to his stronghold; so like the creatures used to frighten children, he lurks out there causing sleepless nights for many a crowned head. But if my brother Conan is set on harvesting his head, then I am with him. And the *Hornet's* crew as well."

The Cimmerian shook his head. "No, Artus, this is not for you."

Artus gripped Conan's upper arm. "Don't mistake me, Cimmerian. I understand revenge. He destroyed your village. He killed your people. He owes you a blood debt, and you'll collect. I know you will. So Khalar Zym is yours, my friend, but his horde is mine."

Conan looked up from the dark depths of the goblet clutched between his hands. "I'd grant you his horde or his hoard, Artus. I yet will. But this is not about revenge."

"No? Do you not wish to see his blood steaming in the gutter? Do you not wish to hear the lamentations of his women?"

"I do and shall." Conan frowned. "For so long I did not even know his name." He stopped, wondering if Connacht had recognized Khalar Zym in the name *Klarzin* and had said nothing. He did not know, but would not have put it past his grandfather to protect him that way. Conan understood and respected such a decision, just as he respected all his grandfather had taught him.

"Khalar Zym wiped my village from the face of the earth

for a tiny piece of a mask." Conan laid a hand on the image of the crest. "Though I do not know why that piece had been entrusted to my people, it had. Whatever the reason, it must have been good. My people died to keep that shard away from him. Their obligation passes to me." *Through my father.*

Artus nodded slowly. "So, you will go after him to take back what is yours, *then* you kill him to avenge your people."

"Not exactly. I will win back the mask. Then I will kill him. But not to avenge. Not for revenge."

"No?"

Conan smiled coldly. "A decade and a half ago I trimmed his ear when I meant to cleave his skull. I go, Artus, to finish the job."

ARTUS STILL PRESSED Conan to make use of the *Hornet* and her crew in his adventure. Conan countered that he did not know enough about Khalar Zym to make any use of the ship or crew. "I do not even know if the information Lucius gave me is true."

Artus had scoffed. "Seeking a woman in the Wastes? Stuff and nonsense of faery stories, but we agree that you must investigate."

Just about the time when the influx of freed mine slaves to Messantia began to be a source of annoyance to the city guard, the pirates quit the alehouse and returned to the *Hornet*. They set sail with the tide to the southeast, to the coast of Shem and up a muddy river where they were able to put Conan ashore with a horse. They agreed he would work his way inland and east, seeking signs of Khalar Zym. They would travel on a parallel course down the coast and rendezvous at the cove nearest the Shaipur outpost.

Though Conan felt regret at leaving Artus and the others behind, those feelings passed after he'd ridden the first mile with a strong horse between his legs. Conan's career as a pirate had well accustomed him to the sea and the life it fostered, but to one born in the mountains, the sea would forever be an alien realm. And the fondest memories he had of that seafaring life were intertwined with memories of Bêlit.

After she died, he had turned his back on the ocean and begun a journey inland. He didn't know where he was going, nor did he particularly care. The ocean had become desolate, a shining waste that drew all things good and bad into its cold, dark depths. He had burned the *Tigress*, making it Bêlit's pyre, so she would not have to endure eternity frozen in still waters.

It had never been his intention to return to the seas, but Artus had prevailed upon him. Enough time had passed, enough dry distance had passed beneath his feet, that he hoped his memories would have faded. Some of them had, but not the ones he'd hoped. Little things, like the creak of planking or the shrill cry of a gull, would spark something. Memories of love would spike through him, then withdraw, leaving him wounded.

And yet from those wounds he slowly healed. He made himself heal. *For her.* Had he allowed himself to succumb to those wounds, he would never have been the man worthy of being her consort.

As he rode inland, his thoughts turned away from things nautical and the memories associated with them. He searched his mind and heart for the true reason he was riding eastward, chasing a story spun by a fat man in the faint hopes of saving his life. He had spoken to Artus truly about wanting to finish Khalar Zym. He thought Artus almost believed him, too. Had he been riding with other men, he likely would not have thought any further about the matter, and would have convinced himself that concluding unfinished business was his only reason to pursue Khalar Zym.

As comforting as that might have been, Conan could not let himself off so easily. He knew in his gut that revenge was not what he sought. Connacht's lesson in futility had never left him. And stories of the continuous raids and counterraids that both Cimmeria and Aquilonia perpetrated on each other, or of the sorties that the Vanirmen undertook against the Cimmerians, or of blood feuds elsewhere lasting for generations; all of these reinforced his grandfather's lesson. While killing Khalar Zym might settle accounts between them, it would doubtlessly leave another thinking he had to seek vengeance against Conan, and so the cycle would perpetuate itself. While Conan feared no man, he did not wish a life of watching for assassins or dueling with anyone who claimed even the faintest of kinship with Khalar Zym.

He flashed on a memory of Khalar Zym's daughter. *What had been her name? Marca?* He cursed himself for being unable to remember, then realized he'd not *wanted* to remember. She had been odd in ways he'd not seen before, and had seen since only in places where things ancient and remorseless slithered around with foul intent. His skin burned at the memory of her tongue's rasp, then he laughed aloud.

"You thought I would be troublesome. By Crom, I pray you are a prophet."

He remembered the sword she'd taken, the one he had made with his father. It had seemed huge then, suitable only for his father's hands. Conan had so wanted to be full grown, so he could accept the blade and wield it to win his destiny.

He frowned. No, he had wanted his father to grant him

the sword. He had no doubt his father loved him and had been proud of him. Corin had looked to a future where Conan would be a great warrior. But he had insisted that his mother, that the both of his parents, had wanted more for him than a life of fire and blood. A life of peace, perhaps? A life much like Corin's?

The youth Conan had been would have rejected that idea, for his father, while known for his strength and skill at combat, was not the adventurer that Connacht had been. Conan had thrilled to his grandfather's stories, and his father had none to match them. It was not that he had thought less of his father than of his grandfather, but it was obvious that they were very different kinds of men. They had chosen different paths, and Conan had equated his life of destiny with his grandfather's adventuring.

And yet my father had been entrusted with the secret of the mask.

Suddenly Conan found himself reexamining his life and his memories of his father. Corin had not just wanted to raise a son who could be a great warrior. He had wanted to raise a son who was capable of accepting great responsibility. When Corin had said there was too much fire in him, he meant more than Conan's immaturity and youthful enthusiasm. He meant that Conan could not yet be entrusted with a secret upon which the fate of the world might hinge.

The day he had been ready, the day fire and ice mixed in him, the day he proved he had been tempered as had that sword, Corin would have granted it to him. His father would have shared the secret of the mask, a secret so powerful and terrible that it kept a great Cimmerian warrior from following his father's footsteps. It would have kept Conan there, too, in the Cimmerian village. *And my son and his son and so on.*

The tempering Conan had been denied in the mountains

of Cimmeria he had gained through his adventures. When Khalar Zym had stolen the mask, Conan could not have understood the nature of the evil it represented. But he had seen things, like the sorcerer Yara, and the horrible excesses that were, for such people, nothing. And while Khalar Zym might have slain Corin simply because he was an impediment to his ambition, Corin had died in the hopes of preventing the deaths of others.

That distinction opened Conan's eyes to the things his grandfather had tried to teach him about the futility of revenge. "Revenge is not part of a warrior's heritage. It is an unworthy indulgence." To be a warrior was to be more than a creature of emotion who struck out blindly and single-mindedly at that which irritated him. Conan could seek revenge, or he could be a warrior, but he could not do both.

And only as a warrior can I be worthy of the heritage my father intended for me. The Cimmerian's eyes tightened. Khalar Zym had destroyed his past, but that was not the same as destroying his future. Khalar Zym did not have that power. Only Conan could do that to himself, and only if he acted in a self-indulgent way that was truly beneath him.

Conan brought his horse to the crest of the ridgeline and looked down toward the Red Wastes. A barren land in which twisted black trees sprouted like thorns from the earth, it had not earned its name from the color of the soil. Men called it the Red Waste because of the blood it had drunk.

Somewhere out there, Khalar Zym hunted.

Conan would find him.

He hoped the land was still thirsty.

CHAPTER 17

ALONE IN HER cabin aboard her father's land ship, Marique knelt naked before a three-paneled mirror. The warm golden light of the swaying oil lamps that hung from the ceiling caressed her alabaster flesh. The woman staring back at her from the mirrors would be judged flawless by any who dared render judgment. Others would declare her perfect, and were she to truly study her reflection, she might agree.

But those others used mirrors to reveal what *was*. In them Marique sought what would be. She never had a clear vision. Just as the voices that whispered to her never made their messages distinct or crisp, so the shadows reflected upon her by the future *suggested* instead of proclaiming, hinted and seduced instead of explaining, and coaxed instead of commanding. She watched, she took it all in, every nuance, letting pleasure and fear mingle within her breast, but never letting them overwhelm her.

Some of what she saw pleased her. Ghost images matched the arcane tattoos which ran from shoulder to shoulder, up her neck, past her ears, and along her high hairline. She'd only seen bits and pieces of them before, but had tracked them down through endless researches in tomes long thought lost by those who should have known better. She'd drawn the images she wanted and showed a legion of tattooists where to place each individual design, then had her father's men slay the tattooists so they could never re-create the designs again.

As she transformed herself to match the spectral visions, her power grew. A smart woman, she realized that she was creating in her own flesh what Acheron's long-dead priest-kings had done in order to create her father's obsession. She did not do this out of greed or lust for power. She did not do it to harness the sorcery that would allow her to rival her father. No, she did it because Khalar Zym would need her if his own efforts failed. When she could do for him what the mask could do, he would not longer need it.

He will need no one but me.

She smiled at that thought, her nipples stiffening, but her smile did not carry to her further reflection. For a heartbeat a dark line drew itself between her breasts. Marique studied its strength and the way smaller, jagged lines shot out from it. She wondered that she felt no pain, and then reminded herself that the mirrors reflected what *might* be, not what would be.

She traced a finger over the shadow and it vanished in the wake of her caress. This pleased her, and her smile did shine in the mirror. She forgot herself for a moment, allowing satisfaction to seize her. She reveled in it, throwing her head back in a silent laugh, then she caught sight of *it* and turned slowly like a snake coiling.

The land ship rode on the backs of eight elephants and rocked gently as it was carried along. Most assumed that her father had ordered the titanic vehicle built as a gross display of his power. That he had was true, in part. He also did it to fulfill obscure prophecies—of which there were far more than there were stars in sky. She always thought of the elephants as *the* elephant upon which the world rested, according to countless faiths and creation stories. It meant her father would be the master of this world, and perhaps more.

Silken curtains covered her cabin's walls and one had slipped to reveal a prize she had almost forgotten. She'd taken it long ago in a Cimmerian village, from a smith and his half-witted, feral child. She'd not thought of the two in many years, and yet suddenly the taste of the child flooded back to her tongue, salty and sharp. The voices had warned her against it, but she'd licked him in defiance. It had been before she had learned that the voices were not just her mother's postmortem mumblings.

Marique rose fluidly and crossed to where the sword hung. Even as her hand approached, before she actually caressed the cool metal, she sensed something. It was almost as if nettles had stung her fingertips. She peered at them to see if her eyes would confirm that explanation. They did not, and when she reached out for the sword again, she encountered no resistance or discomfort.

She was not so foolishly indulgent as to play a finger along the edge. Crude and savage though the Cimmerians might have been, they took pride in their steel and its manufacture. Though she had not cared for the blade at all, it showed no sign of tarnish or rust. She might have plucked it from the village ruins a day ago, or ripped it newly born, directly from the hands of the swordsmith himself.

She did not ask herself why she had taken the sword. Her father—if he noticed at all—had not questioned her about it. He hadn't noticed, of course, since in Cimmeria he had found the piece that completed the Mask of Acheron. At the time she stole the sword, he was basking in the glory of his greatest triumph.

A triumph that had tarnished quickly, unlike the sword.

Reconstruction of the mask had been the goal upon which her father had focused for two reasons. First, it had been an obsession he had shared with Maliva, his wife and Marique's mother. Maliva had brought him knowledge of it through her studies of Acheronian lore. She promised him that the mask, once reconstructed, would provide power beyond imagining, allowing him to raise long-dead legions that would again establish the reign of Acheron upon the earth.

But barbarians akin to those who had created the sword had shattered Acheron and its mask. They had caused the name *Acheron* to be struck from every monument, for Acheronian cities to be buried and their libraries burned. Barbarians who had no use for sorcery did their utmost to make certain no one else *could* use it. Had they pursued that course for another year or decade, perhaps they would have succeeded.

Maliva had collected many volumes of Acheronian lore, copies of which traveled in the land ship's hold, while the originals resided at Khor Kalba. Had her mother been less of a dreamer and more diligent a student, she would have understood that gathering the pieces of the mask were not enough. If she *did* know that, she never communicated it to Khalar Zym because, after Maliva had been burned as an Acheronian witch, her husband had vowed to complete the mask and raise her from the dead.

Marique still recalled the depths of her father's depression when fitting the last piece into the mask had failed to activate it. She had already begun to study the books her mother had so treasured, and was the first to confirm the necessity of a blood infusion to waken the magick, not just, as her mother had believed, enhance it. She'd told her father, and villages were drained dry in the hopes that bathing the mask in gallons of blood would revivify it. He preferentially sought those of Acheronian blood, promising to raise them when he was a god, but it was to no avail.

When that effort failed, her father sat slumped in his throne, holding the mask in both hands, staring at it, asking why it mocked him. Marique, who watched from the shadows, first heard the whispers then. She furthered her studies, an innocent drinking in knowledge so foul it had soured souls which were already as black as night, and driven mad those who had only heard rumors of such things. She pursued clues found in scrolls and by fitting together shattered tablets. And finally she uncovered the truth.

Yes, blood would reactivate the mask, but it had to be *specifically* from the line of the last priest-king to wear the mask and wield its fearsome power. This knowledge seemed to have little effect on her father at first, but over the weeks he returned to himself. He dismissed his armies, promising to recall them when the portents were propitious, and began his long search for the scion of the last Acheronian priest-king.

"Marique. I need you! They have failed me *again!*"

The urgency in her father's voice sped her heart. She'd have run immediately to him, naked though she was, but it would not do for her to appear so before subordinates. She sat and drew on scarlet boots that covered her to her knees. Then she selected a hooded cloak and closed the clasp at her throat. Its silk lining felt cool against her flesh, while the scarlet wool wrapped her in heavy warmth.

She tucked a short dagger into the top of the right boot and prepared to leave her cabin. She glanced again in the mirror and admired herself, then caught a distorted reflection in the Cimmerian blade. She took it from the wall, holding it as she might a short staff, and made her way onto the land ship's main deck.

Her father, tall and terrible, towered over two half-naked men who groveled before him. Bloodstains marked where they had clawed at the deck, and a pale rivulet of urine betrayed the true depth of one's terror.

Khalar Zym turned toward his daughter, his dark eyes flashing. "They say they cannot find her. They claimed to be the best, but they fail me."

Marique moved to her father's side and slipped a hand from within the cloak to lay it on his sword arm. If any glimpsed her nakedness within the shadows, none gave sign, not even the mishapen wretch Remo, who had watched her for years when he believed he was unwatched.

"It is not their fault, Father." She smiled carefully. "We know the trail is cold, two decades cold."

"But they have come this far."

"And now there are elements which work against them." She turned and made for the gangway. "Remo, bring them."

Her father's subordinate grumbled, but did as he was bidden. Guards hastened down the gangway ahead of Marique and the elephant trainers calmed beasts as heavy, booted feet thundered down the wooden planking. Marique made certain to step lightly and to move carefully so it could seem as if all she did was float. Her father, stern and strong, trailed behind her but stopped halfway down, where the gangway twisted back. Arms folded tight to his chest, he would watch from there, so Marique made certain to position herself to great advantage.

Even before she reached the ground, she could feel the magick. She had long since learned all her mother had known, and had studied it all far more carefully than Maliva had been capable of doing. She knew that was a harsh assessment, but she had read her mother's journals and seen her errors in translation and transcription. Had her mother not been so careless, she would have found other ways to grant Khalar Zym the power he sought, but instead her mistakes had doomed his quest.

Marique stabbed the Cimmerian sword into the earth and rested a hand on it. It would anchor her. Though she sensed no immediate malice in the enchantments blanketing the Red Wastes, many were the sorcerers who concealed the lethal in the benign, and many more were the foolish who died because they failed to take precautions. The Cimmerian steel would not ward her per se, but could supply an element to her magick which she doubted another sorcerer would have anticipated.

She crouched, allowing the cloak to puddle around her. Cool air rushed in, exciting her flesh. She slowly reached out with her right hand, fingers splayed, then tucked them in toward her palm as if plucking the warp and weft of some arcane weaving. She felt vibrations, and the voices began to whisper in her head.

As always, they remained annoyingly vague, but none hissed a warning about immediate danger. Marique did not take this as a sign that she was safe, but more as a sign of the enchantment's beguiling nature. That it could fool the voices was proof of its strength, and that others failed to notice it revealed its subtlety.

She clutched the sword's pommel with her left hand. "She

has protectors, Father, *powerful* patrons who deny her to you."

"I am not to be defied, Marique." Khalar Zym raised his face to the heavens. "Your mother has waited too long for her resurrection. We can afford no further delays."

"And you shall have none, Father."

Again Marique played her fingers through the air and encountered more strands of eldritch energy. Some swirled and eddied, like currents in a stream that trapped debris in stagnating pools. These numbered in the dozens, and were the most powerful. She found them rather attractive. They beckoned her on like a melody, to spin her about and out and away, without her ever realizing she had not gone in the direction she desired.

But there were other strands, tiny strands, more fragile than a whisper, as fleeting as a dream upon wakening, and she found them, too. They shied away from her, recoiled, became dead at her touch. The sharp scent of decay filled her head.

Only her grip on the sword prevented her from falling over, nauseous and dizzy. She steadied herself, then smiled. *If this is the game you wish to play.* "We have them, Father."

"Yes, child?"

"These patrons, they are fools. They help the one you seek, and they help others. Had they barred the way to all, we should have been reduced to a pack of curs howling beyond their walls." Marique reached down and gathered a handful of dust. "Because they allow others to seek them, we may find them."

She straightened up and spat into her hand. She mixed the dust and spittle into a muddy paste, then shot a glance at Remo. "Bring the scouts."

The misshapen man wrestled them before her. She dabbed a finger in the mud and used it to draw a sigil over each of their closed eyelids. "If you open your eyes, the magick will be broken. You will die. Do you understand?"

They both nodded.

She stepped between them and Remo and threw her cloak back past her shoulders. She grasped the scouts and turned each to face into the Waste, then smeared another sigil in mud between their shoulder blades. She pressed a finger to the heart of each design, right over the scouts' spines, then whispered a word which, when said louder and with malice, could age a man twenty years before its echoes dwindled to silence.

"Eyes closed. Tell me what you see."

One man shook his head, but the other pointed a quivering finger toward the south. "There, it's beckoning. Blue, a soft blue, tendrils, weaving and flowing. Inviting. Mingling."

Marique lowered her arms, shrouding herself with the cloak. "Do not look where they conjoin, but follow the lines. Ignore the knots, do not get lost in the knots, follow the skein."

The scout who had spoken nodded and started off.

The other, head bowed, half turned back toward her. "But I see nothing."

"I know." Marique nodded solemnly. "One of you had to be blinded so the other could see. Remo, kill him."

Above, her father pointed south. "Do not lose him. Before day flows again into night, we shall have our prize."

CHAPTER 18

CONAN STOOD ON the hillside, shading his eyes with a hand. His horse, reins drooping on the ground, pawed the earth in an attempt to uncover anything even the least bit edible. The barbarian grunted.

He'd spent the night at the top of the hill, and had risen before dawn. He and the horse set off, but as it became light, they'd not gotten very far. Conan could see the tracks leading down the hill and then tracking back around it, but couldn't, for the life of him, remember making any of the turns.

He spat. *Sorcery.* As magework went, it's wasn't the nastiest he'd ever run into. It didn't try to scare him from entering the Wastes. He and the horse could ride into them without feeling any pain. It was just that he got a vague sense of frustration followed by a wave of exhaustion. Trying to go further just didn't seem worth the effort. And, curiously enough, when he let the horse go, they ended up near his hill, with good water and the view of a road that would carry them far from the Wastes themselves.

He suspected, in fact, that if he followed the road and tried to enter the Wastes from another direction, he'd end up near some other campsite of relative safety. It was akin to when his father had placed a sword at his throat, keeping him back from any potential harm in their first duels. Frustrating, yes, but his father wasn't going to let him hurt himself.

But it is worth the effort. Conan took a deep breath and faced himself due west. He spotted a stone twelve feet in front of him. His shadow touched it. He deliberately put one foot in front of the other and in two strides had reached it. Something tried to convince him that he'd gone far enough, but he picked another target and moved to it.

With each step, the Red Waste tried to fight back. It tried to convince him that he need not go any further. But its argument melted in the face of his conviction that he *did* need to go further. In fact, its every attempt to discourage him just encouraged him more. He pitted his determination against that of the sorcery protecting the land, and refused to be stopped.

He glanced at his back trail. It looked as if he'd not gotten very far at all. Hopelessness slammed into him. He snarled. Indulging it was as bad as a warrior indulging in revenge. He would not. It was not part of him or his tradition, so it would find no purchase in his mind or upon his soul.

He turned back to the west and pushed hard, then something broke. He stumbled forward, all opposition gone. Conan wasn't certain what had happened, but he figured it was not good. Drawing his sword, he whistled for his horse, mounted up, and headed west as fast as he could.

TAMARA GREETED THE sun as she always did on the eastern battlements, but found it difficult to find peace. Master Fassir's vision and explanation had confused her. She'd known, of course, about the world beyond the monastery's walls. She'd met monks from Hyrkania and someday imagined being sent on a mission into the outer world. Even so, her very existence had been defined through her relationship to the monastery and her service within the order.

Fassir had left her wondering who she was and why someone might be seeking her. Yes, he had told her it was a madman who wanted her so he could garner power, but that explanation could cover a multitude of possibilities. Unbidden had come to her the idea that somehow she had been a princess, perhaps the twin of some other princess. She'd been stolen and hidden to prevent a civil war. The madman was some renegade prince, perhaps her father's disgruntled brother, come to raise her up and claim that she was the true princess.

She'd known that idea was nonsense, but still it troubled her when a few of the other women who had heard the words of the prophecy teased her about this warrior. They fashioned him into a knight or a noble come to rescue her. That easily fit with her own scenario, which, while devoid of substance, still had the power to enchant.

Tamara drew in a deep breath and forced herself to be calm. She was not a princess, she was a monk. Her master had seen a warrior in her future, but how far into it she did not know. And he had made her promise to go to Hyrkania if so commanded. That precluded her involvement in any civil war. *The source of my blood does not matter. I am Tamara Amaliat Jorvi Karushan, a monk, and that is more than enough for me.*

Smiling at her foolishness, she began to move through her exercises. Away to the south, on the far side of the central courtyard, Fassir watched from a balcony. He acknowledged her with a nod and a quick smile. As he returned to his private thoughts, she closed her eyes and continued with her drills. She flowed from tiger through dragon and into the serpent.

As she pivoted on her left foot, something felt out of place. The ground trembled in an odd way. Two ways, really, a low tremor and a series of staccato beats. She'd not felt its like before, at least not in that intensity or combination. She opened her eyes and glanced over the walls as the first of the riders poured into the monastery.

The riders, encased in black armor, rode down two monks and a novitiate before drawing their swords. Fassir shouted commands, then turned and ran. Tamara immediately sprinted down the stairs and leaped from the lowest landing toward one of the riders. She caught him with both feet in the chest, spilling him from the saddle. He started to get up, but she kneed him in the face and he went back down.

Monks with bows let fly with arrows. One flashed past Tamara's face, thudding into a horse's chest. The beast collapsed, vaulting the rider high into the air. He smashed into the stairs, his body bowing so his heels touched his shoulders, and slumped lifeless. Elsewhere riders fell, skewered by a handful of arrows, yet others continued fighting despite their wounds.

More soldiers, clearly allied with the riders, burst in through the gate. Female archers filled the air with barbed projectiles. Monks curled up around shafts sped deep into their bellies. And then Kushite warriors, led by a giant in mail, brandished oval shields and stabbing spears. A few monks had managed to obtain pole arms and dueled with the invaders. Though the monks had trained for ages to be swift and deadly, the larger spearmen fought with a zeal for slaughter beyond Tamara's comprehension. They needed a lot of killing.

Shocked, she hesitated, and that saved her life. A mis-shapen man on horseback pointed his sword in her direction. "Get her with the others." He reined away as two lightly armored men moved to grab her.

For a moment she wilted in their grasp. As they tightened their grip, she stomped on their feet. One fist swung down, delivering a sharp blow to a groin, while the other went up, crushing a nose. As one man sank to his knees, she slammed the other face-first into the wall, then darted off toward the monastery's interior.

"Where is Master Fassir?" She shouted the question a half-dozen times, but never got an answer. She reached the top of the veranda stairs, looking back from where she and Fassir had spoken the day before. More troops poured into the courtyard, and more monks died, the morning's peace forever shattered.

The slaughter would have been complete at that point, and she would have died with the rest, save for one thing. The staccato rumbling had been the cavalry, but the lower, more consistent thunder had come from a vehicle she never could have imagined existing. The first she saw of it was the stout wooden ram crashing through the battlement above the monastery's gate. That the falling stones crushed monk and invader alike seemed of little concern to few, and of almost none to the man who stood atop the land ship's forecastle.

Arms upraised, clad in black leather armor that devoured the sun's early light, the man seemed more a god than a mortal. He peered down from the heights, surveying all the carnage. The path of a single arrow did not concern him, nor did the flight of a spear. One monk shot at him. The arrow struck the rail by his waist, but the land ship's master gave it no notice.

And a moment later a dozen black-fletched arrows pierced the monk's heart in recompense for his temerity.

For just a moment, as the last stone fell and the land ship squeezed into the gate, the battle stopped. Tamara even stopped breathing. The home she had always known, the place that had been her sanctuary, had been broken by a demigod. He was not, she knew, the warrior of Fassir's vision, but she feared that he *was* the madman of Fassir's tale.

A hand grabbed her forearm and yanked her away from the courtyard. She spun, a hand coming up in a palm strike to the face, but Fassir blocked it easily. "Come with me, Tamara."

"Who was that?"

"It's best you don't know. If you have his name and think on it, he can find you."

She blinked. "How did he find me here?"

"You don't have his name. I do." Fassir dragged her deeper into the monastery grounds, toward the western gate. "We hid you and never thought he might have sought me. I should have sent you to Hyrkania sooner."

She stopped. "I'm not leaving. Our people are dying."

Fassir's voice became edged with steel. "It is for the sake of *all* people that you must go, Tamara. To Hyrkania. Do not hesitate. Do not waver."

A company of twenty spearmen poured into the little courtyard. "We have our orders."

Fassir pushed Tamara toward the western gate and the coach waiting there. One monk sat ready to drive the team of four, and a half-dozen others had mounted up to ride as guards. "Go, Tamara. I prepared the coach against this. Go."

"I don't want to leave you here, Master."

"Deprive me of my fun?"

"Master!"

"Do you trust me, Tamara?"

She nodded. "With my life. With everything I—"

"Then ask no more questions, and do as I say."

The intensity of his stare forced her back. She retreated from him as if half asleep. She did not want to leave, but he had given her no choice. *For the sake of* all *people . . .*

Fassir, his hands open, entered the semicircle of warriors. "Your orders end with me."

Though she knew she should have run to the coach, and though the shouts of the other monks implored her to do so, she hesitated, hypnotized by her master. She had only ever known him as a demanding yet gentle teacher. In exercises, he would bring students to the point where they could seriously injure themselves, then release them and calmly explain their errors.

With the invading spearmen he showed no restraint, and his demonstrations of their errors did not save them from pain. The first of the invaders laughed as he rushed forward, stabbing a spear at Fassir's chest. The old man turned on a foot, letting the spear pass between body and arm. Before the attacker could recover from his lunge, Fassir had flowed forward. He jammed his left elbow into the man's face, then plucked the spear from him. Fassir returned to his spot, spinning the spear with the ease and abandon of a boy idly twirling a stick.

Then he cast it aside. It clattered against the courtyard's cobblestones.

As Tamara climbed into the waiting coach, her master beckoned the rest of the invaders forward. With a clatter of hooves and the cracking of a whip, Tamara fled the monastery and yet allowed herself to imagine that her master still fought and that all was not lost.

CHAPTER 19

MARIQUE STRUGGLED MIGHTILY and succeeded in resisting the temptation to stop in the center of the monastery courtyard to bask in the ebon glow of her father's victory. She told herself that this was because she had significant work to do. Her part in his victory—in their victory—had not yet begun. She hoped he would notice how quickly she fell to her work, advancing even in the face of the monks' continued resistance.

She made slow her advance toward the main temple, flanked by her father's Kushite general, Ukafa. She kept her head high, and brought her right hand up higher. Each finger had been capped with a silver talon of Stygian manufacture. Too delicate to be used to flense an enemy, they had other, more subtle uses. Sunlight lanced from them as Marique thrummed the dying threads of the magick wards that had hidden the monastery. Soon all of the monks' secrets would be open to her.

Ukafa's Kushite spearmen had gathered young female monks onto the temple's top step. A few of the women had been bloodied in combat, but none seriously, as per her father's instructions. Demanding restraint of the warriors had doubtless cost some lives, but the dull ends of spears and the flat of swords had been enough to herd the women together.

Marique was equal parts lioness hunting and empress victorious. Of the dozen women gathered above, three were too young and two far too old to be the one she sought. She did not segregate them, however, since they appeared the most nervous. *Terror is contagious.* Making an example of one would inspire the others to be more compliant, and that would speed her task to completion.

She chose one of possible candidates and approached. The woman shied from her, cringing halfway down to a grovel, but Marique caught her chin in her left hand. She raised the woman up, then tipped her head back. Her right hand came up. She stroked a talon's needle-sharp point over pale flesh, drawing a single drop of blood.

Marique caught the blood on the talon, then delicately deposited it on her tongue. In an instant she knew this was not the one she wanted, but she allowed herself to savor the taste. The girl did have promise, she had power, but not the right type, nor in sufficient quantity. *And then there is the quality of it.* Far too sweet, too light—an offering of weak tea when one sought strong brandy.

Marique smiled. "You are not the one I seek. Go."

The monk stared at her in utter disbelief, then ducked her head in thanks. She darted past Marique, keeping her eyes downcast. Which is why she never saw Ukafa's headman's sword come around. The curved blade took the woman at the base of the skull, shearing through her neck cleanly. Her head slowly spun, her body sagged. Her severed queue writhed like a decapitated snake for a moment, then the woman's head, eyes yet open, bounced down the stairs and rolled up against the body of another dead monk.

The remaining monks drew back a step, but the wall of Kushite shields prevented escape.

Marique paced before them, her silver-sheathed fingers undulating back and forth sensuously. "I look for one among you who is special. In her veins runs the blood of an ancient and venerable noble line. She is descended from the last of the Royal House of Acheron. She is here. I know this. I can smell her. I will taste her. She is among you, and if you have any compassion for your friends and companions, you will make yourself known."

The women glanced at one another, confusion and terror warring on their faces. One, one of the younger ones, bowed her head. "We do not know who you seek, Mistress."

Marique smiled and opened her hands. "There. Honesty. Was that so difficult? Your courage and honesty deserves a reward. Go."

The girl looked up at her. "Truly?"

"Of course." Marique bowed her head. "Go now." She turned and spitted Ukafa with a glance. "Do not molest her. She is free to go."

The Kushite giant frowned, but did nothing as the girl raced past and down the steps.

Of course you don't understand. Subtlety had never been something her father's subordinates appreciated. They had joined him because of simple things. Her father had been stronger than they, and had appealed to their personal vices. He'd promised Ukafa dominion over Stygia and the Black Kingdoms and ceded the western half of the world to the

Brythnian archer, Cherin. Lucius he had tempted through gluttony and doubtless promised Remo to fashion him into a handsome man.

Marique doubted, even if her father gained the powers of a god, that such a transformation would be possible.

But she had learned that subtlety amplified power because it provided access in ways people did not suspect. Yes, the murder of one girl instilled fear—compounding the terror the slaughter below had already ignited. But letting the other girl go free inspired hope. In absence of hope, one might willingly die to defend a friend or a principle, but hope proved corrosive to such bonds when the life of one was to be weighed against the life of another.

Marique looked down the line of monks and caught something in the eye of another. Of the right age and acceptable coloring, the woman brought her head up as Marique approached. Terror retreated from her face almost entirely. She threw her shoulders back and, in profile, reminded Marique of Acheronian queens she'd seen commemorated on old coins.

"You. You are the one."

The woman lifted her chin, her lower lip quivering just a little.

Marique stroked the monk's throat, then tasted her blood. Her eyes closed as the flavor played on her tongue, for at first this one did seem right. Rich, vital, the blood carried strength. This woman had power and knew it. She had tapped into more arcane lore than her masters likely ever imagined she could. And her lineage traveled back along straight lines. She was perfect . . . *almost*.

The tiniest of sour notes ruined it. Subtle, yes, and almost trivial enough to ignore. Marique's eyes opened and studied the woman's face again. Yes, a daughter of Acheron, distantly, and related to the royal house, but not legitimate. Born in the shadows, not to the crown.

Marique spat in disgust. "You sought to fool me."

"No, Mistress. I—"

Marique struck quickly, driving talons into the woman's eyes. Before blood tears could roll down her cheeks, before the woman's hands had risen halfway to her punctured eyes, the poison on the second and third talons had done its work. The woman collapsed, her flesh surrendering quickly to putrefaction, darkening in the sunlight and melting from bone.

Marique pointed at the others with a metal-sheathed finger. "Because I was merciful, do not believe I am simple or can be deceived. You will reveal to me the one I seek, one way or another. He demands it!"

She turned back to point to her father high above the courtyard, but he had abandoned his position. Instead he climbed the stairs behind her, his face set and grim. She turned, her skirt flaring, then sank to a knee. "Father, I—"

"Have you found her yet, Marique? You said she was here."

"I am close, Father."

Khalar Zym grabbed her jaw roughly and tipped her face up. "Your mother waits in a cold void that abrades her soul, Marique. She waits on you. I wait on you, and you tell me close? *Close?* I want her here, now!" He released her roughly, shoving her away, and raised a hand to strike her.

Marique lifted her left hand to ward off the blow, and found her right hand cocked and ready. Her father's armor, which she had helped him don, was not without flaw. *A sword might not find purchase, but a talon?* At his mercy though she was, she picked out three gaps where she could strike and he would flow down the stairs as did the last monk.

And she would have struck had he hit her, but his hand never fell. From the west, a knot of men appeared, wrestling an old, bloodstained monk to the top of the stairs. They cast him to the ground. Their leader, head bowed, went to a knee. "Master, this one sought to prevent pursuit of a wagon that escaped through the west gate. Remo has taken men and ridden after it."

Marique rose and withdrew a step. Though she had never seen the old monk before, she recognized his stink. His essence had been entwined with that of the one she sought from the very first. *He reeks of her even now.* She started forward, her right hand extended, but her father waved her off.

Khalar Zym crouched beside the old man. "Our paths cross again. I had thought you much younger, and hopefully wiser."

The old monk looked up, bleeding from a split lip, one of his eyes swollen almost closed. "You pursue a course of madness, Khalar Zym. A course of evil."

"Evil? You speak to me of evil?" Marique's father straightened up. "You have a convenient memory, Fassir. You know what evils have been visited upon me."

The monk's eyes hardened. "We live here in peace. We do not make war. We do not cause suffering. This is a sanctuary. We value life."

"Ha!" Her father thrust a fist into the air, then brought his hand down, pointing at the women arrayed behind Marique. "You value life. Have you told your disciples how you value it? Have you told them what happened in the forests of Ophir?"

The monk shook his head.

"I thought not." Her father snorted with disgust. "They should know, Fassir, they should know the truth of things, the full truth of them."

Khalar Zym began pacing, his face tightened with fury but his eyes focused distantly. He began to spin for the monks a story—yet telling it more to himself. Marique had heard it many times, told many ways, with her father in moods that ranged from the depths of despair to the heights of triumph. He spun it as a great tragedy—the defining moment of his life. It was the reason he was born and the reason he continued to live.

And yet in every telling, he forgets that I was there.

Marique recalled clearly the baying of hounds and the tramp of heavy hooves as horsemen chased them through the forests. They had left her father's domain, just the three of them, on a mission Maliva had devised. Through her reading of Acheronian tomes, she had come to believe that deep in the forests of Ophir lay a cavern, and within it a Well of Light. Were one to bathe in it, immortality would be bestowed.

Maliva had been too obvious in her pursuit of forbidden knowledge. Her efforts exposed her to enemies who happily fed her information.They invented the Well of Light to trap her, and Marique recalled well the day her mother had joyously discovered clues to its location in documents which Marique had been translating. Maliva had contributed to her own capture through her avarice—and it was only because the taint of Acheronian magick had not clung to Khalar Zym or Marique that they been allowed to live.

Better that we should have died.

When they finally captured Maliva, they lashed her to a massive oaken wheel—so large it might have served to transport the land ship. They secured her to the crossbeams, stretching her limbs until taut, then lit the wheel on fire. Flames sprang up with unnatural speed and supernatural ferocity. Their incendiary caresses darkening her mother's white flesh.

Hair flowing in the heat, then igniting, her mother threw back her head. Marique, in chains, clutching at her father's breast, had turned away, anticipating a scream. Instead, in a haunted voice, strong and free of pain, Maliva damned those who had pursued her.

"I curse you all. You can burn my flesh, but my soul you cannot touch. Husband, resurrect me! Bring me back and you shall be as a god!"

Marique's father held her tighter and his tears wet her hair. Then the wheel collapsed in on itself. Sparks jetted high into the air until they mingled with the stars. Maliva's murderers waited two days for the coals to cool and be raked before scattering the ashes, then set father and daughter free to wander the world as pathetic examples of the wages of infamy.

Khalar Zym's mailed fist slammed against his breast-plate. "All you did to destroy us was for naught, Fassir."

"The monks here had no part in your wife's punishment. They are innocent."

"Her blood may not be on their hands, but there is other blood, isn't there?" Khalar Zym again crouched. "Even as one set of enemies sought my wife, you and your fellow monks anticipated me. Was it a vision, or simple calculation, monk? For you acted even before my wife had died."

"We did what was necessary."

"We? You seek to shuffle blame onto your own master, a man long-since dead?" Khalar Zym rose again and addressed the monks. "Did he tell you what he did? That two decades ago he went into the world and stole a child?"

"A child your agents had taken, though you did not know what she truly was. I rescued her from your evil."

"You did more than just *that*. In fact, I might have admired how you managed it. Incredible skill and stealth, qualities I admire." Her father shook his head. "It was the other that dooms you, old man."

"It was necessary."

"Was it?" He opened his arms. "I seek a woman, pure of blood, descended from the last Acheronian priest-kings. I do not wish to slay her. I merely need some of her blood. A drop, a small vial, nothing she will notice gone, nothing from which she will not recover and be exalted for. For she who provides this would be as a daughter to me. And more."

Marique shivered.

Khalar Zym thrust an accusing finger at Fassir. "To thwart me, this one went and stole a child from my people. He brought her here. But then . . . then he did the unforgivable—that for which there is no redemption. Once he had placed her here, he sought out her parents. He slew them, and her brothers and her sisters, and her grandparents and her cousins. How many were there, Fassir? How many died to lock my wife away in hell? A dozen? Two? Did you ever count? Can you even remember?"

Fassir drew himself up to his knees and Marique sensed in him a purpose. "Every single one, Khalar Zym, from babes suckled at their mothers' breasts to a crone so old and in so much pain that she begged for release."

Marique's father folded his arms over his chest. "Where is the one I seek? Is she in the coach my men are chasing?"

Fassir said nothing.

"Of course she is." Khalar Zym shook his head. "And you're sending her to Hyrkania, aren't you? Don't lie. I see it in your eyes. You didn't think I knew of the monastery there. I've not found it, *yet*, but the road between here and Hyrkania is long. I have many agents watching. You have failed, Fassir. Let that knowledge fill you with regret."

Corin (Conan's father) teaching Young Conan about steel.

Young Conan in the woods,
encountering Khalar's army as they storm toward the village.

Hyrkanian archers from Khalar Zym's army
attacking Conan's village.

Khalar's henchmen Remo and Akhoun in Corin's forge.

Ela Shan and Conan captured.

Fassir telling his vision of a warrior crossing paths with Tamara.

Khalar using his master sword skills during attack on monastery.

Marique tasting the monks' blood,
in search for the Acheronian bloodline.

Conan, now a young man, in pursuit of Remo.

Khalar and the Mask of Acheron.

Tamara attacked by a Sand Warrior at the Shaipur Outpost.

Ukafa and Conan in a wild fight.

Artus and Tamara on the *Hornet*.

Tamara's blood reviving the Mask of Acheron.

Marique in her ceremonial garb,
searching for Tamara among the Acheronian ruins.

Khalar Zym and Conan facing off in the final battle.

The old man looked up. "My only regret, Khalar Zym, is that I was *not* there to watch your witch burn."

Fury pouring from him in an inarticulate scream, Khalar Zym kicked the monk in the stomach. As Fassir bent forward around his middle, Khalar Zym grabbed the monk's head. He smashed it again and again into the stone, dashing Fassir's brains out. Then, chest heaving, he took two steps down and let the blood drip from his hands.

Finally he raised his eyes. "Slaughter them all, man and beast. Raze this place. No stone shall stand upon stone, no well shall be unpoisoned. Fire what will burn, save bodies that you pile to rot, and salt the earth so that for generations to come, this place will stand as a warning against defying the god-king Khalar Zym."

CHAPTER 20

THE CLOUD OF dust raised by pursued and pursuer alerted
Conan to their presence long before he heard hoofbeats or
the rattle of the closed carriage. He rode toward them,
paralleling their course as nearly as he could, seeking a pass
through the hills that would allow him to study them before
he made any decision to intervene. Finally he came over a
low rise as they streamed out of a narrow cut and along a
serpentine road running around the shore of a long-since-
dried lake.

The carriage came in the lead, with a man whipping
lathered horses into a frenzied gallop. A half dozen similarly
attired men, all wearing hooded tunics of rust and homespun
pants of gray, rode behind. Their pursuers, a full dozen men
in black leather armor, with bows and spears, swords and
shields, poured from the cut and lofted arrows toward the
wagon. Dust stained their armor, emphasizing the tentacled

mask crest on their breasts, but Conan did not need that sign
to know they were enemies.

Their leader, a twisted man riding low in the saddle, had
not changed since Conan had last seen him at the forge—
save for perhaps having become even more ugly. He urged
his men on with savage curses. As they split up to engage
the carriage's defenders, he cut to the right, intent on catching the wagon himself.

One of the lofted arrows descended, more by dint of luck
than any skill, and caught the wagon's driver in the back.
He spun, clutching at it, but his legs collapsed. He fell from
his seat and the wagon bumped over him. The wagon
careened onward, outstripping its defenders, the team of
four horses racing white-eyed from pursuit.

Conan set heels to his horse's flanks and the beast leaped
forward. The two cut down the hill, picking up speed, and
came onto the flat scant yards behind the wagon. The Cimmerian urged his mount on, rising in the stirrups, then
leaped into the empty seat and scooped up the reins.

He laughed at himself as arrows whizzed past. Even with
his great strength, hauling back on the reins to slow the
horses would be difficult. If he slowed them, Khalar Zym's
men would catch up. He might be able to control the horses,
thereby preventing the wagon from being wrecked, but hitting a rock or hole at that speed, having a horse break a leg
or fall to an arrow, would bring the wild ride to an end
quickly, and still leave Khalar Zym's warriors to deal with.

A small viewport snapped open and a woman looked out.
"Who are you?"

"Can you drive a team?"

"What? Of course."

"Good." Conan glanced back as two of Khalar Zym's

men came riding fast. He made to hand her the reins through the slit. "Here. Drive."

"What? No. Wait." The viewport snapped shut.

Before Conan could muster a curse at womankind's fickle frailty, the carriage's door swung open. A slender woman, her long hair flying, arced from the interior, her hands anchored on the door. Her feet came up, then she twisted in the air and landed beside him, a smile blossoming on her lips. She snatched the reins from his hands. "Do you wish me to do more than just drive?"

"Try not to die." Conan jumped from the seat to the carriage's roof, drawing off his cloak. He whipped it toward the nearest of Khalar Zym's riders, and then launched himself in its wake. The cloak wrapped the man in darkness, then Conan tackled him, dragging him from the saddle. They landed hard, the soldier breaking Conan's fall and a half-dozen ribs in the process, then the barbarian rolled free, drawing his sword in one flowing motion.

The second rider slashed at the Cimmerian. Conan ducked the blow and struck. His cut caught the rider just above his greave, shattering bone and slicing sinew. The lower half of the man's leg came off, arterial blood pulsing hot and red, while the rider slumped to the left and fell. His foot caught in the stirrup, so his mount raced off, bucking and snorting, struggling to free itself from the dead thing dragging beside it.

Conan turned and kicked the first rider in the head before he could rise. He ran for that man's horse, which had trotted to a stop, and gained the saddle easily. He reined around and quickly took stock of the battle.

The wagon's defenders had given as good as they got. Their efforts cut the pursuit in half. Four of the defenders lay dead, and two clung to saddles despite being pierced by arrows. One of Khalar Zym's men went after them, while the other two started down the road after the wagon.

Conan trotted his horse over to block their path.

One of them raised a spear as he reined up. "Delay us and you incur the wrath of Khalar Zym!"

"I will slay him as easily as I slay you." Conan stabbed his bloody sword forward and kicked his horse in the ribs. The beast leaped forward, then sped toward the enemy. Conan knew better than to charge two armored men, especially when one had a spear and could pluck him from the saddle. But because they had the advantage of numbers, and could easily call their confederates to their aid, if he did not carry the battle to them and quickly, they would regain their wits and trap him.

He raced at them and then, at the last moment, shifted his sword from right hand to left and cut his horse to the right. This forced the spearman to raise his point past his horse's head to keep it on target. By the time it came down, however, Conan had swept past. His sword whipped in. The spearman's shield came up, and Conan's blade sparked from the iron boss. The blade still caught the man in the forehead, denting his helmet instead of cleaving his skull in half.

He spun away, shield flying, spear falling. Conan reined his horse about hard and drove at the swordsman, who'd begun to turn left before he ran into his partner's horse. Conan came around on his right. The man twisted in the saddle, futilely trying to parry Conan's blade. The Cimmerian simply lowered his hand, letting the other man's blade flash past, then stabbed up through his armpit and ripped the blade free.

Conan looked toward where the last of Khalar Zym's men had ridden, but dust obscured his view. Then a black horse with an empty saddle rode free. Conan allowed himself to believe the last attacker dead, so he kicked his horse into a gallop. He gained ground quickly along the road and came around a bend just as, two hundred yards further on, Khalar Zym's hunched lieutenant leaped from his saddle onto the coach's roof.

The barbarian wanted to shout a warning, but the girl would never hear it. *And what could she do?* He urged the horse on faster, riding low in the saddle. *If I cut across the dry lake bed there . . .* But even that would have been of no use because Khalar Zym's minion crept closer and closer. Even if his horse sprouted wings, Conan never could have gotten there in time to save her.

He snarled. *Then Khalar Zym shall atone for your death as well.*

The girl must have heard something, for she quickly cast a glance behind her. Without hesitation, her left foot came up and around, catching the minion square in the chest. He straightened up, arms milling to regain balance. He succeeded, a triumphant expression lighting his hideous face, then the wagon hit a bump and he flew into the air.

He came down heavily, bouncing once, but managed to catch hold of a cleat at the roof's rear. His other hand came up, his fingers crashing through the roof. He dragged himself up, slithering on his belly. Inch by inch he pulled himself after her.

The girl looked back again. She shook her head, then squatted. She tugged at something, then came up again and displayed a steel shaft. She taunted the man with it, then blithely tossed it away.

Before Conan could be certain what she had done, two things happened. The woman leaped forward, onto the back of one of the horses. The wagon slowed as the horses sped on. The wagon's tongue lanced down, stabbing into the road.

Before it splintered, it caused the front wheels to turn sharply left and the wagon hurtled from the roadway.

Of the man on its roof Conan saw nothing until the first bounce. Wheels and bits thereof sailed in every direction. The man arced high into the air as the carriage box started tumbling across the lake bed. It flew to pieces, instantly reduced to jagged fragments. It scattered itself along a twenty-yard path, and the man rolled to the middle of it.

Conan guided the horse toward him and dismounted quickly. Khalar Zym's man took one look at him and scrambled to his feet. He began to run in a shuffling gait, his path haphazard. Conan bent, picked up an iron wheel rim, and hurled it, tangling the man's legs and dropping him to the cracked gray ground.

The minion had rolled to his back and held his hands up as Conan approached. "Mercy, sir, mercy."

The Cimmerian stared down at him, seeing, now twisted in fear, a face he'd last seen warped by triumph and lit by the forge's fire. He pressed the tip of his blade to the man's throat. "You have one chance. Where is Khalar Zym?"

The man hesitated before he answered. Conan knew that hesitation well—civilized men always stopped to concoct lies. "If you seek Khalar Zym, then you can be a very rich man. I can guarantee you that."

Conan's eyes narrowed. "Should I believe your lies, or just backtrail you? I think I am better at tracking."

"Wait, don't kill him."

Conan looked up as the woman approached. "I don't need him. My mission ends where his began."

"Your mission is to take me to Hyrkania."

Conan glanced up toward the sun, then looked at her again. It was a bit early in the day for her to be heat-addled, and she didn't have the look of a congenital idiot. "I do not know you."

"My master knew you. He had a vision. He said a man would come to take me to Hyrkania."

The Cimmerian thought for a moment. He'd believed Lucius was likely lying when he said Khalar Zym was seeking a woman in the Red Waste. Still, Zym's men had been chasing her. The idea that her master had had a vision smacked of sorcery to him, but so did Khalar Zym and the entire Red Waste. "So you are the one Khalar Zym seeks?"

She frowned. "Who's Khalar Zym?"

The minion sucked at his teeth. "Yes, Master, this is the one Khalar Zym wants. He'll pay well for her return. You can be as we are, as we, his faithful, will be. You can be a god, too."

The woman folded her arms over her chest. "I have no knowledge of this Khalar Zym. I just know that Master Fassir said you would take me Hyrkania."

"No, Master, you cannot do that." The ugly man gingerly pushed Conan's sword out of line with his throat. "Khalar Zym is not to be thwarted. If you do not submit, he shall chase you to the end of the earth. He will hound you from Khitai to the Black Kingdoms, and even to the frozen plains of Cimmeria. You must believe me."

"I do believe you, little man." Conan stabbed his sword into the earth and crouched. He held his hands before the minion's face, revealing chain scars traced with dirt and blood. "I remember the last time he was there. I've come to remind him of it, then to ensure that's the last thought that ever travels through his mind."

CHAPTER 21

So used was she to the ritual that Marique could have made quick work of unbuckling her father's armor. The well-worn leather straps were compliant conspirators in what she did, but she did not move with haste. Beneath the armor, beneath the boiled-leather shell, she could feel her father's warmth. She relished it, and took great joy in being of service to him, no matter how tiny that service might be.

Someday he will understand the true significance of all I do for him.

At the moment, however, in his grand cabin aboard the land ship, her father's attention remained focused on one thing: the Mask of Acheron. Unforgivably ancient, the golden brown of aged ivory, with a serpent-scale texture and tentacles arrayed as if rays of the sun, the mask lay between his hands, at once terrible and hideous, yet possessed of a beauty born of its potential. His thumbs caressed the cheeks as he might have caressed a lover's flesh.

As he caressed my mother's face.

Marique removed the armor's back plate and set it aside. She started working on the next layer of buckles, beginning at the top.

"The prize is near, Father. You possess the mask, and soon you shall have the blood to fill it."

"Yes, very soon." His fingers played over the forehead. "It was your mother's dream to wear the mask. Magick flowed in her blood, as it does in yours. She yearned for the power, she sought the secrets of Acheron's forgotten sorcery. Without her and her work, we would not be on this brink."

Marique hesitated, letting a single finger caress the silken undertunic her father wore beneath the armor. His scent rose from within the shell, filling her head, warming her heart. She longed to press her cheek to his back, to linger in his presence. She drew strength from him. She hoped for a second or two of his attention, thinking that would be enough to sustain her forever, and yet knowing it would be but a drop in a vast ocean of desire.

Khalar Zym glanced back over his shoulder. "Imagine, Marique . . ."

"Yes, Father . . ."

"Imagine the secrets she will bring back with her from the realms of the dead." His voice grew from a reverent whisper to a bold declaration. "She will have spent her time well, you know. She will have pierced mysteries that have confounded necromancer and philosopher alike. Even sorcerers who were born prior to the fall of Acheron will bow before her wisdom, the wisdom of a woman who dared venture to a realm that frightens them all."

"Yes, Father . . ." Marique worked at the next buckle. *Does he not remember that I was there? He remembers her death as he needs to. Before the monks it was a foul crime.*

*Now it becomes a bold sacrifice that launched her on a
quest for lore arcane and obscure. Her mistakes, her foolishness, is what led her to her death. Is it sane to assume
she will return any the wiser?*

Her father drew the mask in toward his own face. The
girl felt certain that if it had lips, he would have kissed it.
He stared into the empty eyeholes. "Oh, Marique, can you
feel it? Can you feel the future? With my beloved Maliva at
my side, I shall be invincible! Nations may call forth legions
to destroy us, but I shall harvest them as if they were sheaves
of wheat. I shall trample on kingdoms, I shall reave empires.
All history shall begin with me and dwell forever with my
beloved and me."

"Yes, Father, I believe this." Her fingers stopped. "But,
as you have taught me, as my mother taught me, prophecy
and magick, these are subtle and delicate things. Must we
not plan further?"

Khalar Zym turned halfway around, shifting the mask
so both it and he stared at her. "What are you suggesting?"

"Father, Remo went after the girl hours ago. What if he
does not return with her?"

Her father laughed coldly. "Remo will bring her, or send
word where I can find her. He would rather die than disappoint me, and will sooner soar on invisible wings than fail
me. Put your mind at ease, Marique."

"I wish I could, Father." She turned from him, stepping
beyond his immediate reach. She bowed her head as a penitent
might when begging for mercy. "It is just, I wonder . . ."

"What, girl, tell me . . ."

"The ritual, Father, what if it fails?"

"Fails? It is not possible." Her father strode across the
cabin and replaced the mask in its setting atop a standard.
"Your mother, Marique, she uncovered the ritual. She

translated the lore herself. She knew what she was doing, and went to her death confident that through it we would bring her back. The ritual will not fail . . ."

"But, Father, if it does . . ."

Khalar Zym's eyes blazed hotly. "It will *not!* Maliva *will* return."

Marique turned and sank to her knees before her father, throwing back her chin to expose her throat. Tears, hot, desperate tears, rolled down her cheeks. "My powers are growing, Father. I have my mother's blood—your beloved's blood—flowing through me. I have learned much, Father. I have studied all my mother studied, and more."

Khalar Zym raised a hand. "Insolent child, do not presume you know more than your mother!"

Marique cast her gaze to her father's boots. "Father, I have only ever desired to be a worthy heir to you and my mother. Thus my diligence in studies. I have uncovered secrets, as she did." She reached out and took his other hand and kissed it gently. "Even now, to prove my love to you, Father, I could, I *would,* make them all kneel before you as I kneel."

A low rumble issued from her father's throat. The hand he'd raised in violence came down to caress her cheek. "Yes, Marique, you are like your mother in so many ways . . ."

She smiled against his hand.

He tore it from her and turned away. "But you are *not* her."

Khalar Zym strode from his cabin and abandoned Marique, prostrate and weeping beneath the unseeing eyes of the Mask of Acheron.

HIGH UP IN the Shaipur Pass, overlooking the road that wound its way through the hills, Conan checked Remo's bonds. He'd secured the grotesque man's hands behind him, then bound his feet to a stake he'd driven into the ground. He double-checked the knots, fairly certain the man could not free himself, but completely confident that Remo would do anything in his power to escape.

The woman tapped her foot impatiently. "We are losing valuable time, Cimmerian. We must be away to Hyrkania immediately. My master—"

Conan curled his lip in a snarl. "You have told me ample times, Tamara Amaliat Jorvi Karushan, that your master, the exalted Master Fassir of the monastery at the heart of the Red Wastes, wishes you to go to Hyrkania. I am not deaf. I am not stupid. I do not need to hear it again."

"And yet, here we are." She turned toward the horses. "If you will not take me, I shall go myself."

"You will go nowhere."

She spun, eyes sharpened. "I am not yours to command, barbarian. I am not your property."

"She belongs to my master." Remo's breath hissed from between discolored teeth. "He has sought her for decades. She is his."

"I am no man's chattel."

In one quick stride Conan dropped to a knee beside Remo and pressed a dagger to his throat. "Why does he want her?"

The little man looked up. "She is special. Her blood is special."

Conan looked back at Tamara. She was pleasing to the eye, but so had been the slave women in Messantia. He saw nothing terribly special about her. "Time for the Red Wastes to drink your blood, deceiver."

Tamara held up a hand. "Wait, don't kill him."

Conan stayed his hand.

"Why do you say I am special, that my blood is special?"

The deformed man directed his answer to Conan. "It is true, Master. Khalar Zym needs her blood because she is the last of the Royal House of Acheron."

Tamara laughed. "You're mad. I may have grown up isolated, but even I know Acheron fell millennia ago. Their blood has long since drained from the world."

"The whore lies, Master."

"You can kill him now." The woman snorted dismissively and turned away.

"No, *please*, Master. For her I can get you a king's ransom. What I tell you is true. Khalar Zym has been searching for this one for twenty years."

The Cimmerian again glanced in her direction. "What makes you so certain she is the one he seeks?"

"The monks stole her from his people. He traced her to this place." Remo licked his thick lips. "He will be on her trail again. The man who delivers her to him will be rewarded with anything he desires."

Conan smiled, and assumed that Remo's corresponding smile meant that the captive imagined Conan was dreaming of gold and jewels. "Then we shall wait for Khalar."

"A wise choice, Master, very wise. I will arrange everything. I shall be your agent. I shall deliver your message."

Conan stood and returned the dagger to its sheath on his belt. "Yes, you will."

He walked over to where the woman was putting a saddle on one of the horses. As she ducked down to grab the cinch strap, he plucked the saddle off the horse's back and tossed it with the rest of the tack. "We are waiting here."

She straightened up, making no attempt to hide her anger. "Apparently I have not made myself clear to you, barbarian. I, Tamara Amaliat Jorvi Karushan, have been charged with a sacred duty. If you will not take me to Hyrkania, then you are not the man from the vision. I shall make my own way there. Do you understand me?"

Conan chuckled, which inflamed her further.

"Why did Master Fassir not see you were an idiot?"

"Why do you believe I am stupid?" Conan folded his massive arms over his chest. "I, at least, know from whence I am come . . . and I do not need *four* names to fix myself in the world."

"Do you even have one? Do you know it?"

"Yes."

"Yes?" She raised an eyebrow. "And you haven't thought fit to share it with me because . . . ?"

"You have have told me your name five times now. I feared I would have to repeat my name five times for you to remember it."

Tamara stamped a foot. "Tell me your name."

"Conan."

"Conan? That's it?"

"It is all I need."

She scrubbed her hands over her face. "It's not even a civilized name."

"Civilized like Khalar Zym?"

Tamara started to answer sharply, then thought better of it. "He destroyed the monastery, Conan. It was horrible. He is not a man you wish to wait for. Please, I implore you, I beg you, take me to Hyrkania."

The Cimmerian met her gaze openly. "Khalar Zym found you at the monastery. Do you not think he will track you to Hyrkania, too?"

She paused, nodding. "Yes, but it is a long journey. Something may stop him."

"Yes, Tamara Amaliat Jorvi Karushan, something may. Something *will*." Conan smiled. "I am that something, and I shall stop him soon."

The monk shook her head. "I amend my statement. You are not just stupid, you are insane, too. Have you not heard anything I said? He destroyed a monastery full of monks trained as warriors. How can you hope to stand against him?"

Conan laughed easily. "You hide behind four names. He dreams of resurrecting Acheron. You both are proud of civilization, and look down upon me, for I am barbarian. But understand this: civilization is an illusion. What he did to your monastery was not civilized. It was savage. It was barbaric. You mean that as a curse, but I do not take it as such."

Conan turned from her and looked away to the north. "Before I had the first hair on my chin, I met Khalar Zym. I drew his blood. Me, a barbarian child. Four years later I was among the barbarians that overran the 'civilized' outpost of Venarium. I have traveled throughout this world, seeing many things that call themselves civilizations, dealing with many men who counted themselves civilized, and none have beaten me. Khalar Zym shall not beat me."

"There is no doubting, Conan, that you are a great warrior; but Khalar Zym is—"

"Khalar Zym is a man." Conan rested a hand on his sword's pommel. "I shall remind him of that fact."

Tamara stared at him, then shook her head. "You do not understand."

"Fear not, Tamara. Get some sleep." Conan smiled happily. "I have a plan."

CHAPTER 22

MARIQUE KNELT ALONE in her cabin, her lamps unlit and the portholes shuttered as firmly as possible. She wanted no light, for she desired to avoid all chances of seeing her reflection in the mirror. She could have covered the looking glass with a shroud, but somehow that seemed to anger the voices. She could not have endured their sibilant whisperings, especially when she knew their comments would ooze ridicule.

She'd stripped wall hangings to stuff even the tiniest light leak, and took it as an omen that the only ray which pierced the darkness pinned the Cimmerian sword to the wall. The dark hilt and pale blade reminded her of her mother, bound to the giant wheel before it had been set ablaze. She stared at it through half-lidded eyes, not daring to catch a full reflection of her face in the metal.

Marique hated herself for thinking it, but she was coming to pity her father. Not that he had become old and infirm, not that he was any less glorious than he had been on the day he completed the mask, but in that his obsession nibbled away at his reason. It blinded him to other possibilities, other realities, and to the potential for destruction that lurked in the world.

She could not imagine how he missed that truth. Her mother had been just as certain of the validity of her path, and look where it had led her. In retrospect, he had fashioned her death into a necessary trial he'd had to endure. He'd reshaped their life together into some sort of mythic journey that forced Maliva to endure time in the grave. It was a challenge that she alone had embraced because it was the only means by which she could grant Khalar Zym the power for which he had been born. He would resurrect Acheron as he would resurrect her.

But he had completely forgotten that this was not the way it had begun. Was he of Acheronian blood? Perhaps. Her mother's records had been vague on that point. True, he was a princeling—a minor one, and a renegade at that—of Nemedia, and some Acheronian blood did run in his veins. *But only so much as a single scratch with one of my talons would drain it.* Still, from her mother's perspective, that had been enough to make him worthy of elevation. The Acheronian heritage truly ran through her, as she sprang from the loins of those who had long inhabited a distant Acheronian outpost. Maliva's parents had been cast out for doing something so foul that even the Acheronians could not sanction it, and the child they had borne had found in Khalar Zym an ambitious man with a taste for tales dark and arcane.

Though Marique had not been there when the quest began, more than once her mother had confided in her their plans. She and Khalar Zym would piece together the Mask of Acheron. They would use blood to further invigorate it.

Through the mask, Maliva would lay claim to the full panoply of eldritch Acheronian sorceries—and her mother imagined that even things long forgotten would be revealed to her in full once she wore the mask. She would have the power. She would be the goddess-empress, and Khalar Zym would rule as her mortal consort.

Yet, when death claimed her, her father had reimagined their plan. *Or remembered it as it had been told to him, his beloved wife having never confided the truth to him.*

Marique decided that this latter circumstance was the case, lest she be forced to imagine her father a complete fool. While his obsession did delude him, it had not rendered him wholly without genius. He had destroyed the monastery in the Red Wastes, a feat unimaginable to those who knew of its existence. Its sister in Hyrkania would fall to him, too—before or after he found the girl and brought his beloved back to life.

She started down the dark road of imagining her mother's return—an arduous journey she had often taken and never enjoyed—but a sudden crash from above saved her from such dark thoughts. Something had slammed into the land ship. She bolted from her cabin and up a companionway, slipping past Ukafa's bulk and into her father's cabin.

Full sunlight poured through the gaping hole in the deck above. Her father sat on a barbaric-looking throne, clad only in breeches and boots, staring at the stone that had snapped oak planking, but failed to pierce the cabin's deck. A rope had been wrapped around it, then tied to a man's ankles, much as a corpse might have been bound before being tossed into the sea. The man's broken body lay twisted on the deck.

Remo!

Marique knelt by his head. Death had not made him any more handsome; nor could it have made him any more repellent.

Khalar Zym lifted a finger. "Do not bother, Marique. I know who it is."

She teased a slender strip of cloth from between Remo's lips and drew it out slowly, like a fakir producing a silk for wide-eyed children. It matched the color of the female monks' robes, save where blood had been used to write upon it. Even before she recognized the first word, Marique could feel the power. She wanted to taste the writing, just to be able to savor it, even though that act would tell her nothing new.

"It's her, Father, the one you seek."

It took a moment for him to tear his gaze away from the mask and focus upon Marique. He showed no enthusiasm, no haste; more a languid sense of ennui than anything else. "Of course."

The girl stood, stretching the cloth out between her hands. "There is a message, in her blood."

His eyes closed and his head tilted back, his face a serene mask. "Yes."

" 'I have the woman. The Shaipur outpost. You have two days. Come alone.' "

Nothing in her recitation had mattered until those last two words. Khalar Zym's eyes snapped open. " 'Come alone'?"

"Yes, Father." She held the strip of cloth in the sunlight so he could read it.

Khalar Zym sat forward, elbows on knees, hands on chin, and for the first time in too long, his eyes sharpened as if he had awakened from a dream. " 'Come alone.' She has a protector. Not one of the monks, but a new player. Remo must have told him how I valued her, yet he demands no ransom. Who, Marique, would dare? One of the Hyrkanian monks would have whisked her away and left Remo tacked to a tree as a warning. And if it were those who slew your mother, they would have killed her, then fallen upon us to destroy the mask."

Khalar Zym looked up past her to Ukafa. "Stop our advance. I wish to see the place from which this stone was hurled."

The Kushite bowed his head in a salute. "As you desire, Master."

Khalar Zym smiled. "Prepare yourself, daughter. What we shall find will be unique."

"Yes, Father?"

"Yes. A very foolish man has injected himself into a game fit for gods." Khalar Zym's eyes narrowed. "A bold move, but his last, and one certain to end in pain."

TAMARA LOOKED AT her companion and decided, one last time, to risk his tying her to the saddle as he had promised before. "Conan, I have told you I think your plan is brilliant. You send Khalar Zym to the Shaipur outpost and we ride to Hyrkania. We have a string of fine ponies. We will make it 'ere the next full moon rises. The monks in Hyrkania will not have much, but they will give it all to you."

The Cimmerian shook his head. "I am not simple, Tamara. Had I wanted gold, I could have sold you to Khalar Zym and saved myself a long ride with a chittering companion."

She hissed at his rebuke. "But you cannot believe he will come to the outpost alone. Even *if* you are able . . ."

Conan shot her a hot glance.

"Your pardon . . . even *when* you slay him, that will not stop his subordinates or cause his raiders to disband. From the pass, you saw the troops who travel with him."

The Cimmerian shook his head. "I care not about his minions, though I have had the measure of two of them.

They are cowards who only grow bold in his shadow. When he is dead, their courage will drain with his blood. My desire is to stop him."

She cocked her head and pressed a hand between her breasts. "You could do that by killing me."

Conan reined back, stopping, and fixed her with a harsh stare. "A civilized man might consider that course. I will not. I do not know if you are the last person of the Acheronian line. I do not care. Khalar Zym's ambition resides in his breast. When I split his skull, when I still his heart, when I smash that mask . . . *then* it will be over."

"Until then, I am but bait?"

Conan laughed and started riding forward again. "I saw you fight, woman. Khalar Zym sees you as bait. Your master made you more than that."

"And how do you see me, Conan?"

"As more." The Cimmerian smiled in a manner which irritated her. "I have a plan. In it, you are my *silent* ally."

KHALAR ZYM CROUCHED, tracing a finger through a footprint high on a ledge overlooking the Shaipur Pass, and Marique studied him carefully. Already one of his troopers had fallen quite by accident, confirming that the ledge was the point from which Remo had been launched. That man's misfortune saved Khalar Zym from having to toss a man from that height, something her father would not have hesitated to do.

Her father studied the footprint keenly, a hunter assessing spoor. It had been forever since she had seen that in him, and it pleased Marique no end. Khalar Zym glanced down and back at the much broader shelf a dozen feet below where she waited with the others. A trail led back around the promontory to a small valley in which they'd already discovered traces of a campsite and more footprints. Her father nodded slowly, then stood.

"He is a tall man, and heavy. Very strong." Khalar Zym pointed at the path he'd taken to ascend to the ledge. "He climbed up here with Remo over his shoulder. I imagine he broke Remo's neck before carrying him, but he's a very good climber. Born in the mountains, no doubt."

A thrill ran through her. *Cimmeria is full of mountains.* She bent, finding another of the footprints, but a swirling zephyr vanished it before she could touch the track. She listened for whispers, but caught only the hiss of the wind.

Khalar Zym opened his arms and raised his face to the sun. "I wish, Marique, your mother was here. I shall bring her, once she is back. From here I can look down to see the instrument of our victory, and out to see the world that will be ours."

"Yes, Father."

He looked down at her. "Have you more sense of the woman, Marique?"

"Yes, Father." Marique pointed toward the hidden camp. "She slept there. Remo, too, and apart. Their essence yet resides where they bedded down."

"And what of her protector?"

"You read more in his tracks than I can read in his essence, Father. She has powerful blood. Remo reeked of hedge wizardry meant to cure his many ills; but the man, nothing. Other than lingering impressions of hot curses uttered in the name of a cold, uncaring god, nothing."

Khalar Zym leaped down to her level—a dangerous maneuver, but one he dared, certain as he was of his destiny. "What would your mother tell me of him, Marique?"

She would miss even the tracks in the dust, Father. The

girl shook her head. "Far more than I could, Father. She would express caution."

Khalar Zym's expression shifted to an impassive mask. "She would not doubt me, Marique . . . as you apparently do."

"No, Father, no." Marique immediately dropped to her knees and kissed his boots. "She loved you as do I. Caution is only that you should not waste your valuable energies to capture the girl. Please, let me do it for you, to prove my love. I will bring her to you, I will."

"I am certain you would, Marique. And I do love you for that." Her father chuckled lightly. "But the challenge was issued to me. I have no intention of going alone, but I will go. I must see with my own eyes the man who would presume to command me. But fear not, daughter mine, for your love endears you to me; and for that reason, I grant you the honor of being at my side."

CHAPTER 23

CONAN PACED THE sandy courtyard of the Shaipur outpost with the fierce economy of a panther. The outpost had been established many centuries before atop a cliff overlooking a natural bay with deep blue waters. The kings of Argos had intended it to house tax collectors who could discourage smugglers, but the smugglers paid better than the kings. As the land around the outpost became exhausted, the outpost could no longer sustain itself. The people fled, taking with them most anything of value, and pirate raids successfully ended the smuggling trade.

Of two things Conan had been certain when he stuffed the note written in Tamara's blood into Remo's mouth and dropped him. The first was that the falling rock would not kill Khalar Zym. Civilized men might have added to the note some paean to the glory of Fortune, hoping the stone would crush the life out of his enemy. Conan had no doubt that while some gods were capricious enough to interfere with the affairs of men, Crom was not. For him, the only satisfaction would be watching Conan slay or be slain. While Conan never minded a bit of luck here and there, those who counted on it always ran out of it when they needed it most.

Second, Conan knew that Khalar Zym would not abide by the admonition to come alone. The man had no honor, therefore could only be trusted to act dishonorably. He was, however, vain. Tamara had described him in his ebony armor, appearing at the monastery as if he were some god of the underworld. Such a man would believe that Conan—simpleton that he must be for issuing such a challenge—expected him to come alone. Khalar Zym would, for the sake of appearance, come to the outpost and meet Conan in open combat. This would give Conan his best chance at slaying the man.

Conan had prepared his battlefield well. Opposite the entrance, at the top of stairs on the balustraded outpost, Tamara stood bravely. A rope had been looped about her waist and appeared to bind her hands behind her, and her body to the worn stone pillar against which she leaned. On either side of her burned torches in sconces, giving her the appearance of a sacrifice intended to appease some ancient and terrible god.

The folds of her robe hid a dagger. If Khalar Zym got past Conan, she was prepared to pin the madman's tongue to the top of his skull.

Conan looked to the west and shook his head. *What fools these civilized men are.* Khalar Zym had sent troops ahead—most likely his female archers—to take up a position near the ruins of the western wall. Even if they had not knocked over some of the piles of rocks Conan had set up to warn him of their advance, the dust they raised as they slipped into position would have given them away.

Their arrival heralded that of their master. Khalar Zym entered through the long-shattered main gate, pausing at the top of the stone ramp leading down into the courtyard. Clad in black leather armor and purple skirts that contrasted sharply with the dusty beige of the outpost's walls, he surveyed the ruins and deliberately avoided catching Conan's eye. His gaze measured the place not as a combatant might, but as a conqueror come to survey a far-flung shard of his empire.

Behind him, clinging to what little shadow existed in the sun-washed outpost, lurked a woman. In her, Conan recognized the strange girl he had seen in his father's forge. The Cimmerian shivered as he recalled the rasp of her tongue and her whisper. Khalar Zym might have grown to be evil, but she had been raised in it, steeped in it. Killing him alone would not end the threat to the world.

Khalar Zym plucked a small leather bag from his belt and tossed it into the sand. It clinked and gold coins spilled out. "You are bold, northerner. I admire valor, even when it is in service to a doomed cause. There, take your reward."

Conan shook his head. "I do not want your gold."

The man in black armor studied him for a moment. "An ambitious man. What do you wish? Jewels? To replace Remo at my right hand?" He glanced over his shoulder at the woman. "To win my daughter and become my heir? You exalt yourself."

Conan drew his sword.

Khalar Zym's face lit with surprise. "You wish to kill me?"

Conan beckoned him forward with a hand.

Khalar Zym sighed. "I had so hoped for more. So many people have wanted to kill me. It becomes tedious, and I really haven't the time for it." He raised a hand. "Marique, my pet, show me how much you love me. Kill him."

THOUGH SHE WISHED to take a moment to luxuriate in the warmth of her father's words, Marique fell to obeying his command in an instant. In her left-hand palm lay a half-dozen shards of clay plucked from the fortress's crumbling outer walls. Upon them, using one of the Stygian talons, Marique had drawn the image of warriors, and covered them with venerable glyphs of considerable power. She closed her hand into a fist, crumbling them into dust, then opened her hand and blew.

The dust spread into a cloud that rolled down over the courtyard. The barbarian drew back, apparently intelligent enough to recognize sorcery, but not nearly bright enough to understand it would be his undoing. The dust plunged into the courtyard sand, mingling again with the earth that created it, and the sand itself rippled. The Cimmerian studied the patterns, shifting this way and that, tracking them and seeking a position from which he could fight.

A shiver ran through Marique. She'd not known he was a Cimmerian, that impression had just come to her. But now, as she watched him, this magnificent man whose muscles rippled under flesh bronzed by the sun's kiss, she understood that he was *the* Cimmerian. She sniffed, hoping for more than dust, for a hint of his scent. *He is special.*

Her stomach twisted. It took her a moment to understand the emotion. Fear, but fear as she had never known it before. This man could slay her father. And though she hated that thought, she did not call out a warning. For in the wake of fear came a thrill as she watched her father work his way around toward the woman, blithely unconcerned that his destiny danced with naked steel in the courtyard below.

CONAN PULLED BACK, watching the movement within the sand. Whatever lurked there, the things moved as sharks through the water in the aftermath of a sea battle. Conan leaped across their paths, seeing how quickly they could turn, then spun and lashed out low, expecting to split the skull of some saw-toothed serpent or venomous blind worm.

He found his target, but instead of slicing through its head, he cut cleanly through both skeletal shins. His blade met less resistance than it might have done with a human foe. Worse yet, as his sword passed through, sand flowed down from above, and up from below, closing the cut without the hint of a scar. The sandlich slashed back at him with a curved dagger blade made of glass, which shattered when Conan blocked the cut. The sandlich spun away, but the blade grew back.

Conan took one step toward it, but the warrior, its death's-head grinning, melted back into the sand. Another rose behind him, its shadow his only warning, and the sting of a dagger his reward for sloth. The Cimmerian whirled, again aiming low. He expected his foe to melt away, and he was right. His blade carved the skull up from down, leaving a small pyramid of dust to mark its passing.

Conan's eyes narrowed. He had the sandliches' measure now. Though he had no use for sorcery, he'd had ample experience of it. The two he'd faced had strange sigils inscribed in breastbone and forehead. While these doubtless gave them life, they also provided him with targets to destroy them. *And once them, then Khalar Zym. Or, perhaps, the daughter.*

Two of the warriors jetted up through the sand, one to each side. Instead of cutting at them, Conan dove forward, tucking himself into a roll, then came up and spun. Both of them came in slashing; what had been dagger blades had grown into long swords, similar to the one Khalar Zym wore. The Cimmerian smiled, ducking both slashes, then lunged, piercing one's breastbone glyph. It evaporated as Conan broke the other's sword, and he allowed himself a quick glance at Marique. *They shall not stop me.*

MARIQUE FROZE FOR a heartbeat as the Cimmerian's hot gaze met hers. Her sandliches should have dispatched him easily. They'd slaughtered countless enemies when she'd used them before. Then, in a flash of insight, she understood the barbarian's smile and why he looked at her. Her sandliches fought in the style of her father, but only at the level of *her* understanding of swordsmanship. All she knew of it was what she had gleaned from watching her father dispatch enemies. She was no match for the barbarian in that realm.

Will my father be?

She could not bring herself to imagine her father any man's inferior, but dared not chance that he was. From a small pouch at the back of her belt, she drew a small brass device shaped like a dragonfly and a small vial sealed with wax. She flicked open a panel on the dragonfly's thorax, scraped the wax from the vial, and poured a thick, black liquid into the hollow body. She snapped the panel shut again. The wings glistened as the poison oozed out to cover them.

Muttering words she'd learned from her mother when the dragonfly had been given her as a child's amusement, she launched it into the air, and sent it into orbit around the outpost.

"CONAN"

The Cimmerian turned at Tamara's cry and bounded up the steps three at a time. Khalar Zym had reached her side. She'd slashed at him, and he'd recoiled from her attack. She moved to press it before he could draw his sword, but one of the sandliches had risen to grab her ankle.

Khalar Zym drew his curved sword and stepped back, allowing Conan to meet him on level ground. They circled for a moment, each eyeing the other. Khalar Zym finally nodded, and beckoned Conan forward with the same casual gesture the Cimmerian had made before.

Conan darted in, thrusting low, then bringing his blade up for a cut at Khalar Zym's groin. Zym parried the blade out and up in a circle, steel skirling. Conan drew his blade back as they passed, then whirled and slapped, knowing his blade would hit flat. Khalar Zym had not expected that, but still turned and avoided most of the blow. Nonetheless, the blade caught him over the ear, knocking him back and sending him stumbling down the steps.

Khalar Zym's hand came up and fingers probed his ear. They came away bloody. He looked from his hand to Conan. "Who *are* you?"

"You left a boy in Cimmeria holding a chain. You stole something from his people."

Recognition washed over Khalar Zym's face, but in its wake came a dismissive snort. "You'll have to do better than pinking my ear, boy."

Conan, intent on pinking the other ear as well, and

thrusting steel through the skull to link them, flew down the stairs at Khalar Zym. The Cimmerian's sword came up in an overhand blow. Khalar Zym blocked it, but staggered back two steps. He thrust, hoping to drive Conan back, but Conan beat the blade aside and lunged again. Khalar Zym retreated, a line on his armor revealing how close Conan had come to opening an artery.

As Conan engaged Khalar Zym at the outpost's heart, Tamara engaged two of the sandliches. With a dagger in one hand and a torch in the other, she fended off the sorcerous creatures. One ducked beneath a swipe with the torch, but Tamara's front kick crushed the sigil on his breastbone. She leaped away from the second, moving up toward the outpost's seaside wall.

Khalar Zym drew back, becoming less arrogant in his stance. Conan knew better than to mistake that as a retreat. He waited, knowing the man who had destroyed his village would have to prove himself the superior warrior. Zym obligingly drove forward, a stamp feint raising dust, then lunged. As Conan went to parry, Zym brought his blade up and over. That thrust missed and Zym sailed past, giving Conan an easy shot at his back.

Conan hesitated for a heartbeat. Zym's twin blades parted, one twisting around and locking into place at the other end of the hilt. As the man whirled, the second blade passed through where Conan would have been. The blow would have cut him from hip to spine, and before he fell, the second slice would have taken his head.

As Khalar Zym came around, Conan parried his slashing blow low, then whipped his left fist around, catching the man in the face. Zym spun away, flailing to catch his balance. He went down to a knee and continued to twist around. He regained his feet, swaying drunkenly, then spat blood from a split lip.

Before Conan could close, he caught a glint of light in the corner of his left eye. For a moment he thought it was an arrow and twisted away. It still sliced him, a flesh wound, nothing more, on the neck. It plunged past and into the dirt, a metal dragonfly, which Conan stomped on contemptuously.

"Enough games, Khalar Zym. It is time for you to die." Conan took a step toward the man, but suddenly the landscape shimmered strangely. Khalar Zym's shape blurred and wavered as if he were a heat mirage. The man lunged and Conan parried, but it came slow and Zym's blade cut him over the thigh. Numbness began to spread over Conan's left shoulder, a tingling descending that arm.

The Cimmerian reeled back, falling at the foot of the steps. Khalar Zym loomed above him, twin blades whirling. "Now you join your misbegotten clan, Cimmerian."

"Touch him, Khalar Zym, and I throw myself from the battlement."

Khalar Zym hesitated and Conan scuttled back up the steps. Though he could only see her as a dim outline, Tamara stood there on the wall, tall between crenels, a burning torch held aloft. "If he dies, so do your plans."

Khalar Zym retreated to the middle of the courtyard. "Well played, monk."

"Master Fassir taught me well."

"Alas, not well enough." He raised a hand. "Cherin, your archers. Varminting points. Take her."

Around the western wall appeared the female archers, bows drawn, arrows with thick, blunt points nocked.

Tamara's voice gained urgency. "Now, Conan!"

Though the world blazed in some spots and grew dim in others, though his limbs quivered and his tongue had thickened in his mouth, Conan sped into action. He lumbered up the steps, or so it seemed to him, though, in reality, thick thews made short work of the distance. Bows thrummed and a few arrows hit him like punches. More had hit Tamara and she fell inward toward the courtyard, but still she had the presence of mind to pitch her torch to the left, through the hole that led into the bowels of the outpost.

Conan and Artus had once explored the outpost as a potential sanctuary for their corsairs. It had been thoroughly looted and in need of an abundance of repairs. It would not suit them, but in it they located several tunnels filled with a viscous mixture of naptha and oil that the Argosians had once used to project fire onto attacking ships below. Since their arrival at the outpost, Tamara and Conan had filled urns and casks with the stuff, placing it where Khalar Zym would most likely hide his troops, and laying a trail to it that led back to a number of holes like the one into which Tamara had cast her torch.

As she fell inward, Conan rose to meet her. He caught her around the waist, gained the top of the battlement in a step, then launched himself into the air. Behind him, in a series of explosions, fire geysered up and gushed out. Archers screamed and a few fell toward the sea. Others launched arrows that sped past. But of his plunging fall into the water, aside from a brief glimpse of the *Hornet* coming around the headland and into the bay, Conan remembered nothing.

CHAPTER 24

MARIQUE REACHED THE wall beside her father, having dodged blazing puddles and the thrashing of burning bodies. A ship—smaller than her father's land ship—had rounded the headland and had deployed two longboats. Corsairs pulled at oars, heading for where the monk was managing to keep the Cimmerian afloat.

Her father, a trickle of blood running down the side of his face, slammed his fist against the wall. "She is getting away."

Marique laid a hand on her father's forearm. "We shall get her, Father."

He turned on her, fury knotting his features. "We? *We?* Her escape is *your* fault."

"My fault?"

"Yes, your sorcery has failed me . . ." His eyes became slits. "Your *weakness* sickens me."

Marique fell back, clutching her stomach as she might

have had her father shoved a foot and a half of steel into her belly. "My weakness?"

He stared out at the sea again. "You know it is true."

"My weakness?" Anger entered her voice, tinged with ice. "It is *I* who found her for you, Father."

"And you could not do as I asked. You could not kill the barbarian as I asked. So now she flees. My archers burn and the two of them swim to that ship." He thrust a finger toward the east. "So, what does your sorcery tell you now, Marique? That they will sail up the River Styx and, from there, overland to Hyrkania? Or perhaps they will skirt the Black Coast and sail to Vendhya and go north from there. Maybe all the way to Khitai and then west? Will that be it?"

"Father, I can track her, but you know that I cannot predict . . ."

"Then what good are you to me?" He turned, a hand raised to slap her. "Your mother was not weak. She could have predicted."

Marique clenched her jaw. *Could she? Could she indeed?* Marique wanted to shout the obvious at him: that her mother had *failed* to foresee the trap that led to her own death. *Where was the strength of her magic when* that *happened?*

Outrage raced through Marique. She forced herself to look out at the ocean. Pirates were already pulling the Cimmerian's unconscious body into a longboat. What an amazing constitution he had, for the poison, even with so tiny a scratch, should have felled him in two steps or three. Even wounded and wavering, he had fended her father off—proving himself to be the better man.

The moment that particular thought entered her head, Marique's vision of the future shifted. She had always believed that they would succeed in activating the Mask of Acheron. It would allow her father to draw Maliva back from the dead, but that did not mean that the mask was good for nothing else. Marique knew far more of the ways of the mask than her mother ever had. With it activated, on his face, and he in full command of its magicks, Khalar Zym would become invincible in battle. No force could stand against him. He would be able to summon the wisdom of Acheron's finest generals, direct the magicks of its greatest necromancers. Compared to that, the things her mother might offer would be but the snarls of a puppy in a company of wolves.

But my father is not the only one who could wear that mask. She allowed herself to imagine Conan wearing it, with her at his side—or rather, with him as *her* consort. With her magicks and his skill, not only would Acheron rise again, but it would expand far beyond the borders it had once known. Her father's dreams of power and glory would fade in comparison to the reality Conan and she could create.

Khalar Zym turned cold eyes on her, a fingertip probing his busted lip. "So silent, Marique. I would take this as a sign of your being appalled at your weakness, but you are not at my knees, begging my forgiveness."

"Do you wish to know the depth of my *weakness*, Father?" Marique turned, and with a crooked finger summoned the acolyte who bore the standard upon which hung the Mask of Acheron. The man came forward, stumbling, the mask swinging. Two of Ukafa's burly spearmen moved to stop him, but sandliches sprang up and hamstringed them with quick cuts. The acolyte flew up the stairs even more swiftly than the barbarian had done, and slammed into the wall.

The Mask of Acheron hung past the battlements, dangling above sea and stone.

"*This* is how weak I am, Father. Watch my sorcery shatter

the mask and scatter the pieces into the sea." She looked at the soldiers who had filtered into the outpost. "Watch me burn the eyes from your warriors, snap their spines, and boil brains within skulls. And ask yourself, Father, once I have done all that, will you *dare* to call me weak?"

Marique watched him. *Show me one sign of your own weakness, Father, just one sign . . .* She looked for a lip to quiver, for a bead of sweat to rise on his brow. She wanted a muscle to twitch, his pupils to contract, his mouth to hang open, just a bit. Anything to show that he knew that she had grown past him, past her mother.

Give me that sign, and I shall destroy you.

Instead his head canted to the side, only a degree or two, in a sign of curiosity. A smile tugged at the corners of his mouth. "Oh, Marique, so much of your mother's fire, so much of my spirit . . . they have melded in you in ways unexpected. You make me so proud."

Her grim expression eased.

"You must forgive me for scolding you, beloved daughter. We are *so* close to everything we have sought. Being able to rebuild our family, to recover our heritage." Khalar Zym turned his back to the sea and the sight of the monk as she was taken aboard the pirate ship. "And you will forgive me for testing you."

"Testing me?"

"Oh yes, Marique." He focused distantly. "My longing to have my wife returned to my side has not blinded me to the difficulties of the future. The task we set ourselves of restoring Acheron is not one which two alone can accomplish. I have driven you hard, Marique, and today the hardest of all. Never have I questioned your love for me, but being as close as we are, now, I had to assure myself that you were committed to realizing our entire goal. Resurrecting your mother is but one part of it—a minor part—and you shall be a major player in all the rest."

The girl frowned and gestured toward the outpost. "This was a test?"

"Yes, and you proved yourself, Marique." Khalar Zym smiled. "When I *allowed* the barbarian to strike me, when I *allowed* it to seem as if I was in danger, you reacted. You attacked him, unbidden. You worked *with* me to defeat him . . . and so shall you work with me to defeat *all* of our enemies."

He reached out and caressed her cheek. She raised a finger to his broken lip, repairing the torn flesh with a whisper, ignoring the fact that Ukafa had pulled the standard back from the battlement. "I love you, Father."

"I know." He slid his arm around her shoulder to guide her out of the burning outpost. "Come, we return to Khor Kalba to continue our preparations."

"But, Father, we don't have *her*."

"This shall not be a problem for long, I trust, Marique, will it?" Her father gave her a squeeze. "I want you to use your unique and valuable gifts . . . your very *strong* gifts . . . to find the woman for me again."

"Yes, Father, I shall." Marique nodded solemnly. "And at Khor Kalba, we have just the creature we need to bring her to us."

CONAN SHIVERED AS consciousness teased him with its return. The world moved around him, but resolved itself into a steady, rhythmic motion. Combined with faint creaks and tang of salt air, he concluded that he was aboard a ship. He tried to move an arm and wasn't certain he'd been able to do so. Still, he felt no band around his wrist, nor heard

the clank of chains, so he assumed he was not in the hands
of his enemies.

As more of his senses returned, with them came an
awareness of aches and pains, and general stiffness. The cut
on his neck burned still, but not with poison. The unguent's
scent reminded him vaguely of the poultice Connacht had
used to preserve his hands so many years before. Other nicks
and cuts he found through the tightness of stitches. The
wounds hadn't been deep that he remembered, and had they
been, cautery would have been used to close them instead
of needlework.

A gentle hand laid a cool compress on his forehead.
Another cloth dabbed at the wound on his neck. Soft words
in distant whispers reached his ears, and his mind reconstructed his world. On a ship, a woman attending him, her
hand so gentle, her voice warm for him. *My beloved . . .*

When he opened his eyes, even the feeble candlelight
burned them. He began to tear up, but not quickly enough. He
could not recognize the woman perched on the edge of the
bunk, but he knew who she was *not. She is gone, Conan, long
gone.* A tremor shook him, then all strength fled his limbs.

Tamara pressed a hand to his chest. "Don't speak, Conan.
Don't try to move. The poison gave you a fever. It's only just
broken."

He blinked away tears. "How long?"

The monk smiled. "You don't listen very well."

"How long?" He tried to make his words forceful, but he
could barely muster a whisper.

"Two days. There has been no sign of them." Tamara
nodded sincerely. "Artus has set course for the east, to
Hyrkania."

Conan shook his head and tried to sit up. "No."

She restrained him with a light hand. "Once I am safe, there is nothing more to fear."

Conan sighed. He wanted to explain to her that as long as Khalar Zym lived and had the mask, she would never be safe. She would argue that her master had directed her to Hyrkania, and he would explain that her journey and his mission were not intertwined. He had to go after Khalar Zym and destroy the mask.

But weakness betrayed him. He surrendered to her ministrations and exhaustion. *First defeat the poison, then the one who uses it.*

IT TOOK ONE more day for Conan to crawl from the bunk, and that over Tamara's protestations that he would faint and his stitches would burst. He just growled at her, and the woman proved she had some sense by not trying to stop him. She showed she had more by not laughing when he bumped his head on the companionway ceiling as he stumbled his way to the main deck.

Thank Crom it's night. He straightened up and drew in a deep breath, resisting the temptation to shade his eyes from the harsh moonlight. It splashed silver over the waves and he smiled, remembering many an evening watching it, content with his life as a corsair.

Artus looked down from the wheel deck. "So the dead have risen."

"How long are we out of Shaipur?"

"Three days, but becalmed for the last half." Artus shrugged. "Trade winds will be shifting soon. I'd rather not chance the Styx. So what will be your pleasure? Vendhya or Khitai?"

Conan slowly trudged up the steps and stood beside his friend. "Someday both, but not for me, now."

"But the girl said . . ."

The Cimmerian patted Artus on the shoulder. "You can take her to Hyrkania, and may all the gods speed that journey. But me, you'll be putting me ashore as soon as we find a place where I can buy a horse. Khalar Zym has to be bound for Khor Kalba. I'll happily kill him there."

"That will be quite the undertaking for one man, Conan, even such as you. Let us come with you."

The Cimmerian shook his head. "It is not your fight, Artus."

"Either you are lying to me now, my brother, or you are lying to yourself." Artus waved a hand toward the shore, which was but a distant black band beneath the starry sky. "You tell me that Khalar Zym must die and the mask must be shattered so he cannot raise Acheron. You claim preventing this is a responsibility you inherited through your father. But I ask you, were Khalar Zym to succeed, what would his empire mean to me, mean to this motley pack of sea wolves?

"One empire from mountains to sea, from ice to the Black Kingdoms? Would there be room for corsairs and adventurers? No, save perhaps in arenas where men die for the amusement of nobles. No freedom. No wealth to be won, no wenches to be bedded. My parents were slaves, but not I, and I shall die fighting Khalar Zym's empire."

The barbarian's head ached. Conan could not tell if Artus was right, or if he'd been lying to himself and indulging in dreams of revenge. Ultimately it did not matter, because either answer still pointed to the same necessities.

"You are wise, Artus, perhaps wiser than I." Conan exhaled heavily. "You can help me, but it will not be by traveling with me."

Artus folded his hands over his chest. "Go on."

"If I fail, the girl must be hidden in Hyrkania *and* the world must know the danger it faces. Upon you I rely for both of those things."

The Zingaran's expression tightened. "You cannot assault Khor Kalba alone."

"I don't intend to go alone. And I don't intend to make an assault." Conan smiled. "Remember, Artus, before either of us were pirates, we were both thieves. A thicf will do what pirates can't . . . and pirates will be free to save the world."

CHAPTER 25

CONAN STOOD ON the main deck a day later, the sword in his hand whistling through the air. He'd lost his sword at the Shaipur outpost. The *Hornet*'s armory boasted a fine selection of weapons plundered from the world over. As sailors were wont to do, they wagered on which they thought the Cimmerian might choose.

He tried a half dozen, almost instantly rejecting anything saberlike that resembled Khalar Zym's sword. While the sabers were fine weapons, and curved cutlasses worked well aboard ship, both served best when the fighting allowed for grand slashes. He wanted more reach than afforded by an Aquilonian short sword. The closest blade they had to the one he lost needed a new grip. Finally he settled on a long sword, which gained in length what it surrendered in width. *Had this been my blade at Shaipur, I might have spitted him.*

Conan studied the blade once more, then turned to face

Artus. "Raise an edge on it, open the toe of my scabbard so it fits, and I am set."

Artus smiled and accepted a small pouch of gold coins from the first mate. "I thought that might be it."

"And 'twas your teeth that gnawed the grip on the broadsword."

The Zingaran shrugged. "Tang was weak and cross hilt too small."

"True." Conan smiled. "Artus, I had him. So very close."

"The gods were not amused enough." The corsair's eyes narrowed. "Are you certain you're well enough to go after him?"

Conan spread his arms wide, stretching massive chest muscles. "I will be fine by the time the gods are amused enough to blow us to the coast. I swear, Artus, you are as bad as Tamara."

"I care for you as a brother, Conan. She cares as well." Artus smiled easily. "You saved her life."

"And she mine." Conan shook his head. "You must promise me she will be safe, Artus."

"I will not disappoint you. Still . . ."

"Yes?"

"There is no reason you cannot get her to Hyrkania and await Khalar Zym there." Artus held a hand up. "No, Conan, do not try to convince me this is the only way. He *needs* her. He will pursue her."

The Cimmerian shook his head. "I am not one to lie in wait, Artus, you know that."

"True, but if a brother may point out the obvious to a brother, you seem to run faster *from* her than *toward* him."

Conan growled at Artus, but before he could say anything, Tamara appeared from belowdecks, adorned in bright red and blue silks. She wore a broad smile.

The Cimmerian snapped at her. "You look like a harlot."

Her eyes flashed. "Yes, and apparently I'm the only woman you have met who isn't one!"

Conan stared at her for a heartbeat, then turned away, his new sword singing through the air. One sailor laughed and the Cimmerian spun, looking at him over a yard of steel. "Artus, give her leather and armor. She handles herself better in a fight than you scum. Keep civil tongues in your heads and you may live long enough to see the proof."

TAMARA LOOKED AFTER the withdrawing barbarian, then to Artus. "I don't understand."

Artus perched himself on the rail as Conan climbed up to the wheel deck and disappeared from sight. "Most people look at him, a northern barbarian, and they think he's simple. And 'tis true that strong currents run through him. When action's demanded, he's the man who acts instead of thinking . . . but he's cunning, too. I've seen that over my time with him, and it's that time, going on a decade here and there, that maybe lets me see."

She pressed a hand to her throat. "Then perhaps you can enlighten me. The Conan I've seen has the constitution of a bull and the disposition of a mule. He's fearsome in combat and yet capable of . . . Khalar Zym's aide, the one we captured, Conan snapped his neck as if it was nothing."

"From the barbarian point of view, the man was already dead. After all, had he been any sort of warrior, he never would have surrendered. He would have died on the battlefield." Artus shrugged. "And his willingness to bargain, this unmanned him further. The man, I'm sure, thought he could pull the wool over Conan's eyes. Not the first to make that mistake, and certainly not the last—though all of them tend to share the same fate."

She glanced up toward the wheel deck but could not see Conan. "So, he is a man who kills, and that is all?"

"You know that is not true, woman. Conan is a man of great passions. Wine and women, plunder and adventure; these are passions of his. But he is fiercely loyal. You've saved his life. He shall never forget that, and never let harm come to you. Know that as well as you know the sun rises in the east."

Tamara nodded. Conan was completely unlike the people she had known growing up. In the monastery, their training allowed them to channel their emotions into constructive things. While they did develop martial skills, they studied them to defend themselves and others. Conan's passions flowed in the entirely opposite direction. *Master Fassir was a creature or order, but Conan . . .*

The instant she sought to contrast them, she immediately saw that which they shared. Master Fassir, too, had his passions. He loved the people of the monastery. In taking her in, he had proved his love for the people of the world. Master Fassir had dedicated his life to thwarting Khalar Zym in one way, and so Conan, in another, was devoting himself to the same task.

Tamara reached out and caught Artus's forearm. "You are his friend, Artus. Tell me, his life, is it one that makes him happy?"

The Zingaran scratched at his chin. "He is one who may not have been born to ever be happy. Where others first taste mother's milk, he had her blood. Born on a battlefield was he, and never quite so happy is he except when fighting."

"Never?"

Artus sighed. "Conan and I are not joined at the hip, little one. There are times he is away. When he returns, perhaps he is less melancholy. It is not the way of men to ask after these things."

"That is foolish." She turned toward the stairs, but Artus caught a handful of silks and restrained her. "Let me go."

"No, Tamara. You seek to mend that which cannot be mended. Not now." The corsair laughed easily. "Get yourself below. Get yourself into proper dress, battle dress. If that won't bring a smile to his face, I sincerely doubt there is anything else that will."

IN THE DEEPEST depths of Khor Kalba, restless waves splashed up through a massive iron grate filling a cylindrical cavern's floor. Shadows obscured the upper reaches. Chains attached to cages filled with skeletons or skeletally slender prisoners hung down from the darkness. The other ends attached to massive cleats, allowing attendants to raise and lower cages as required.

The iron had been worked in a pattern that recalled the arms of a squid. Marique had liked it from the first because of its tantalizing symmetry. Her father had seen it as an omen confirming the rightness of his choice of Khor Kalba. He seemed to have forgotten that it was Marique who had discovered that the current construction had been built over Acheronian ruins. And, indeed, nearby excavations had unearthed much which increased her knowledge of necromantic lore.

Marique picked her way along a haphazard path like a child wandering through a garden. She chose carefully the runes upon which she stepped, and how hard she stepped on them. The sounds her boots made, the cadence of her steps, and the very notes produced by each individual rune wove a powerful magick.

Finally she reached the center point. From the small sack on her belt she withdrew the limp body of a cat—one of many feral creatures infesting Khor Kalba. She'd lured it with cheese, then snapped its neck. She disemboweled it, read the liver, then packed it up with a small bit of the cloth bearing the monk's blood and another missive that Marique had written herself. She looked down through the hole centermost in the grate, then dropped the cat and watched as it disappeared into the depths.

A minute, perhaps two, passed, then the water became greatly agitated. It splashed up through the grate, though it never touched Marique. Then it settled, several feet lower than it had been, and she walked from the center uncaring what tune her steps played.

Her father awaited her at the edge. "Well?"

"It is done. Your troops shall reach their ship unseen, and the girl will soon be yours."

CONAN STOOD AT the aft rail, staring at the sea. He felt the breeze and heard the gulls. The tang, their cries, took him back to the *Tigress* and the time he had spent with Bêlit. He had tried very hard to avoid those memories, but he could not. Though Tamara and Bêlit could not have been more different, when he had wakened from his fever to discover Tamara tending him, he had at first thought she was Bêlit.

I wanted her to have been Bêlit.

He shook his head, but his father's words came to him. "When you find that one woman, Conan, the one who fires your heart, who makes you feel alive and makes you want to be a better man than you are, never let her go." But he had. He'd lost her to an ancient evil, and though he knew himself to have been lucky to have survived at all, guilt restrained him like an anchor chain.

Artus appeared on his left at the rail. "She means well, Conan."

The Cimmerian growled.

"Let me rephrase: she means you no harm." The corsair faced him, leaning on the rail. "I actually think she wishes you well."

Conan nodded. "I was sharp with her."

"Were words a sword, there would have been no healing that wound. It is not my place to ask . . ."

"No, it's not."

"So I shall just tell, then. You forget, Cimmerian, I knew you when you were a sneak thief, and not a very good one. You made up in audacity what you lacked in skill, and the only reason fences did not turn you over to the city guard is that you'd take a tenth of what you could have gotten for the wares you sold them."

"If this is meant to cheer me, you are failing, brother."

"It is meant to remind you, brother, that I have seen the youth you were, and the man you have become. No, don't give me *that* look. I don't presume to know what goes on in that thick skull of yours, and I don't pretend to know what adventures you've had outside my company." Artus spat into the sea. "I do wish I knew of your previous life as a corsair, for it was there you changed. Not unexpected, the loss of carefree youth . . . but something replaced it."

The Cimmerian stared at the distant horizon. "I was born to battle. Courage and cunning are what Crom gives us, and I have made the most of them. Of comrades and companions I have had legions. Most have died. Many I have mourned. A few, however . . ." *One . . .*

Artus remained silent, letting the distant crash of surf on

shore devour Conan's words. In that one act the Zingaran revealed that he was a true friend, and likely knew the Cimmerian better than anyone else alive.

Conan looked sidelong at him, then finally turned to face him. "I have no fear of death, Artus. I cannot think of a time when my death concerned me. But I wonder, sometimes, if Death uses me as bait, much as I used the girl. Does Death allow me to survive so that others will follow me into his realm? My friends do not live long. Survive another year and you will have known me longer than did my father. And my mother, well . . ."

Artus rested scarred hands on Conan's shoulders. "I am your brother, Conan. I'll see you into a grave or the other way around. It does not matter. If I follow you, it is not because I believe you will make me immune to Death's touch, but because you open the way to adventure. Already, Conan, men sing of you, and of those who you have known."

Conan nodded. *The Song of Bêlit* had become popular in Shem and he'd even heard it sung once in Messantia. "There are more pleasant ways to become immortal."

"Are there?" Artus laughed and pointed off toward Khor Kalba to the north. "Immortality is what Khalar Zym desires, and his way is none too pleasant. His way is decidedly unpleasant for those who stand between him and his goal. Most men would never dare oppose him because they fear for their lives. But if they do not oppose him, they do not have a life."

"So you have told me."

"So, perhaps now you will listen."

Conan nodded. "I will."

"Good." Artus ran a hand over his jaw. "One thing about those we leave behind, Conan. We never know what they would want, but we can be sure what they would hate."

"Yes?"

"For their death to become our death. They live in our memories." Artus smiled. "Our lives make them more vital. Your glory is their glory, your victory is their victory. Live as they would have lived, live as they would have desired you to live, and you will be worthy of their lives forever."

The Cimmerian nodded. "Over the years, Artus, you have become much wiser."

"No, Conan, I've always been this wise." The Zingaran's laughter rose to the stars. "It's just taken you this long to realize it."

CHAPTER 26

TAMARA HAD NO difficulty finding Conan belowdecks. She followed the ringing rasp of whetstone on steel. As expected, the Cimmerian sat in his cabin, working an edge onto his new sword. He did not look up as she approached, but she knew he was aware of her. Even when she paused in the hatchway before his cabin, he did not acknowledge her.

She rapped lightly on the wooden bulkhead. "Is my attire suitable?"

He looked up, the light in his blue eyes visible despite the cabin's dim interior. His gaze raked her up and down. From the ship's stores she'd chosen tall boots of brown, which matched a sleeveless leather bodice. Beneath that, she wore a pale green man's shirt—the bodice covered three stab wounds that she intended to stitch up later. Its tails covered her to midthigh. Leather skirting hung from a wide belt, affording her some protection without the sacrifice of mobility.

The Cimmerian grunted. "Good."

Tamara waited for more, but he'd returned his attention to the sword. She swallowed hard, then looked at him. "Conan, we need to talk."

The barbarian glanced back up, pain washing over his face. He'd clearly rather be testing the edge on his sword—and from the looks of it, either on her or his own throat—than chatting with her. He drew in a deep breath, then nodded. "Talk."

"What I had on before, the silks, I did not choose them because I wished to dress as a harlot." She chewed her lower lip for a moment. "In the monastery, we led a very disciplined life. Everything was prescribed and done in accordance with strict rules. Twice a year we would have festivals in which we would celebrate the lives of those who had passed. We would dress gaily and remember them at their best. When I sought other clothes, it was the first time I'd had a chance to truly realize how much I had lost. I did not think what you and others might think of me. I was thinking of them, the people I lost."

Conan grunted.

"And I am sorry, Conan, for the remark I made." Tamara frowned. "Your comment stung me and I struck back. It was not worthy of the person I was raised to be. I beg your forgiveness."

The Cimmerian set the whetstone aside, but left his sword resting across his thighs. "It did not sit well to see you dressed as a slut. I have seen you fight. I have seen your dedication—*insistent* dedication—to the wishes of your master. You dishonored yourself and your master when you dressed in silks."

"I understand."

"And I could have phrased things better."

Tamara leaned against the bulkhead. "I did not truly mean you did not know any women other than harlots."

Conan smiled. "Yes, you did. You are perhaps not too far wrong."

"But there is your mother . . ." Tamara looked up toward the main deck. "Artus told me, not much . . ."

The Cimmerian shrugged. "He told you what I know, which is not much. She bore me on a battlefield. She named me. I do not remember her."

Tamara hugged her arms around her belly. "I do not know my mother either. Or my father. I was rescued while an infant by Master Fassir. The only life I have ever known has been destroyed. I'm not even sure why, save for the insane dreams of a madman."

"Khalar Zym destroyed a village." Conan held up a thumb. "All for a shard of bone no bigger than this. He killed everyone—or thought he did. I'd all but forgotten him until I ran across Lucius and, from him, found Remo chasing you. He has this Mask of Acheron and some warped dream of using it to conquer the world. It was my father's duty to protect that shard. It is mine to get it back, or pursue a more direct solution to the problem."

She shivered. "The Mask of Acheron . . . now things begin to make some sense."

The Cimmerian's eyes sharpened. "What do you know of it?"

"Only what I have been taught, Conan. Evil roots itself in the world in dreams and devices. The Mask of Acheron was a dream that became a device, and then returned to being a dream. The priest-kings of Acheron created it, fed it the blood of their daughters, and reaped great power through it. They built their empire upon the agony of millions.

They celebrated, their joy made greater by the lamentations of those they oppressed."

"So I have heard in legends."

She smiled. "Master Fassir taught that evil is a fickle mistress. Those she raises high, she raises high only to dash them more magnificently on the rocks of despair and failure. Evil concentrates power, but it also concentrates the core essence of those who wield it. The invincible warrior needs a magick sword because, deep in his heart, he fears being defeated. That fear becomes his weakness, his downfall. So the Mask of Acheron will expose Khalar Zym's weakness."

The barbarian nodded, a low growl rumbling from his throat. In the half-light Conan became something more than she had seen before. Though he was still physically magnificent, with muscles etched in shadow and burnished with golden lamplight, it was the play of emotions over his brooding features that revealed his depth to her. He had actually listened to what she had said, and was considering it. Behind those cerulean eyes, he reevaluated all he knew of Khalar Zym.

Conan smiled, and she took heart from the sight. "A man who would be king has no need to surround himself with minions. Khalar Zym relies upon them and his witch of a daughter. Yes, he believes he needs her magick, the magick of Acheron, to accomplish his ends."

The monk nodded. "There, you have it. He's never had magick, never controlled it, and believes it is his only path to power. Just as he thinks himself a lesser man without it, so he must judge all men without it to be inferior as well. Gaining the mask will raise him to the pinnacle of power, and yet will blind him to the abilities of mere mortal men."

"You may need to change again, Tamara of the four names."

"Yes, Cimmerian?"

"The robes of a philosopher would suit you."

She laughed. "You were thinking the same thing."

"Hardly." He raised the sword and studied the edges. "I was thinking that in all my travels, I have never met anything of sorcery born which could touch me, that I could not touch with steel and come away the better for it. If Khalar Zym's empire will be built on a foundation of sorcery, then cold steel will shatter it."

He nodded at her, then picked up the whetstone. He whisked it along the blade twice, then looked up again. "Something else . . . ?"

"When you lay there, and I was tending your wounds. When you were fevered . . ."

His expression froze. "Did I speak?"

"Some, yes, but in a hill dialect I have no way of understanding." She gave him a smile she hoped would be reassuring. "When the fever broke, and you came awake, and I was there at your bunk. . . I was not the one you expected to see."

"No." He glanced down, hesitating. "You are not my grandfather."

"Conan, you don't need to lie to me."

The Cimmerian looked up, regarding her coldly. "If I do not need to lie, then why would I?"

The vehemence of his words, and the way he deliberately thickened his Cimmerian accent, shocked her. Tamara took a half step back, raising her hands, using the heartbeat this afforded her to recover herself. "I need to explain."

"You need to go."

"Conan, you need to *understand*."

He looked up but said nothing.

"My past has been wiped away. At the moment I met you, all I knew was that everyone I had known was being slaughtered, and I was being sent away. I was not allowed to defend my home against invaders, and *everyone* there was dying to protect me . . . even though *none* of them beyond Master Fassir knew why. Had you not come upon the scene, they would have taken me. Even now I would be hanging by the ankles from chains in Khor Kalba, my blood draining into that mask.

"And then, from Remo, I learned that I am the last daughter of the Acheron Royal House. It meant that whoever I thought I was, was an illusion. Khalar Zym wanted me for my blood. You wanted me as bait. And though you were willing to treat me as an equal at the Shaipur outpost, and even though you confided in me your plan, I did not feel I served you well."

The barbarian grunted. "I had seen you fight. You are an ally. We are here, so your effort was what we needed."

"You may think so, Conan." Tamara's eyes sparkled for a second. "You are a terrible weight to drag through the water, but that is all I felt I had done. So when you were ill and I had a chance to ply what I had learned in the monastery of the healing arts, I was determined that you would not die. I owed you that much and . . ."

Conan nodded. ". . . and I was your only link to your past."

"Yes. And by caring for you, I proved that who I had been was not an illusion. I was Tamara of more names than a barbarian needs, not some vessel bearing the tainted blood of an infamous lineage. Unless I kept you alive by my skills, I was nothing, just a very frightened woman all alone."

The Cimmerian stood, setting his sword and whetstone aside. Tamara imagined, for a moment, that he would come and take her into his arms. She wanted that, desired it, hungered for his warmth and strength. And for just another moment, it appeared as if he might do exactly that.

But then he half turned from her and studied the shadows in the corner of his cabin. "I have been alone for much of my life, Tamara Amaliat Jorvi Karushan. There are times when that makes life simpler. Others create obligations and demands. Others fail. Avoiding all that creates a life of freedom.

"But it does not always make life *easier*. Artus is a loyal friend, who watches after me even when I do not watch after myself. I have known few such people down through the years." The Cimmerian's head came up. "And perhaps I have been such a friend to too few people. I was born to war, Tamara, and for one with my destiny, to travel alone is better than traveling with ghosts."

A chill ran down Tamara's spine. She had always been alone, but she had never *felt* alone. The other monks and Master Fassir had become her family. Conan's family had been peeled away, person by person. A lesser man would have let those losses cripple him. Conan merely shouldered them and carried on.

He faced her. "You and I have an obligation to each other. To the world. We are linked by a chain not of our forging, but created by Khalar Zym. He has severed you from your family, and me from mine. But he has brought us together. We have each other, and I believe that means that unlike him, we are not alone."

"But his daughter . . ," Tamara's eyes narrowed. "No, no, I see your point. Had he a true family, if he were not alone, he'd not be pressing a quest to re-create a past that was stolen from him."

"So he does those things to others which had been done to him. His family was taken, so he took mine, took yours, took others, and will take more." Conan gave her a half smile. "But you and I, we will not let that happen."

"No." Tamara reached a hand toward him, then let it drop. "I want to ask you to remain with us, to take me to Hyrkania. I will not."

"Because you know I will not agree?"

"Because I fear you might, to be a good friend to me, to assuage my fears and, thereby, allow Khalar Zym to kill more people."

"You do not need me to keep you safe, monk." Conan laughed. "I would only keep Khalar Zym safe from you."

"I hope that is as you say, Conan." Tamara glanced down, hiding a smile. "And I pray we never have to learn if it is the truth."

CHAPTER 27

THUMP!

The Cimmerian came instantly awake catlike, and reached for his sword. It had not been a loud sound, or one particularly pernicious, but it had been out of place. He slid from his bunk and on bare feet padded his way up the stairs to the main deck, and again up to the wheel deck.

The helmsman had vanished, and save for water splashed between the wheel and taffrail, nothing appeared out of order. Bare steel in hand, the barbarian ran to aft rail and looked down, expecting to see the man's body floating on the placid surface. He saw half of it, and only by the dint of its being silhouetted against a massive, malevolent golden eye.

What in the name of Crom! He turned back and already dark forms swarmed the main deck. Kushites with spears and shields, Khalar Zym's light infantry with leather armor and swords, and even a few archers who climbed into the ratlines. A knot of men ran directly toward the companion-way leading belowdecks.

Conan hammered the ship's alarm bell with his sword's pommel. "To arms! Rise now, or die in your berths!"

He vaulted from the wheel deck to the main and cleaved one man from shoulder to hip with a slash. Conan then spun and threw himself feetfirst down the companionway. He caught a man in the back, between the shoulders, and pitched him forward into the others. Conan landed heavily on the stairs and lost hold of his sword, while the others crashed below him. It didn't matter. In the ship's close quarters, a sword would be useless, whereas the dagger he plucked from a downed warrior's belt would answer very well.

A bass voice barked a command. "Get the girl to a boat!"

From the shadows rose the Kushite general Conan recalled from his village. Snarling, the man rushed at him, reaching out with thick-fingered hands. Conan dodged left, letting the dagger in his right hand trail. The edge scored a line along Ukafa's leather breastplate, but the larger man spun away before Conan could shift his wrist and draw blood.

The Kushite drew his own knife and crouched. "I have killed lions with this blade, Cimmerian."

"And in the Black Kingdoms, I was known as Amra." Conan relished the way recognition widened the man's eyes. "But this lion is not yours to kill."

The two of them moved through the mid-deck, cutting around pillars, tucking hammocks hung from rafters. The sailors who had slept there had fled to the main deck. From the sound of it, a massive battle raged. Bodies slammed to the deck above, reverberating like thunder in dark depths. Here and there blood seeped down, invisible in the shadows, though its scent overrode the stink of sweat and bilgewater.

Ukafa lunged. Conan twisted, spinning inside the man's

thrust. The Cimmerian forced Ukafa's arm against a stanchion. Something snapped and the Kushite's dagger sailed free, but the larger man entangled his fingers in Conan's hair and whirled him away. Conan flew across the deck and slammed into a post, wrapping around it then spinning off again, his knife vanished.

He came to rest against a bulkhead for an eyeblink, then twisted. Ukafa's kick snapped planking. Conan kicked to the side, catching the Kushite's planted leg, and spilled him to the deck. In a heartbeat he pounced on Ukafa's back and struck him three times, each a mighty blow, to the side of his head and face.

Roaring, Ukafa heaved himself from the deck and slammed Conan into the deck above. He lowered himself to do it again, so the Cimmerian slipped back, jamming both feet against the giant's right heel. Ukafa began to fall. Conan grabbed his right wrist, twisting it to snap another bone, then flung the Kushite through a bulkhead.

Ukafa came up, eyes tight with rage, fists balled. He limped forward, lips peeled back, revealing filed teeth. "I should have slain you in Cimmeria."

"Not even then could you have managed it." Conan took a half step toward him. "This lion is your last."

The Kushite drove at him, arcing in punch after punch. Conan ducked the lefts and blocked the rights, driving his elbow into the man's broken forearm. The armor made it impossible for any blows to damage his body, so Conan concentrated on his head. Stiff right hands slowed Ukafa's advance. Left hooks twisted past slow rights to batter his head around. As the man sought to bull-rush him, Conan gave ground, then stopped and drove the Kushite back.

Had another man—a *civilized* man—been watching, he would have told the tale of the fight simply, and imparted to the Cimmerian a variety of motives. He might suggest, for example, that breaking Ukafa's arm was related, in some small way, to an injury the giant had done to Conan's father. And the way Conan drew the man on, then beat him back, would be attributed to the Cimmerian's desire to teach Ukafa a lesson, to prove who was the better man.

But this was not a battle of civilized men. It was barbarian against barbarian. Conan's vision had long since drowned in a sea of blood red. He did not think, he *felt,* he *knew.* If he withdrew, it was only because he wished to deny Ukafa the benefit of momentum. If he struck and drove forward, it was to exploit weakness. Instinct and survival drove him, pride prodded him. Here in the darkness belowdecks, in the underworld of the *Hornet*, Death looked to sup, and Conan refused to be consumed.

Finally, after Conan ducked a blow and delivered two in return, the Kushite slumped against a post. He clung to it to remain upright, for to fall was to die. Conan lashed out with a foot, snapping the man's head into the post. The Kushite collapsed, and then, in the darkness, Conan found his knife and harvested the man's head.

"Conan!" Tamara appeared before him out of the shadows. She bore a poniard dripping blood. "Two of them came for me. They'll come for no others."

The Cimmerian looked up. "There's more that need killing." He stalked off in search of his sword and found it at the stairs. Then he ascended into battle with Tamara in his shadow. Khalar Zym's men had forced the *Hornet*'s crew back toward the forecastle, Artus at their center. Kushites closed on them with spears raised. Archers in the ratlines drew back arrows.

And Conan laughed. "You did not wait for me, Artus."

"I've just played the good host at this party, Conan, awaiting you, the guest of honor."

Conan bounded across the deck, sword singing and reaping lives. From one of Khalar Zym's dead archers, Tamara appropriated a bow and arrows. She skewered her counterparts, leaving them hanging tangled in rigging before they could twist around and find her. And the *Hornet*'s crew, with Artus's sword flashing at their forefront, cut a swath through Khalar Zym's men.

Several went over the side, scrambling for strange boats that, to Conan, most closely resembled clamshells. Each could carry two dozen or more people, and the first survivors to reach them sought to pull the halves closed. Leather gaskets appeared to make them watertight, though as later experimentation proved, the wood burned easily enough. Still, the Cimmerian saw neither sail nor oar, so had no idea how the invaders had traveled to the *Hornet*.

Artus, fresh from helping the rest of the crew toss bodies to the circling sharks, could shed no light upon the mystery of the burning clamshells. "Save for being small, and lacking any propulsion or steering mechanism, they appear to be quite nice."

"I wonder." Conan returned to the wheel deck and looked over the aft rail. Aside from five sharks circling the ship, he saw nothing. *Is it a trick of the light?* He hoped it was. He much preferred believing that sorcery had propelled the little boats than that they had been dragged along by a creature with eyes the size of a shield.

The Zingaran shaded his eyes with a hand. "Sorcery to track the girl and get the boats here?"

"Probably."

Artus beckoned Conan into his cabin and pointed to a map spread out on a table. "Cove up the coast, near that other set of ruins we've explored. We'll be there in a couple hours. We can take on water and leave with the morning tide. From there, you can find a village, steal a horse, and head to Asgalun. We'll make our way to—"

Conan held a hand up. "Don't tell me. Don't decide yourself. Just as you sail along, throw dice and let them decide."

"A wise plan." Artus nodded. "And I know, even if he were to capture you, you'd tell him nothing."

"Not whilst alive, but his daughter has something of the necromancer about her."

"And we will alert people as we go that Khalar Zym would make himself emperor. Most won't care, and some will hire on with him. Let's hope that those who opposed him in the past will rise again."

Conan smiled. "And you'll take good care of the woman, yes? You'll be as good a friend to her as you have been to me?"

"I shall guard her life as if it were my very own."

"Thank you, Artus." Conan studied the map again, measuring the distance to Asgalun and then to Khor Kalba. *A handful of days to make the trip . . .*

"Have you given a thought, my friend, as to where I shall meet you again?"

"Hyrkania, Artus." The Cimmerian tapped the map with a blood-encrusted finger. "And if you need me sooner, I shall find you."

Conan left his friend and descended into the ship. He paused in his cabin to set aside his weapons. He intended to clean them and oil them, whetting away nicks and burrs. Before he could gather his tools to work, however, he caught scent of something odd. He moved along the companionway and stopped beside the opening to Tamara's berth.

She knelt, naked, before a low, makeshift altar. Two sticks of incense burned on it. Three gold coins had been arranged in a triangle. A small bit of cheese had been set at the triangle's center. A small bowl with bloody water and a damp cloth sat on the deck beside her left knee. The lamp-light washed her hair and back in gold, from her shoulders to the flare of her hips.

She reached out and drew the incense smoke over her. Conan knew the scent well: myrrh. It overrode the stench of death. She bowed her head so smoke billowed over it. Spreading her arms, her palms facing the sky, she prayed in low tones.

"Mitra grant that my actions have been right and pleasing to you. I took life to save life, I imprisoned evil in death so others could be free. Judge not my companions by their actions, but by the content of their hearts, as they help me do thy will."

Her head remained lowered, but cocked slightly, as if she were listening for a reply. Conan remained still and held his breath, lest she detect his presence. Though she betrayed no sign of knowing he was there, he felt certain that she did. Despite that feeling, he could not drag himself away.

"Mitra, I beg thee for the strength to overcome any taint of my blood, from my actions or the sins of ancestors aeons past. Confirm me in my purpose. Point me to peace in your service."

The sincerity of her words surprised Conan. His own god, Crom, invited no such intimacy. He pitched infants into the world screaming and waited their recitation of their life after they died. He expected them to make the most of his gifts, and their failure was of no interest to him. Similarly Conan had dealt with many men—be they commoners, kings, or high priests—who professed devotion to gods and then, in turn, blasphemed in preference to worship, claimed all glory to themselves, and placed all blame for adversity on the gods. As he had come to discover was the case with most civilized men, they paid lip service to the gods, and relied on selfish motives to govern their behavior.

Tamara's voice rose just a bit, her throat tightening. "With your gentle wisdom, bless this man who protects me. Lift his burden of pain, as you do mine. As it is your will, abide by my wishes. I am yours forever, heart and soul."

She drew her hands toward her body and wrapped her arms around her middle. Then she began rocking forward and back. The myrrh smoke swirled around her, fragrant threads creating a ghostly cocoon.

Conan watched until the incense burned to nothing and she ceased moving. Were it not for her chest rising and falling, he might have thought her dead. He entered her cabin silently and scooped her up in his arms. He laid her on her bunk and checked that none of the blood she'd washed off had been hers. He wrapped her in a blanket, then stole back to his cabin.

As she had found peace in her prayers, so Conan found it in caring for his weapons. He washed and oiled them, scraping away all tarnish and rust. He wiped them clean of oil, then held each blade over a lamp's flame. Soot blackened the steel so no reflected moonlight would reveal it. He similarly blackened a cloth so he could darken his face as needed, then opened his sea chest, pulled out a mail surcoat, and repeated the process with it.

He prepared his weapons for war with the same sincere devotion Tamara had showed in her prayers. Not because Conan worshipped war, but because he had been born to it. It occurred to him, with a degree of grim satisfaction, that as long as wars raged, and men like Khalar Zym sought to elevate themselves over others, he would never truly be alone. War might be a fell companion, but it was one he knew well. *And as long as I know it better than my enemies do, I shall not fall.*

CHAPTER 28

MARIQUE STARTED, NOT because she had not expected her father's reaction, but because she had underestimated his fury. He banged open the bronze doors to her chamber and marched in as if he were already a god. Anger had flushed his face purple and sharpened his features into a fearsome mask.

"What have you done?"

She folded the light purple tunic and laid it on top of a saddlebag before she turned to face him. She kept her expression serene, hiding her racing heart. "I am doing as you ordered, Father."

Her answer stopped him. Shock softened his features, but only for a moment. He pointed toward her chamber's floor. "Akhoun has told me that the Beast That Lurks has returned. Neither Ukafa nor any of those who accompanied him have come back. Their submersible coracles are lost. They failed, you failed! The girl is gone. Your mother is gone."

"Calm yourself, Father."

"I cannot be calm, Marique!" His clawed hands rose toward the ceiling, his angry words filling her domed chamber. "Ever have I been patient with you. For your sake. For your mother's sake. But now . . . now that we are so close, so very close, you have failed me. *Again!* How am I to feel calm, Marique? Where do I find a wellspring of peace?"

"Here, Father." She beckoned him to a side table which had been topped in forgotten times with a mosaic map of the Acheronian empire. The coastline had changed. Rivers flowed in different courses, but the mountains remained the same and created suitable landmarks for navigation. A rounded crystalline bell had been fitted over the top of the table. Beneath it had been trapped a single insect.

Khalar Zym's rage simmered. "An old map of an old world."

"A world to be made again anew, Father. That's what you want. And the monk, she is of old blood." Marique smiled casually. "This is why we had trouble locating her. The monk Fassir changed her, hid her, so that as we looked for an ancient bloodline in a modern world, we could not find it. But when we look for her blood on a world in which it was born, we find it."

"How?"

"Is it not obvious?" Marique pointed.

"A bug on the ocean, daughter, does not cheer me."

"A *hornet*, Father. The ship she is on is the *Hornet*. Right now it lurks here, off the coast. The scrap of cloth still bears her essence and puts her on the ship, but not forever." She glanced at the baggage on the bed. "I go with a handpicked squad to ride and to retrieve her."

Khalar Zym shook his head. "From Khor Kalba to there will take four days, and that would be riding horses to death."

"Yes, Father, but you forget. I am my mother's daughter."
Marique laughed. "With the magick at my command, what
was once a horse will no longer be, and riding them unto
death and *beyond* will make all the difference."

Khalar Zym threw his head back and laughed, anger
drained from his voice. "Very clever, beloved daughter. Proceed. But mark me. Return without the monk, or fail to bring
her here for the ritual on the night of the moon's death, and
all the sorcery in the world will not save you from my wrath."

TAMARA STOOD ON the wheel deck, dressed as a pirate
should be, with her long, dark hair dancing in the dying
day's breeze. She watched Conan below as he bid his fellows
farewell. She'd awakened in her bed, naked but wrapped
tenderly in a blanket, and knew who had done her that
kindness. Her ritual had provided her some peace and more
clarity, though the latter only extended so far.

She hoped that by standing there, standing tall and looking every inch as a corsair should, she would give Conan
heart. She wanted terribly to beg him not to go—not because
she feared for her safety on the *Hornet*. Not only would her
skills with a knife and bow save her from unwanted attention, but Artus had declared her the little sister he'd never
had and had suggested, none too subtly, that the rest of the
crew should do likewise.

Unspoken was the fact that to fail in that regard would
be to face her wrath, or his wrath, or Conan's wrath, in no
particular order.

No, Tamara feared for Conan. Oddly enough it was not
because she doubted his skill with arms or courage—she
had never seen a man so fearsome in combat. Though she
would never have wished them to oppose each other,

she would have felt certain that even Master Fassir would fall to the Cimmerian.

It was instead his grim fatalism that caused her anxiety. All of the pirates appeared to go through dark moments, but Conan dwelt most comfortably there. Quick and clever and vital as he was, in those moments of quiet where she found peace, he retreated into melancholy. Tamara worried that there might come a time when he could not find his way back.

But she smiled bravely when he looked up at her. "May the gods speed you, Conan."

He nodded once, solemnly, then shouldered a supply satchel and headed down the gangway to the abandoned stone pier by which they had dropped anchor. Without looking back, the broad-shouldered barbarian marched to shore and started up the nearest hillside.

Artus looked up at her. "Well, woman?"

"What, Captain Artus?"

"I like the sound of that, '*Captain* Artus.' You poxed dogs remember that." Artus plucked a rolled piece of canvas from his belt. "The Cimmerian forgot his map. I'd send a man, but they all need to be filling our water casks. I need someone fleet to catch him."

Smiling, Tamara leaped to the main deck. "I'll gladly . . ."

Artus extended the map to her, but did not yet let go. "We sail with the tide. Be back by dawn."

"Aye, Captain."

Artus smiled. "And if you have a chance, Tamara, tell him he'd best meet me in Hyrkania, or I will hunt him down."

EVEN BEFORE HE caught sight of her, Conan knew it was Tamara. She made more noise, deliberate noise, than an advancing company of freebooters. He paused on a sandy switchback, the breeze teasing long blades of sea grass, and smiled as she turned the corner. Beyond her, on the beach, Artus waved.

She held the map out to him. "Artus said you forgot this."

Conan patted a folded piece of canvas at his belt. "You'll have to take that back. He's forgotten I made my own copy."

Her face fell.

"But not yet, Tamara."

She closed the distance between them and slipped her hand into his. "You'll think me silly, but in all my time at the monastery, I never had to say good-bye."

The Cimmerian resumed his hike up the hillside with her in tow. "People must have died."

"Yes, but you knew that you would never see them in this life again. There was no wondering as to their fate. No anticipating a return, or hearing bad news." She shook her head. "I would not have thought it so hard."

"Hard are the times when you never have the chance to say good-bye." They crested the hill and turned inland. There, just on the other side of the hill, lay another cove similar to the one where the *Hornet* anchored. At this one, however, the beach had risen to bury ruins, leaving visible only two massive statues. White sand covered them to the waist. They stared blindly at the ocean, and the fanglike stones that warded the cove and kept all ships at sea.

Tamara stopped. "Who were these people? Did they think they could conquer earth and sea?"

"Perhaps for a time they *did* conquer earth and sea."

"And now all they know is ruin." She squeezed his hand, then looked up into his face. "Do you think our lives are part of some grand plan?"

Conan shook his head. "I do not know. I do not care.

I live, I slay, I love, I call no man master. If there is a purpose to life beyond that, it means nothing to me."

Tamara's gaze met his openly, with no guile or hidden intent. She raised his hand to her lips and kissed it. "I want nothing of you, Conan, save that, for this night, you do not have to pass it alone."

Two dozen yards along the path and back up a bit, they found shelter in the ruins of what had once been a watch-tower. A cleared floor and a small stack of firewood revealed that other travelers had used it before them. The Cimmerian kindled a fire and Tamara spread out a blanket. She shed her clothes, then freed him of his.

It was not the first time he had seen her naked, but that morning, aboard the *Hornet*, it had been entirely different. Now her long hair fell forward of her shoulders, but did not conceal her full breasts with their dark nipples. Her body tapered at the waist, then flared gently through her hips down into long, slender legs. Her face, though half shadowed, had a regal beauty that insisted she must be of nobility, and her slender hands, which caressed his chest, testified to her femininity.

Conan took her in his arms and kissed her, deeply and passionately, but she broke the kiss and forced him to lie down on the blanket. She knelt at his feet, then worked her way up his body, kissing each of his scars, solemnly and slowly, the intimacy of her caresses all the greater for their simple innocence.

She was not the first woman he had bedded since his days on the Black Coast. He could not remember all of them. He had sought their company to hold ghosts at bay. He'd thought to bury Bêlit's memory and the pain in the anonymity of hot couplings. That effort had failed, for the hollowness of the acts resonated within the void in his heart, mocking with their shallowness the depth of what he had once had.

But Tamara . . . she saw him differently than the legions of whores and concubines. She continued kissing him, but when her lips met a scar on his left hip, he flinched.

She looked up. "Did I . . . ?"

Conan shook his head. That wound he'd taken aboard the *Argus*, as Bêlit and the *Tigress*'s crew had overwhelmed the smaller ship. She'd made him her consort and king. She had danced for him and then, later, kissed that same scar.

Tamara's eyes glistened. "She must have been very special."

Conan nodded.

Hot tears anointed the scar. "And so fortunate to have won your heart."

The Cimmerian reached down and drew her up. His fingers slipped into her dark hair and he brought her mouth to his. He kissed her fiercely, as if it were the last kiss he might ever give, then crushed her to him.

Theirs was not the sloppy, clumsy lovemaking of children, nor the passionless joining of bodies performing for pay or duty. At first it was frenzied and urgent, because of the primal hunger that united them. Khalar Zym's machinations may have thrown them together, but this union was of their choice, for them and them alone. And through it, and as it settled into a more sustained course, they confirmed their existences. It gave each of them a piece of the other, a slice of time shared, that guaranteed they would never be alone. Without regret, and yet with great joy, they came together again and again and, eventually, with hungers sated, lay entwined in the dying firelight.

He held her so she could not escape, but she made no

attempt to do so. Instead she traced fingers over his myriad scars like a palm reader tracing the lines of his hands. She kissed the scars, though this time more quickly and playfully, wistfully, then snuggled in with her cheek pressed to his chest.

"I shall be thinking of you always on your journey, Conan."

"Three days to Asgalun, and another to Khor Kalba."

"Artus said that if you did not meet him in Hyrkania, he would hunt you down. Will you meet him?"

He pulled back, and looked her full in the face. "I will find him. I shall need to know that he brought you to safety. If, for some reason, he failed, then I shall have to know who to kill."

She kissed his lower lip. "He will not fail, Conan. On the tide he shall bear me safely away."

With another woman, these words would have been an invitation to ask her to come with him, but he did not take them as such. Tamara did not look at him quizzically, wondering why he refrained. She smiled and nestled deeper into his arms.

He kissed the top of her head. "There are hours before the tide, Tamara. I shall return you to the ship soon, and see you off. Then I am bound for Khor Kalba, to see you free forever."

CHAPTER 29

TAMARA DISENTANGLED HERSELF from the safe warmth of Conan's arms and silently pulled on her clothes. She sat there for a bit, watching him, listening to him murmur in a dialect she did not understand. She chose to assume it was Cimmerian. It gave her great pleasure to imagine that their passion had left him untroubled enough that he could revisit a peaceful time.

Mitra, thank you for granting him peace. She smiled and resisted the temptation to softly kiss his brow. She did not wish to waken him. She would have welcomed his pulling her back to him, and to sharing intimacy with him, but for both their sakes she had to be away and to the *Hornet*.

Though she was taking her leave of him, she did not feel she was abandoning him. What they had shared, this consummation of their relationship, made positive a thing fashioned by the desires of evil. Prior to the previous night, they were simply people Khalar Zym had drawn together by dint of his avarice. They had been running in parallel courses, but now they were a team. Though their paths would split apart—and part of her believed she would never see the Cimmerian again—their purpose and effort were united. Until Khalar Zym had her blood, his plan could not be fulfilled, which gave Conan ample time to put an end to Zym's planning for all time.

Tamara left their shelter and worked her way back along the sandy path. In the light of the waning moon's sliver, she watched silver waves caress half-buried statues. There would come a time when the sands would fully cover what the ocean had not eroded. So it would be with the stories of Khalar Zym, and how he sought her, but how she, with Conan, destroyed him. Their efforts, for good or evil, would be forgotten.

She did not think that a bad thing. The sun and moon rode through the sky, uncaring of the travails of men. Tamara had no idea who had built the ruins below her. She did not know the name of the sorcerer who had raised the stone teeth to close the bay. She was willing to grant that having that knowledge could not hurt her cause, and might help it, but in the steady progression of the aeons, who these people had been and what they had done were immaterial.

Tamara came over the hillcrest and down the other side, smiling happily. The night's chill nibbled at her, but she could still feel her lover's warmth. Girlishly she skipped down part of the trail, laughing lightly to herself, allowing her this excess of joy simply because it balanced the horror through which she had so recently lived.

The whirring buzz was the first clue that something was amiss. The sound was not wholly out of place in the jungle. Something flew past her, then came around again. It was only when the sound centered itself on her that she realized she was a target.

She spun, her first instinct sending her back toward her lover, which was when the mechanical insect hit her shoulder and stung. Tamara slapped at it, shattering delicate wings and scattering bronze gears. *Too late*. Fire burned through her flesh and her right arm immediately went numb. She staggered back several steps, tethered to gravity, then twisted and fell in the sand at the mouth of a path that led deeper into the jungle.

She struggled to get up, but her right arm collapsed, leaving her on her belly, staring up at Marique and the nightmare creature upon which she was perched.

Part of the animal defied description. Tamara told herself this was because the insect's poison affected her ability to reason. But the rational part of her mind knew this was untrue. Part of the beast was beyond understanding. Though she saw its forequarters clearly, with the shiny black reptilian scales covering what resembled a horse, and the forehooves that had been split and transformed into a raptor's claws, the creature remained indistinct behind the rider. A shadowed form only, it seemed a thick protoplasm which reflected the night's sky—though each star became a bright spot on a long thread that twisted and stretched to infinity. Though she was fading quickly, she realized the beasts—for there was more than one—were dying. The magick that had changed them was killing them, and for Marique not only was this not a concern, it was an active source of pleasure.

Marique pointed her quirt at Tamara. "Two of you, fetch her. We are to be away."

Rough hands jerked her up. They tossed her over the shoulders of one beast and tied her into place. Until Marique leaned down to sniff her hair, Tamara did not know upon which beast she had been placed. The witch's sibilant whisper chilled her.

"You are now mine. I shall deliver you to my father. You

will make him great." Marique chuckled lightly. "And you shall make me greater."

Tamara tried to reply, but her tongue had become a dead thing. She could only listen as Marique dispatched a half dozen of her riders to kill Conan. "Bring me the barbarian's head; I have a use for it. If you return without it, I will find an unpleasant use for yours."

TAMARA'S ABSENCE REGISTERED in Conan's consciousness the second he came awake. It, however, was not the reason he'd wakened. Something was amiss. He felt it. He'd heard something and he did not need to identify it before he filled his hand with steel and rolled to a crouch in the shelter's corner. Another man, naked save for the shadow that cloaked him, might have felt vulnerable. While Conan would have preferred to have pulled on his mail and his boots, his current condition did not inspire fear—as it would not have inspired fear in a tiger setting itself to hunt.

Only the distant surf broke the silence. All the jungle creatures remained quiet. Anticipation grew like storm clouds on the horizon. That he was being hunted Conan did not doubt. That meant that Tamara was in danger; but her safety was not his primary concern. To do anything to help her, he had to survive; and survival, for Conan, meant killing his enemies as quickly as possible.

In the darkness beneath a vine-screened window, the Cimmerian grinned. Who would Khalar Zym have sent to kill him? His best troops—at least, the best of those yet alive? Proud men, city-bred men whose sense of confidence came from the superiority of numbers and the livery they wore. Driven by fear or visions of profit. They had the confidence of hunters, the arrogance of civilization.

But they are only men. Mortal men. It is time to show them what this truly means.

Their caution betrayed them. One man crept up to the window beneath which Conan crouched. He used a dagger to move a leaf aside so he could spy the shelter's interior. Conan waited until the blade stopped moving, then stabbed his sword up and back. The point hit. Something popped, something cracked, then the Cimmerian hauled forward on the blade. He pulled the man—transfixed through the eye—in by that window, and left him thrashing his life out on the dark floor.

The other assassins came for the doorway, knowing only that their fellow had disappeared within. They'd not seen enough to decide if he had plunged in after their prey, or something sinister had befallen him. The first two burst in, one ducking low, the other leaping, so that any cut intended to bisect a man would miss both.

But before they had reached the doorway, the Cimmerian had gone out through the window. His first slash cut a man's spine at his pelvis, leaving him to scream in terror as he collapsed, the lower half of his body dead. The barbarian's second cut carved deep into a thigh, hamstringing an assassin and severing an artery. He spun down over his companion, shouting in panic, and Conan vanished into the jungle.

He did not go far, and though he secreted himself in a thicket, ignoring the painful caress of thorns and nettles; his concealment was not intended as defense. Conan had hunted in jungles before, and had been hunted by men far more used to these conditions than Khalar Zym's assassins. A legion of Picts would have made less noise than the trio of men pursuing him. Savage tribes throughout the Black Kingdoms had sought Conan through rain forests and savannas, coming closer to discovering him than did these civilized men.

Had it been in his nature, the Cimmerian might have pitied them, but the wolf does not pity the sheep. The lion does not wonder if an antelope is loved or will be mourned. These were the concerns of civilized men, thoughts they used to insulate themselves from reality. For civilization was but a slender mask concealing savagery. Though desperation and a desire to live might strip it away, and while these assassins might choose to abandon it, Conan, the hunter, would not give them that chance.

Remaining low within the brush, Conan waited for one of them to slip past. The Cimmerian stabbed out, slicing through the back of the man's boot, severing the tendon. Going down to a knee, the man thrust blindly into the thicket. Conan grabbed his wrist and dragged him deeper, where the man struggled against thorns while the barbarian opened his throat.

He did not stop to imagine the others' reactions to what they heard, or their reactions when they discovered the body. Had he any strategem in mind, he might have chosen to climb a tree and leap down upon them. Any of that, all of that, smacked of trickery; and trickery was what the hunted used. All Conan really needed was to keep moving, restlessly and relentlessly.

So he did, pausing only briefly to listen for his prey. One made far too much noise in an obvious ruse to attract him. Conan circled higher and around. A hunter wanted higher ground, and Conan found the assassin waiting. *Not high enough.*

The distraction masked the dying man's sigh. Conan had approached from the left, and as the man spread branches to peer through, the Cimmerian thrust deep into his armpit. He felt the man's life flee through tremors communicated by the steel linking them. He laid the man down, sliding his sword from him, then again moved through the jungle and back to the shelter.

There he tugged off the thigh-stuck man's helmet and grabbed a handful of greasy hair. Looming large, he yanked back. "Scream for your friend."

The wounded soldier needed no more encouragement. "He's here, he's here!"

A careful crashing sounded through the brush. Conan released the soldier and moved down to a sandy circle. He waved the last assassin toward him. "It is done."

The man approached, his blade held high and back in the manner of sword schools scattered across Hyboria. He stamp-feinted, kicking a sand plume at Conan. When the barbarian did not give ground, the soldier lowered his stance, brought his blade forward, and the two of them locked eyes.

Something his grandfather had told him returned unbidden. "Some men believe that being skilled at swordplay is the same as being skilled at killing." Conan let his sword's tip waver and descend, imparting a tremble as if fear trickled through his belly. Then he lowered his sword and stood fully upright. "Prove you're a man, or die playing children's games."

Whether stung by his words or provoked by Conan's abandoning his guard, the soldier attacked. He slashed toward the left, his blade poised to slice open the Cimmerian's belly. Though that cut had not even tasted flesh, he began to shift so the return would take Conan's head off cleanly.

But faster than the man could have imagined, Conan shifted his sword from right hand to left and effortlessly blocked the cut at his middle. He lunged forward, catching the man's throat in his right hand. He lifted him up, letting him dangle, then tightened his hand. Steely fingers crushed the man's windpipe. Conan tossed him to the ground and listened to the strangled whistle he made while struggling to draw breath.

Conan killed the other two, then got himself dressed. He dragged the other bodies from the jungle and severed all of their heads. He pitched the bodies down into the rock-warded bay, then bound the heads together by their hair and dragged them along the path Tamara's tracks had taken. He crouched where she had fallen, fingering a piece of bronze machinery and the sliver of a wing.

That Khalar Zym had taken Tamara had been obvious, but the tiny piece of machinery meant that the daughter wanted him to know of her hand in the abduction. Why Marique had done this really didn't matter—far more noble creatures were wont to mark their territory. Her motives did not concern him. He would not be distracted by them. His mission had not changed. He was to kill Khalar Zym and destroy the Mask of Acheron—and did not particularly scruple over the order of accomplishing those tasks. That Marique might also need to die had always been a possibility, but Conan saw no reason to assign her any priority.

He stacked the heads into a pyramid and stuffed the small machine part into the mouth of the uppermost head. He faced it toward the northwest. When the girl did not return to the ship, Artus would send out scouts. They would find the skulls and read the signs as easily as Conan did. Without the girl to convey to Hyrkania, the pirate would set himself to the task of warning others about Khalar Zym.

Conan took a moment to study the trail Tamara's kidnappers had taken. He'd not seen spoor like that before, and the distance between individual tracks suggested strides two or three times as long as those of a horse. Keeping to the coastal road and cutting inland, they'd reach Khor Kalba quickly enough—and far more quickly than any man trailing them on foot.

He followed another set of tracks back into the jungle and located the place where the assassins had left their mounts. Bridles and reins hung from the trees to which they had been bound. Saddles sat in the middle of black puddles upon which falling leaves floated, and up through which rose white bones that appeared to be etched by years of weathering. How the creatures had died he really could not assess, save that several skulls sat in puddles slightly removed from those of the closest body. It suggested that the mounts had been somehow linked to the assassins. What he had done to the assassins had been done to their mounts, and he did not find himself regretting that.

He was a Cimmerian. Other men might have wanted a mount to carry him along the coast and eventually through mountain passes. He had been born to the mountains. Turning his back to the sea, he headed inland and up. He moved through the mountains with the ease of a raven winging its way through the sky. And while he did eventually steal a horse, it was only after no mountains stood between him and Asgalun, and straight roads sped him on his way.

CHAPTER 30

THE WORLD SWAM in and out of focus before Tamara's eyes. The poison had rendered her largely senseless during the ride. She actively sought to forget what little of it she recalled. The mounts had made blasphemous noises as they traveled, a soul-rending screeching with all of the shrill notes of steel etching steel, but in no way sounding regular or right. Arrival at Khor Kalba had not made things better because though the poison's effects were slowly draining, her body felt as if she were still on the move.

Four robed acolytes surrounded her as she marched through Khalar Zym's domain. The hallways were so wide and the ceilings so high, she imagined she'd shrunk to the size of a child's doll. That seemed a more plausible explanation than believing in a giant race that needed such space, or the arrogance of man believing he deserved it. The floors and pillars had been carved of black marble, worn smooth by countless feet and yet colder than the darkest winter night.

Ahead of her Marique stalked through the hallway. She moved with the prideful ease of a house cat within its own domain. She raised a hand as she came to massive iron doors, and they parted before her as if they were servants withdrawing before their master. Their retreat revealed a cavernous room that once had possessed a stately elegance; but its time had since passed.

The room had been transformed by the addition of statuary and other artifacts of times best forgotten. Elder gods crouched on thrones, their webbed feet crushing beneath them the skulls of screaming children. Mosaics had been pieced together on the walls, depicting ancient rituals that involved more bloodletting than religious devotion—though a devotion to bloodletting was not hidden. Here and there, the Mask of Acheron appeared, sometimes worn, always venerated, and clearly feared.

Tamara thanked the gods that she could not see more. She stumbled into the chamber and collapsed at Marique's feet.

"Behold, Father, I have returned with the girl."

Khalar Zym slowly roused himself from a daybed. He had been staring intently at the mask. He moved easily enough, but was clearly reluctant to tear his eyes from that most valuable relic of Acheron. Wearing a dark robe, he strode across the floor, his hooded eyes, clearing gradually. He smiled, but it was the same smile with which he'd stared at the mask, not a pleasurable response to the arrival of his daughter.

He dropped to a knee and took Tamara's jaw in his hand. He turned her face left and then right. "So, elusive one, you have joined us finally."

Tamara tried to shake her head, but she lacked the strength, and even the attempt made the world spin. "You are mistaken. I am no one. I am not the one you seek."

Khalar Zym glanced up. "Does she tell the truth, Marique?"

Marique stroked a Stygian talon against Tamara's neck, eliciting a sharp cry. She withdrew it, a drop of blood hanging there. "Would you care to taste, Father?"

He shook his head.

Marique greedily sucked the blood off the talon, then licked the droplet that had risen on Tamara's neck. "Hot and sweet, Father; the fullness of Acheron's Royal House pulses through her."

"Excellent." Khalar Zym stood. "Preparations are almost complete, and shall be by the eve of the Dead Moon."

His daughter hissed in Tamara's ear. "Yes, when the tide has ebbed, and the ruins are dry, when the moon is eager to rise from the grave, then shall Acheron be brought forth again."

Khalar Zym reached down and stroked his daughter's cheek. "You have made me proud, so very proud, Marique."

The sorceress purred.

Tamara, despair welling up inside her, bowed her head and sobbed.

CONAN MOVED THROUGH the fetid alleys of Asgalun, choosing his path by diverting ever deeper into shadow. He could feel the eyes upon him, measuring him. From him thieves could not hear the ripe peal of gold coins in a pouch, just the purposeful jingle of a swordman's livery and the soft rustle of mail. Most of the watchers dismissed him because of his size alone. Others for the quick certainty of his step. Though he did not belong in the thieves' quarter of the city, he was not drunk, not a foppish noble seeking adventure and stumbling about without purpose. Those who studied him knew that, at best, attacking him would be a lethal exercise that promised little return for their efforts.

The Cimmerian moved into a tiny courtyard and drove straight at the door beneath the sign of the seven daggers. He pushed the dark, oaken door open and ducked his head to enter. The Den of Blades spread out and down before him; lit poorly, a labyrinth of tables, benches at various levels, and shadows. Hard men and harder women filled it, but none favored him with a glance. To do that would betray concern, and no one here had any concerns in the world.

At least, none that could not be dealt with through a knife in the back, or some tincture of black lotus in a goblet of spiced wine.

Conan read the room as a wolf would read a flock of sheep. He didn't see Ela Shan, but that did not bother him. Thieves seldom kept schedules and he didn't know if the small man had even made it back to Asgalun. But someone in the room would know, and that someone appeared to be a fat Argosian perched back in the corner halfway between the bar and the hearth.

He made for the fat man directly, well aware that he was violating customs and protocols. As a young thief in the Maul, he had learned them and understood them, then dismissed them as silly laws imposed by the lawless on other outlaws, a mere parody of the rules of the civilizations upon which they preyed. Had they imposed them to mock those who despised them, Conan would have understood and abided by such laws. But their intent came from pride and pretense, and for that Conan had no use.

He towered over the fat man. "I am looking for a thief."

"Looking for a thief, are you?" The fat man spread his arms wide, contempt twisting his features. "You accuse us, here, of being thieves, then?"

The Cimmerian's expression sharpened. "I seek Ela Shan."

The fat man's jowls quivered with laughter. "And who do you think you are, barbarian?"

Conan caught the man by the throat and lifted him from his chair. He raised his voice. "I seek Ela Shan."

The fat man's face became purple. His nostrils flared. All around Conan, knives slid from sheaths. Table legs scraped and benches squeaked as they were pulled away. Steel sprouted in shadows and silence, save for the pop of the fire and the fat man's wheezing.

"Stand away, you fools." Ela Shan appeared from a darkened doorway off to Conan's left. Dressed in black velvet finery chased with silver threads, and looking as if he had bathed within the day, Ela Shan presented an image that Conan almost failed to recognize. The furtive glances, the haunted eye; they had vanished, and he'd even gained a few pounds—not counting the weight of the half-dozen knives he had secreted over his person.

Ela Shan pushed aside bared blades and moved to the heart of what would have been the killing ground. "This is Conan. This is the one of whom I have told you. I owe this man my life, and now all of you owe me yours. Before Bovus"—he nodded toward the fat man—"could have dropped back into his chair, the Cimmerian's blade would have appeared and have rent most of you in twain. And before Bovus's chair collapsed beneath his girth and he hit the floor, the rest of you would have been down and staring at him with dying eyes."

He turned around and smiled at Conan. "You can let Bovus go now. He's arrogant and ignorant, but that's hardly cause for you to strangle him."

Conan released the man, and true to the prediction, his

chair crumbled and spilled him to the floor. Laughter erupted and drawn steel retreated. Ela Shan waved Conan forward along a newly cleared path, to the bar and a waiting flagon of foaming ale.

The thief smiled. "I'm glad you've found me. There has arisen a job for which a man of your talents would be—"

Conan shook his head. "You said you owe me your life. I am here to collect."

Ela Shan raised an eyebrow. "Yes?"

"Khor Kalba. I need to get in."

"Don't even think it." Ela accepted a cup of dark wine from the innkeeper. "There, I've saved your life. We're even."

"You said there was no lock you could not break."

"There isn't."

"Then you *can* get in."

"I could, Conan, but you do not seem to grasp what I am telling you." The thief scrubbed a hand over his face. "Khor Kalba is a fell place, my friend. It was built to be an impregnable fortress, and no one has ever taken it. But it has fallen many times, riven from within, the factions killing each other. And each new owner rebuilds, adding more locks, more traps, more passages and devices which he hopes will keep him safe. They never do, but they remain to destroy any thief who is foolish enough to enter. And no thief would enter, since there is nothing there worth plundering."

"There is now." Conan nodded grimly. "A friend. A woman."

"A lover?"

"Someone who saved my life. I pledged to keep her safe, and Khalar Zym now has her. He will kill her."

Ela Shan exhaled slowly. "Were it for all the gold in the world, I would not join you, Cimmerian; but my debt to you means I am indebted to her as well. Come, my friend. We will dare that which daunts all other thieves. Two nights hence, we will penetrate Khor Kalba, and carry away that which its master values most."

MARIQUE WATCHED FROM the shadows as the slaves guided Tamara into the marble basin filled with steaming water. Lilac blossoms floated in it. Marique allowed her gaze to linger on the monk's naked body, searching her pale flesh for any bruise or blemish. No imperfection marred the woman's beauty as she sank into the water and the slaves began to wash her.

Marique had clipped a lock of the woman's hair and sniffed it. Sweat and grime, yes, and even the foul lather of the beasts they'd used to transport her clung to it. But beneath that was something more earthy, musky, and strong. The scent of the barbarian. Marique recognized it from when she had tasted him so long ago.

As Tamara was bathed, other slaves brought platters of fruit and viands, delicacies from throughout the world. Tamara, sedated, ate mechanically, as she was bidden, and sloppily drank wine. The bathers washed spills from her, then took her from the bath and dried her with scarlet towels. They led her to a padded bench and seated her in the center. Two slaves brushed out her hair while another half dozen attended to her nails. All the while the woman faced forward, staring distantly at an empty wall.

Marique came around and plucked a blueberry from one of the platters. She sniffed at it, then made to fling it away. But she stopped and instead approached Tamara. She pressed the berry to the woman's red lips. Tamara accepted the berry and chewed until it had been reduced to something that barely required swallowing.

The slaves withdrew as robed acolytes entered the chamber. They stood Tamara up and stripped her of the towels. They then bid the woman step into a scarlet gown, which she did. They bound her into it, then let her sit again.

Marique waited until they had departed before she slid onto the bench. "My mother wore that gown on her wedding day. It flatters you."

Tamara's jaw trembled, then her lips parted. "I am not your mother."

"But you will be." Marique laughed. "Do you know why they bathe you in lilac water? It was my mother's favorite. Do you still taste blueberry on your tongue? Another of her favorites. They will serenade you with the music that she loved. They will tell you tales to which she thrilled. And do you know why?"

Tamara said nothing, but a tear glistened in her right eye.

"My mother will take you—not as your barbarian did, but even more completely. You are a vessel, Tamara. Now they fill you with things my mother will remember. Things that remind her of the joys of being alive. When my father summons her from beyond the grave, your soul, your essence, will drain out and she will flood into you. Up through your toes and your legs, up through your loins and belly and breasts. She will course up your neck, filling you . . . filling you until she turns your pretty blue eyes pitch-black."

The monk shook. "I would rather die."

"You will, Tamara, you will . . ."

The chamber door opened and Khalar Zym entered. A smile grew on his face and it took a moment for Marique to realize that, yet again, it was not for her.

He stopped and held out a hand. Tamara resisted, but her hand rose to his, then she stood. He walked around her, admiring her. When he came around again, when Marique could again see his face, his smile had broadened and filled with love.

"So perfect you are, Maliva, my love."

Marique turned from him and fingered a lock of hair. "She is not my mother."

"But she shall be, Marique. Her death will herald your mother's return . . . and the return of Acheron's glory. Maliva's sorceries will melt flesh from the bones of kings. Together we, my beloved and I, shall cast *all rivals* into an ocean of blood."

"And what of *me*, Father?" Marique rose, turning slowly, a cold edge seeping into her voice. "Am I to be cast aside? Will you find me weak? Will you find me flawed? Will you forget all I have done in your name?"

Khalar Zym raised his chin, regarding his daughter through slitted eyes. "Do you think I could forget the one who brought me this vessel? Do you think I have forgotten how you found the last shard of the mask? Just because I love your mother so much, it does not mean I love you any the less, Marique."

He reached out for her with an open hand. "Our enemies will drown, my daughter, in a boiling crimson sea. But you, Marique, the product of our union, you will be raised up. You will reign as our princess."

Marique took his hand and allowed him to guide her to Tamara's side. They flanked the monk and stared at their reflections in an obsidian mirror. "Smile, my cruel angel. Soon we will be a family again."

Marique nodded slowly, seeking shadows in the reflection, listening for treacherous whispers; but she found neither. She smiled and, for a heartbeat, felt almost embarrassed, as a child might. "Yes, my dear father, yes. A family once again."

CHAPTER 31

KHOR KALBA ROSE from the coastal plains defiantly, its bold black lines mocking the ocean's ability to dissolve even the strongest stone. At the low-tide mark, barnacles and other signs of sea life made themselves visible, but only the most hearty. As Ela Shan and Conan picked their way over algae-slicked stones, pale crabs scuttled away. The two men headed for a large outflow pipe that stank of things noxious, of the creatures that throve in such filth.

Beyond the castle walls, a half mile farther along the coast, lay a stone formation looking very much like the skull of a giant clawing himself free of the earth. It appeared as if the moon's dark disk was rising from within it. A bright fiery stream of magma flowed over the giant's tongue and spilled far below to sizzle and hiss in the ocean. It seem to Conan as if the giant could not digest that which lurked in its belly and was vomiting that evil upon the earth.

Ela Shan crouched in the shadows beside the outflow.

"The iron grate is new—at least, newer than Khor Kalba. Your Khalar Zym is not completely stupid."

The Cimmerian moved forward and grabbed the black metal bars. He'd be hard-pressed to pull them apart. Still, there was no other way in.

Ela Shan's hand landed on his wrist. "Give me a moment. No lock may withstand me, and iron bars I find particularly offensive."

When they departed Asgalun, Ela Shan had exchanged his finery for dark clothes that made him all but invisible in the night. Over his doublet, in lieu of armor, the thief wore a vest of many pockets and sheaths. Conan estimated that the small man likely carried more steel by weight than he did, but the vests pockets contained yet more. The thief drew a small vial from one pocket, broke the wax seal, then used a bit of shell to smear the viscous liquid from within at the base of two bars.

Both the shell and the metal began to smoke. The thief tossed the bottle and the shell aside into the sea, then drew back upwind of where the potion worked. "You don't want to breathe any of that."

Conan nodded and crouched beside the thief. "How long?"

"Close. Foaming like a rabid dog, that's what we want." Ela Shan pointed toward a crusty patch on one of the bars. "The things that grow there produce an acid that etches the metal so they can sink roots in it. An alchemist believed it would let him change dross into gold, so he concentrated it. He had an accident and now, lacking hands, he's willing to trade the secret of his formula with people who will perform services for him. I scratch his back—well, I provide people for that—and—"

The Cimmerian rose and delivered a sharp kick to one

of the bars just above where the acid had done its work. The bar parted with a wet crunch, the sound of a soaked cable snapping. The second broke more easily. Conan waited for Ela Shan to wash the edges down with cupped handfuls of water. Conan then grasped the bars and was able to twist and spread them enough to permit passage.

Ela Shan kept to the side of the round conduit to avoid splashing through the stream of raw sewage in the middle, but the Cimmerian had no such option. Even with his head bowed, his shoulders brushed against the top of the pipe. Glowing lichen provided an eerie, pale green light to illuminate their path.

Beneath the first line of walls they discovered a narrow passage extending to the left and right, with the floor sloping upward. Ela Shan could have slipped into it easily, but for Conan it would have been a very tight squeeze. Evenly spaced along it, brick-lined chimneys extended up into darkness.

The thief shook his head. "In other places I've used a crossbow and grapnel for ascent. The last thing we want now, however, is for some fat-arsed guardsman to plant himself on a head and hear us coming up at him. Deeper in we'll find more chances that are shorter climbs, and in portions of Khor Kalba that have gone unused for a long time.

As they pushed on, the tunnel broadened, as did the flow through it. Two more tunnels joined it at a collecting pool, and their path continued on straight across. Fetid bubbles rose to the pool's turgid surface, bursting through a filthy brown layer. Conan probed with his sword. "It's not deep."

The thief restrained him with a hand to the chest. "It doesn't need to be." He fished a small box from one of his pouches and poured into his hand what appeared to be salt crystals. He tossed some of them before him, into the pool, as would a farmer sowing seed. As they sank, they began to glow a lurid purple, marking an uneven path.

More importantly, dark shadows moved within the water, jerking sharply away from the light.

Conan frowed. "What manner of sorcery—"

"Not sorcery, my friend. Magick can always be detected." Ela Shan moved along the path, spreading more crystals before him. "A different form of the lichen provides the light, and oil of the red eucalyptus provides most of the crystal. Not many creatures can abide it, and as long as there is light, the path is safe."

Conan followed the thief to the other side, then stopped as they reentered their tunnel. "The water is colder."

The thief crouched. "Fresher, too, much fresher. There must be a bigger channel, a massive one, that draws colder water from the deep. Why they'd need it, however, I have no idea."

The Cimmerian remembered the baleful eye he'd seen on the *Hornet*. "I do."

"Yes . . . ?"

From above, distant yet powerful, drums began to pound. "It's begun. Let's move."

"Conan, what are we facing?"

The Cimmerian turned toward the thief, his face taut. "I hope you have more of your crystals." He turned, and plunged into darkness.

MARIQUE PACED AROUND Tamara, admiring and hating her at the same time. Tamara stood there in Maliva's gown, her hands and ankles bound with long chains. The set of her shoulders and the way she raised her chin reminded Marique of her mother. *At the end . . .*

"I do believe you are properly prepared."

Tamara's eyes flashed. "Do you not wish to drug me again, Marique? After all, I might try to escape."

Marique's right hand rose, the Stygian talons sharp and bright. "Such a precaution might please me, but I would not have my mother addled when she takes your form. But you thought yourself clever, didn't you? You want me to drug you so my mother will fail."

Tamara said nothing.

"But failure is not something we shall know this night." Marique went to the throne room's window and pointed to the courtyard below. "Already, fighting men flock to my father's banner, filling his ranks. Word has gone out. And trust me, child, any that even barely resemble your Cimmerian will be killed. He may have escaped my assassins, but he will not arrive in time to rescue you."

"I care not for rescue. It is enough he kills your father and destroys the mask." Tamara smiled slowly. "And he *will* kill your father. He would have done so at Shaipur save for your intervention."

Marique let pride smother the spark of fear in her belly. "Nothing will stop my father."

She turned and took the Cimmerian sword from the stand where it rested. She meant to brandish it triumphantly, but when she touched the cool metal, she felt a spark of fear reignite in her breast. That Conan and the blade were linked had never been in doubt. He had had a hand in its creation. She glanced at the metal, seeking illumination in its reflections, but saw nothing. This reassured her for a moment, before she realized that she should have seen a reflection of her right hand, the hand holding the blade.

Is he that close? Marique snorted and lifted her gaze from the blade. "Did you know I met your barbarian as a boy? I took this sword from him."

The monk's upper lip curled in a sneer. "He said nothing of you. You were not memorable."

"Oh, I remember him." Marique licked her lips. "I tasted him long before you ever did. I'm told that Cimmerian steel is sharper and *harder* than any other . . . that when it cuts, the pain is close to *pleasure*. I know it will please you."

Tamara did not reply.

"It will please me as well, Tamara." Marique glided in, whispering in the monk's left ear. "You see, once you are my mother, I shall make your Cimmerian mine. He shall be my consort. As you have known him, I shall know him. What was once yours will be mine, and you, little Tamara, will fade from the world's memory."

Tamara turned, her voice low. "I will kill you."

"You will never have the chance."

"If I do not, I will make certain your mother *does*."

Marique hissed, then withdrew to the chamber doors. She shouted at the soldiers and acolytes lining the corridor. "Strike the drums. Come guide your goddess to her destiny. Any man who fails in his duty will know my wrath, and terrible indeed it shall be."

TWENTY YARDS FURTHER along, the tunnel became much steeper. Conan cut right and Ela Shan left onto narrow walkways that paralleled the spillway. They raced up steps and the tunnel broadened out before them. A massive iron grating worked in a tentacular design covered a deep pool from which water splashed at the bottom of a cylindrical cavern. Cages on chains hung from the shadowed heights, and stone steps combined with drawbridges twisted around the cylinder in a double helix, leading up to Khor Kalba's main fortress.

Conan took all this in with a glance, then focused on the

giant rising from a stone throne across the cavern. Chains swathed the man, taking Conan back to Cimmeria, to his father's forge, and the last of Khalar Zym's minions. *Khalar Zym's last lapdog, Akhoun.* As Conan and the thief started up the steps, Akhoun hauled on chains and drawbridges rose, trapping them.

The giant pointed at the interlopers. "Kill them, now!"

Other men in leather harnesses brought weapons to hand. By dress and location they marked themselves as torturers instead of warriors. They carried whips and red-hot branding irons, rushing around the grate's perimeter. So used to having terror on their side as they plied their trade on their victims, they advanced without realizing just how dangerous some men can truly be.

Ela Shan worked his way up the stairs, hands flashing. Blackened steel spikes and sharp-bladed knives flew. One torturer reeled away, blood spurting from his opened throat. He stumbled onto the grate, then went to his knees. As he struggled to get back up, a gray tentacle rose from the water, curled itself around him, and pulled him under.

Conan roared forward, his sword coming up in an arc that opened a man from hip to shoulder. He fell back, slowing another man. A third torturer lunged with a branding iron. Conan sidestepped it, then took the man's arm off at the elbow. The Cimmerian caught the branding iron in his left hand, then backhanded another man with the glowing end. The man stumbled back, then fell through the grate, bobbing for a heartbeat before disappearing beneath the water's dark surface.

Akhoun brandished a heavy mace, whirling it in time with the drums' resonant pulsing. He moved along toward where Conan had won through the torturers. "Come, Cimmerian, you will trouble my master no more."

Conan went for him, and would have fallen into a trap save for Ela Shan's cry of warning. One of the thief's throwing knives clattered against the grate. Conan turned toward the sound, then ducked as a tentacle swept through the air. As it came sweeping back, Conan sliced at it. Though the cut was a full six inches in depth, it was but a scratch to the monster, which watched Conan through the grate.

Akhoun's laughter boomed through the cavern. "My pet will never let you harm me."

Conan darted two steps forward, then one back, as the beast attempted to grab at him again. "Coward!"

"Smart, not craven." Akhoun opened his arms. "The Dweller will be more kind to you than I."

"Conan, get ready."

His left hand firmly wrapped about a chain, the Shemite thief leaped from the stairs and arced out into the middle of the cavern. His right hand came forward and down. A glass bottle broke against the grating edge, at the central hole. Smoke began to rise from the metal as the thief sailed away again.

The water roiled and Conan sped forward. Akhoun glanced toward his pet, and saw the golden light of its eye slowly fading away; then he turned toward the barbarian. He raised his mace, his mouth open, his roar giving voice to the pain the creature must have felt. He darted forward, intent on Conan. The two combatants hurtled toward each other, one blow aimed high, the other low, with no thought to defense given by either man.

Conan's blade sliced across Akhoun's belly, opening him from navel to hip, front to spine, as the Cimmerian passed beneath the giant's left arm. Blood gushed and a pale rope of intestine spilled out. Yet before death could claim him, Arkoun's mace struck.

The weapon's iron head should have crushed Conan's skull, and likely would have save that a flailing tentacle brushed the mace at the highest point in its arc, diverting and slowing it. The club fell, its haft striking Conan on the shoulder. It knocked him down and sent him tumbling against the chamber wall. He rolled and came halfway up before impact with the wall dropped him onto his ass.

Akhoun stood there, staring down at his ruined belly. A hand reached toward his guts, as if to stuff them back inside. He took a sidling step toward the Cimmerian. The pure venom in his eyes overrode the shock on his face.

Then two tentacles swept out, ensnared him in their coils, and yanked him from sight.

Conan scrambled to his feet and ran to Akhoun's throne. He released the chains that had pulled the drawbridges up, then ran over and joined Ela in his ascent. Below, the water still splashed and things moved in it.

"What did you do?"

"Five years' worth of venom from spitting cobras. The thing's not dead, just blind."

"That's more an assassin's tool than one for a thief."

"If I used it on other than watchdogs, it might be." Ela raced ahead and reached an iron door. "You can feel the drums through here."

"Open it."

"Lock's rusted shut, but one of these others will work. The one across the way will be more accommodating." They ran to it and Ela Shan had it quickly open. The two of them burst into a small garrison chamber and each slew a sleeping man. They moved into the corridor, then found the servants' stairs and worked their way up, killing everyone they could find.

Finally they reached the uppermost level and burst in through the open doorway. The fact that no guards had been posted had warned them that they would find no one. Conan ran to the window and looked down. A long procession had begun with a man in golden armor riding at its head. Behind him came acolytes carrying banners, and Conan imagined that the one at the procession's center bore the Mask of Acheron. More riders, in long robes, with Marique among them; then a crude cart with a woman bound to a post, her back straight, her head high.

Tamara.

Ela Shan joined him. "It looks as if they are bound for that mountain. We can get there easily enough, but look at the companies he has arrayed on the road. We couldn't possibly slaughter them all."

Conan turned and clasped the thief on both shoulders. "Our debt is settled."

The thief chuckled. "Do not think you can abandon me in the midst of an adventure, Cimmerian. I, too, am not without honor."

"And I have a favor to ask of you."

"Yes?"

"You said this place was full of traps and dangers."

"More of those than there is treasure."

"Good." Conan glanced out the window again. "I can get to that mountain. I can slip past those guards. I will destroy Khalar Zym and his mask. But . . ."

"But were the unthinkable to happen, you want him to return to a stronghold that will consume him."

Conan nodded grimly. "Make this a place of death."

"It would make me more of an assassin than a thief, but that old career is getting boring." Ela Shan smiled. "I shall do as you ask, friend Conan. I likely won't kill him, but I shall slow him down. And that might give the world a chance to make this his mausoleum."

CHAPTER 32

FROM HER PLACE of honor Marique studied those working below her. Four acolytes had bound Tamara to the ceremonial oaken wheel, linking her chains to it. She hung there as Maliva had once hung. *As she will again.* Displaying strength that belied their slender forms, the acolytes lifted the wheel and settled it in a wooden collar that had been fitted across a ragged split through the heart of the skull mountain. Scaffolding had been constructed around it to provide a platform for the ceremony, but down through the opening and off into the distance, one could easily see the river of fire that rose to pour out of the skull's mouth.

Marique felt especially proud, for in the lava's red-gold glow could be seen ruins, ancient ruins that dated back to the Acheronian period. The coast where Khor Kalba now rose had once been home to a grand city in the heart of a plain. The shattering of Acheron's power had fractured the land as well. The sea had greedily devoured what it could,

and men supposed that the city had been completely consumed, but much of it had been preserved. Marique's
researches had located it, and she had convinced her father
to excavate the ruins near Khor Kalba. Within the ruins
Marique had uncovered material the existence of which her
mother had only dreamed about, and with this material, she
had been able to construct the ritual that would bring Maliva
back to life.

She had spent much time in those ruins, fearing at first
that she might have been wrong, and later because the voices
that spoke to her did not like the ruins. Despite this, Marique
directed the recovery of the statuary and mosaics that filled
her father's throne room. He had seen her delivery of them
as an act of homage to the god he would become. While she
was still subject to his rages, he always forgave her because
she was, after all, the first to worship him.

Marique wondered, at times, what he would think if he
knew that she had recovered many more things within the
ruins. Dark things. Foul things. Things that defied description. Things that had moved through dimensions untouched
by time, to somehow become lodged in the sea-gnawed city.
She collected them, arranging them in the largest of the
galleries that lay hidden in shadow. She could only guess at
some of their names, and at the unspeakable relationships
that existed among them. And though she recognized most
as gods, Lesser and Elder, Great and Hidden, she refrained
from worshipping them.

Instead she arranged them to be *her* first worshippers.
For while her father would be made a god, he would only
ever see her as a princess. That was an error he would not
be the first god to make; and her taking her rightful place
in the pantheon would not be the first act of divine rebellion.
Though she loved her mother and father dearly, she was

fully aware that they had used her as a means to achieving their own ends, and so she would use them as a means for her to become that which she had always been meant to be.

Below, two acolytes blew on ivory horns carved from mastodon tusks. The bass call reverberated through the sacrificial cavern. Marique felt a familiar thrill running through her belly. Outside, warriors snapped to attention. They stood on either side of the roadway, ready to welcome their new queen. Maliva would make them over into the creatures Acheron had relied upon for centuries. Their limbs would be straightened, the forms made more powerful. They would cease to be human, and would not notice or care. They would be handsome, if the shadowed murals below were any clue, and alien.

She thought briefly of Remo, whom she had seen skulking through the ruins from time to time. He'd seen the murals. It was his wish to be transformed. He believed—or at least had presumed to hope—that Khalar Zym would choose him as Marique's consort. And the true pity was that his wish might have come true, though his transformation would have rendered any conventional understanding of their relationship moot.

Her father appeared and the horns blasted again. He had donned golden armor, which shone with unnatural brightness within the cavern. It had been modeled on that worn by the last priest-king of Acheron, and the ruins themselves imparted energy to it—the tribute of ghosts who longed to honor near-forgotten glories. His twinned serpentine blades rode in the scabbard at his left hip. He walked to the platform, his steps sure, his eyes bright—every bit a warrior and a ruler. He took up his place at Tamara's left hand, his back toward Khor Kalba, then surveyed the gathered faithful as a god might survey an assembly of his high priests.

He opened his hands. "Now is the time in which great wrongs are righted. Through this woman and her sacrifice, my wife shall return, and through her shall we return Acheron to its glory. All of you, whether from far Nemedia or Turan, from the deserts of Stygia, the dank jungles of Keshan, or the jeweled cities of Aquilonia, you all have shared with me a secret. The blood of Acheron runs through our veins. Some of us had it introduced by rapine. Others of us fled when Acheron fell. Some of us never knew until recent times of our heritage, and others have worked for centuries to bring this day to fruition.

"The day of our redemption is at hand!"

That statement was Marique's cue. She turned to an acolyte and accepted from his hands the red silk-wrapped Cimmerian sword. She descended a short set of stone stairs and approached her father's left side. She could not keep a smile from her face, but whether it arose from pride in her father, or because she knew that all of them would soon be on bended knee before her, she could not say.

Marique unwrapped the blade and raised it high, red silk hiding her hand and flowing, bloodlike, down her arm. "As a victorious barbarian's sword once shattered the Mask of Acheron, a vanquished barbarian's sword—one made by the hand of the last guardian of a mask shard—shall revive it."

Khalar Zym took the naked blade from her, and as he did so, her smallest finger brushed the sword's bronze pommel. It stung, as if a metal burr had slid into her flesh . . . but she knew it was not that at all. *The barbarian is close.* She smiled. He was not close enough. Nothing could stop her father now.

Khalar Zym studied the blade, then washed it in the smoke of a censer. As the acolyte bearing that censer moved to waft smoke over Tamara, two other acolytes tipped the wheel forward. Tamara hung by her chains above the fiery river far below, her long hair idly buffeted by rising currents. The last acolyte moved onto the platform, bearing the mask on a golden ceremonial tray. Marique took the tray from him, and moved to her father's right hand.

Again he raised the sword above his head. "By lusty Derketo and the serpent lord Set, by Dagon and Nergal and gods we shall return to their rightful places . . . with this blade I do seed the mask with the blood of its ancient master."

With the delicacy of a parent brushing an errant lock from a child's cheek, Khalar Zym laid the sword's edge against Tamara's collarbone and slid it forward. The woman gasped and blood flowed. It trailed down from the cut to the fullness of her breast, then dripped off, hot and red.

On bended knee, Marique raised the tray and let the blood splash over the mask. The droplets did not spatter as might have been expected, but were sucked into the mask as if it were thirsty silk. What had been a hard-edged puzzle of bone and reptilian leather drank the blood. Tiny bubbles frothed along the breaks caused by the shattering, then those fissures sealed themselves. Desiccated flesh grew more supple. Tissue swelled, taking on a deeper luster. The patina of age faded and vitality suffused the mask.

And there, for the first time, one of the tentacles twitched. It was not a strong motion, but it was not a trick of the eye either. Then another one moved, and another. The motions became deliberate. One tentacle tested itself against the tray, lifting the mask for a heartbeat, then letting it thump down again. Marique felt it through the gold, and heard it, and when she looked up, in her reflection on the golden tray's edge, she spied a goddess.

She turned, and her father, bloody sword in one hand, secured the mask in the other. The tentacles caressed his hand. Marique did not know which she envied more: the tentacles for being able to touch her father in way that lit his face so, or her father, for holding, pulsing and alive there in his hand, the culmination of his dreams,

"Ancient ones which burn beneath us, unspeakable art thy names." Ecstasy in full possession of his expression, Khalar Zym lifted his face to the heavens and laughed aloud. "Behold your new master, and despair in his lack of mercy."

He stared at the mask in his left hand, then slowly raised it to his face. The tentacles, as if feeling his breath, bent themselves toward him. As he pressed the mask against his flesh, they wrapped around his head. Their tips plunged into his skin, through his scalp and cheeks, along his jaw. No blood welled from the wounds because the mask's flesh and his flesh became as one.

"Yes, of course, yes." Khalar Zym turned toward Marique. She rose and held the tray between them as if it were a shield. "Fear not, daughter. I have always loved you. I always shall. I can forgive you anything."

A chill ran through Marique. She bowed her head. "My father is most kind."

"He is." Khalar Zym's voice grew slightly distant. "But I shall not always be your father."

He turned, extending his open hand toward Tamara. "Maliva, my queen, hear my call! I summon you from the depths of the deepest hell. Swiftly return, my love, and bring with you all knowledge forgotten and damned. Now is the time for our eternal rule to begin."

On the other side of the wheel, the censer clanked to the decking. The acolyte's body fell one way. His head rolled and bounced off the platform. The acolyte beside him began to bleed from the forehead, in a line that ran down his nose. His eyes rolled up as if he were attempting to see what had happened, then he jerked forward, rebounding off the wooden collar, having been propelled by a booted foot.

Khalar Zym snarled. "Who dares?"

"That mask is not yours, Khalar Zym. Nor is the power that goes with it." The Cimmerian crouched low, blood running from his blade. "I've come to take the piece that is mine, and to send you to join your wife in hell."

CHAPTER 33

CONAN FLICKED BLOOD from his blade and stalked across the platform toward the man who would be a god. One of the acolytes let loose with a blast on his ivory horn—a blast Conan aborted with a harsh glance. The other acolyte pulled back, and his retreat spurred the ritual's observers to join him, giving the fighters ample room to engage each other.

Khalar Zym raised the Cimmerian great sword and struck a guard, as if he were once again a minor Nemedian prince dueling at court. Conan came at him directly, both hands on his long sword's hilt. He did not feint or waver; he came on directly. When Khalar Zym lunged, hoping to spit him, Conan battered aside the blade his father had made and struck. He caught Khalar Zym above the right ear, striking sparks from the mask and drawing blood that the mask greedily drank in.

Foul green energy pulsed forth, sending a cold wave of

numbness down Conan's arm. Khalar Zym fell back and the very earth itself shook. Planks snapped. The platform sagged, spilling half the visitors off into the fiery abyss. Stones crumbled and began to fall, then a loud crack sounded from behind the Cimmerian.

"Conan!"

The Cimmerian turned and leaped toward the ceremonial wheel. The wooden collar around it had broken. His gaze met Tamara's for a heartbeat, then the wheel dropped down, as if falling down a chimney, taking her with it. Conan ran to the edge, fearing all he would see was her body dwindling in the distance, a blackened shadow against the molten river below.

But there, twenty feet down, the wheel's pins caught. On either side of the crevasse two statues faced each other, kneeling, arms spread. The black basalt figures, one male, the other female, regarded Tamara with blind, pitiless eyes. The wheel slowly spun in the space between the statues, Tamara's fate resting in the laps of forgotten gods.

Conan leaped down and landed with feline precision, one foot on a god and the other on the wheel. He hammered a manacle with his sword's pommel, popping it open, then slashed the chain binding Tamara in half.

"I will have you out in a heartbeat."

She smiled at him. "And then for getting us out of here, you have a plan?"

Before he could reply or reach her other manacle, the Cimmerian looked up. Khalar Zym landed across from him and stomped on the wheel. It came up and over, spilling Conan back against the basalt goddess's breasts. "Tamara!"

A chain slithered through a bolt. "I'm free, Conan. There's a ledge."

"Find a way out."

"I won't leave you."

"I won't be far behind."

Khalar Zym shouted back up the chimney. "Marique, find her. She cannot escape." He then reached down and pressed his left hand to the wheel. His hand glowed, not the green emanating from the mask, but the dark violet glow that pulsed from deep within some of the ruins' recesses. Purple witchfire spread over the wheel, consuming nothing. Instead it appeared to stabilize the platform.

Khalar Zym straightened, then stepped onto the wheel. "Come, Cimmerian. You shall be the first sacrificed to my glory. Forever shall be remembered your name."

Conan joined him, contempt in the grin he wore. "I don't want to be remembered—just to make certain you're forgotten for all time."

TAMARA RAN ALONG the ledge and onto a broader avenue of soot-blackened ruins. To the right and downstream of the fiery river was the platform from which she'd fallen. She wasn't certain she could get back out that way, and was positive that people would try to stop her. To the left, the avenue paralleled the river, and slowly curved off to the right before making a broader sweep back to the left and inland. Below and before her, ancient bridges crossed the burning flow.

She saw footprints in the dust near her feet, so she ran along left. Since everything at her right hand was on the coastal side of the ruin, she peered through doorways, hoping to see the night sky through a crack, or perhaps catch a hint of a breeze from the sea. She ran along quickly and then, toward the back of a long, dark space, she caught a flicker of light. Carrying the length of chain still bound to her right wrist, she made for it.

Halfway along, the room exploded with light. Tamara found herself in a forest of obscene statues—graven images that mocked and blasphemed. They'd been gathered together in tableaux which defied description and could only have amused a very sick mind.

And down through the aisle between them strode Marique, her head held proudly high. She spread her hands, Stygian talons bright on the right, a sharp poniard in the left. "Welcome to my realm. Do you like it?"

"Not in the least." Tamara dropped the chain and slowly started looping it around her forearm. "Show me the way out of here."

The witch smiled coldly. "If I do not?"

"I'm not drugged. I'm not in chains, and you don't have a cadre of guards to restrain me." Tamara's eyes became slits. "You can't stop me, and if I need to prove I'm not lying, you'll pay the price in pain."

THE TWO MEN moved around the wheel, swords occasionally licking out like serpents' tongues, to contest the space at the wheel's heart. The blades rang together, the Cimmerian steel all the sweeter for its masterful construction. The peal and the echoes brought back memories of Conan's father wielding that same blade, and a slow fury at Khalar Zym's unworthiness to use it began to rise in Conan.

Conan came around the wheel, knees bent, shoulders forward, always keeping his weight even and his balance under control. He pushed forward, poking low with the long sword, then withdrawing the blade before Khalar Zym could parry. He blocked the man's return cuts with ease.

Khalar Zym's frustration grew. The mask writhed impatiently on his face. Conan did not wonder if the mask remembered the barbarians who had come to destroy it before. It would be enough that Khalar Zym did. It would get him thinking about insignificant things, about Conan being from Cimmeria and being the only man who'd drawn his blood in duels.

"Damn you, Cimmerian!" Khalar Zym's face twisted in a demoniacal snarl. "You have troubled me too long. It is time for you to die."

The man-god advanced quickly, stabbing low and coming high. Conan retreated before him, working his way back around the wheel. They'd come all the way around, Khalar Zym quickening his pace, when Conan stopped. The Nemedian lunged, but Conan leaned left. The Cimmerian great sword passed between Conan's body and arm. He clamped down on Khalar Zym's wrist, binding it tight to his side, then hit him twice with a fist, hammering that bleeding ear.

Khalar Zym pulled back. Conan stripped the sword from the man-god's hand, letting his own long sword fall away, and reared back. He planted a front kick against Khalar Zym's breastplate that slammed the man-god back against the ebon idol's chest. Khalar Zym rebounded onto his knees and caught himself before he could pitch headlong into the abyss.

"Damn you, Cimmerian." Khalar Zym raised a fist wreathed with arcane flames. "Damn you to *hell*!"

The man-god's fist fell.

The wheel exploded.

MARIQUE REGARDED THE monk with new eyes. "Should I be amused by you, or angered?"

"If those are your only choices, you're an idiot." Tamara

drifted forward more quickly than Maliva's gown should
have allowed. She let a foot or so of chain slip into her hand.
Then she whipped it around, lashing out. Before Marique
could move, the chain tore the dagger out of her hand. The
blade ricocheted off into the darkness below the cruel gods.
Then Tamara's fist came around and Marique saw stars. She
found herself flat on the ground with the monk heading out
the side passage.

Marique tasted blood. *She struck me. She dared* strike
me! She came up on all fours like a cat, then started after
the monk. *You will pray that I let you die!*

Marique bolted through a short passage, then down a
flight of stairs that spread out into a small courtyard. Back
when the sun shined on the city, it had been a garden, but
the molten river had long since nibbled away the edge on
this level and all those below. Opposite the courtyard, she'd
arranged a half-dozen statues of horned gods, thinking eventually to consign them to the flames, but at the moment she
was pleased to have them there to witness her victory.

Tamara turned, her back against the little garden's wall.

Marique spat blood. "No one dares to strike me. No one."

The monk smiled. "I'll be happy to do it again."

"You don't understand, my dear." Marique raised her
right hand and, with her index finger, inscribed a burning
sigil in the air. "You learned to fight. I taught myself to *kill*."

At a whispered word, the Acheronian sigil flew directly
at Tamara. The monk dodged, impressing Marique with
both her speed and agility. Neither mattered, however, as
the sigil hit her in hip and spun her around. She slammed
into the wall and bounced off it, dropping to her hands and
knees, her head down.

Marique marched over and grabbed a fistful of her hair.

She yanked back, stretching the woman's throat. She raised her right hand, the claw full of Stygian metal glinting gold in the hot river's glow. "And kill you I shall."

Tamara looked up. "But if you kill me, you kill your *mother!*"

Marique laughed. "Who do you think it was who let my mother's enemies take her in the first place?"

The monk gasped in horror.

Marique grinned.

Her hand rose high and descended . . .

. . . And the Cimmerian great sword took it off cleanly at the wrist.

Marique spun, staring at the blood spurting from the stump, and the barbarian crouched with his back to the gods. She started to say something, but then the monk was again on her feet. Tamara spun and caught Marique with a kick to the belly. The witch flew from the garden, plummeting toward the river, but a stone post one level down stopped her. It snapped her spine, crushing her heart against her breastbone, then burst up through her chest. Impaled, she slid down its glistening length and stared up into the darkness.

Conan and Tamara appeared above her, having descended to that level. They wore pitiless expressions. Marique would have smiled at that if she could. Then they vanished.

Then her father came into view, blood smeared on the side of his face, his sword in hand. The mask displayed shock when he saw her. He jogged over and sank to a knee. "Oh, Marique."

She tried to smile. *You can resurrect me. You can make me whole. Please, Father.*

Khalar Zym looked down. "I have loved you always, daughter mine. I would have loved you forever, but this proves that things were as I feared. Unlike your mother, you

are simply too weak and, therefore, must be surrendered to
Death's embrace."

CONAN FOLLOWED TAMARA through the labyrinthine
Acheronian ruins. They descended another level to get past
a point of collapse, then worked their way up two more as
the crevasse turned inland. And there, on the other side, he
caught sight of what he took to be a sliver of night sky.

"We have to get across."

Tamara pointed to a bridge. "There."

Hope speeding them, they raced to the wooden bridge. It
consisted of three spans, the middle resting on two columns
that the river had not yet eroded. They darted across the first
span, which, while a bit rickety, held them above the molten
rock. Heat rose from it, but the wood had not charred. Odd
sigils had been worked into the wood, and Conan wondered
if it had been sorcery which had preserved it.

They had gingerly made their way over the second span
when Khalar Zym appeared at the far end. Conan turned to
Tamara. "Go. Get free. I'll stop him."

"No, Conan, come." She grabbed his hand. "We can get
away." She pulled and her hand slipped from his as she
stepped on the third span.

A board cracked and she fell.

Conan lunged and caught the chain as it unspooled from
her forearm. The chain jerked tight, grinding his shoulder
socket. He felt her strike the stone column twice. He pulled
back and looped a length of chain around his wrist, but the
slat he was using for leverage began to splinter.

"Tamara."

"I'm here, Conan. My shoulder. I can't pull myself up."

"I have you."

"But for how long, Cimmerian?" Khalar Zym sheathed his swords and approached with arms wide. "Beside me, none are equal. Beneath me, all must submit. Before me, all are sacrifices to my glory!" He closed his eyes, basking in the sound of his own voice as it echoed through the ruins. "Maliva, I summon you here!"

Tamara jerked at the end of the chain. An ill wind rose off the lava, lifting clouds of bright embers to swirl like stars through the air. They fell on Conan's hands and face, singed his hair, and sizzled against his flesh. "Tamara?"

"He's summoned her, Conan. I can feel her entering me."

Khalar Zym chuckled and the mask glowed a malevolent green. "Once again, a Cimmerian boy is caught holding a chain."

"Let me go, Conan. Drop me. I cannot fight her."

"No!" Conan, on one knee, stabbed the great sword into the railing at the base of the second span. It sank through the wood, splitting a sigil, and struck stone, anchoring him. Muscles bunched and quivered. Pain shot through his shoulders. "His evil kills no more."

"You're on one knee already, Cimmerian." The man-god pressed his hands together. "I offer you what I offered your father. Kneel before me and you shall live."

"Conan, I can feel her. She's mad. Worse than the daughter. Drop me!"

"What will it be, Cimmerian?"

Conan, chest heaving, looked at Khalar Zym through sweaty locks of black hair. "Do you want to know why I could beat you when you wielded my father's sword?"

Khalar Zym's eyes tightened. "Tell me."

"He did not make this sword for a boy . . . or a god. He made it for a man." Conan tightened his hand on the hilt.

"A Cimmerian, born to war, who would someday *slay a god*!"

Conan jammed the blade toward the far side of the bridge. As his father had done when levering ice to cool off a hot-headed son, so Conan levered an aged span of bridge off a tall pillar, and spilled a god toward a hell from which he would never escape. Yet even before Khalar Zym could fall, the realization of doom trapped in his horror-filled eyes, that same blade came up and around in a silver blur. It caught Khalar Zym one last time over the right ear and passed fully through his skull. It shattered the Mask of Acheron as it went, consigning master and device to the molten stone below.

The sword stroke released more magickal energy, which shook the ruins to their heart. Lava splashed below, over-running what had been the river's banks. Stones fell. Terraces collapsed. A huge boulder tumbled down and smashed the bridge's first span to flinders.

Conan stood and hauled Tamara up from the hole. He held tightly for a moment, then retrieved his father's sword. Together, they tested the planking on the remaining span, but soon gave this up as pointless since falling rocks posed more of a threat to the bridge than breaking boards did to them. At the far side they had to cut back toward the platform as collapsing terraces cut them off from the opening they'd seen.

They burst from the cavern mouth and Conan immediately moved Tamara behind him for cover. While most of Khalar Zym's troops were fleeing back toward Khor Kalba, two companies had remained. The man-god's elite guard stood poised with swords drawn to oppose Conan, while fresh recruits huddled in their shadows much as Tamara sheltered in Conan's.

Conan shook his head. "Your master is dead. His dreams

290 MICHAEL A. STACKPOLE

are lost. How many of you wish to die for promises that will never be kept?"

The elite guards' captain took a step forward. "Some of us fight for duty and honor, not plunder or power."

A soldier who had lurked behind him stepped halfway around, then pressed a dagger to the throat of Khalar Zym's man. "And some of us, Captain, fight for our friends." Behind him, the other recruits similarly threatened Khalar Zym's last company.

Conan roared with laughter. "Artus! What are you doing here? You were supposed to be warning the world about Khalar Zym."

"I whispered in the ear of one Shemite merchant, so the rumor is halfway round the world by now." The Zingaran shrugged. "We actually hadn't intended on fighting, you see . . . We just wanted to let you know we sail for Hyrkania with the tide, and didn't want you to be late."

EPILOGUE

CONAN STOOD ON a hill overlooking a desolate Hyrkanian plain. Tamara stood beside him and Artus waited at the base with the horses. The sun beat down mercilessly, and heat made the land shimmer—though the Cimmerian was certain that the shimmer was not from heat alone.

Tamara smiled. "Yes, Conan, the monastery is out there. I can feel it. I can find my way through the wards."

"So you will go."

She reached up and rested a hand on his shoulder. "I have considered what you suggested, but I feel I must."

He nodded. "You are very loyal to your master."

"It's not just him." Tamara took his hands in hers and turned them over, exposing the chain scars. "Master Fassir told me about Khalar Zym in a roundabout way. He said that there were madmen in the world who saw patterns as portents in almost anything. Those sorts of men were the kind who kidnap children and make other children orphans. He left the monastery to save me from the consequences of such a madman. His burden passed to you. And now I must accept it *from* you. Somewhere, out there, will be a child who is sought as I was sought. As Master Fassir saved me, so I shall be able to save that child."

"That child will be very lucky." Conan smiled. "And the world as well, for your effort."

Tamara squeezed his hands and looked up into his eyes. "You could come with me."

"I do not need saving, Tamara Amaliat Jorvi Karushan."

"The monastery is a place where you can find peace, Conan."

The Cimmerian pulled her into his arms and gave her a kiss, then released her and took a step back. "I was not born for peace, Tamara. I am a Cimmerian. I have a sword at my side, a horse to carry me to conquest, and enemies who need to be slain. It is my life, my friend, and I could never know any greater joy."

ABOUT THE AUTHOR

MICHAEL A. STACKPOLE is an award-winning novelist, screenwriter, podcaster, game designer, computer game designer, editor, and graphic novelist who is best known for his *New York Times* bestselling novels *I, Jedi* and *Rogue Squadron*. This novel is his forty-fourth to be published. He is currently finishing work on *Of Limited Loyalty*, the second in the Crown Colonies series. You can learn more about him and his work at his website: www.stormwolf.com.